"Who are *you*, Lainie Farrell?"
Nick murmured, touching a
finger to her bare shoulder.

She tried to smile. "No one you'd want to know."

He turned her to face him. "You're wrong. I *do* want to know you. In every sense of the word."

It was nothing but the simple truth. He *did* want to know this woman. And if that meant slowly seducing her, if it meant taking his sweet time and winning her over one word, one touch, one promise—one kiss—at a time, then that was what he would do. Even if it killed him.

It wouldn't, of course. *Succeeding* would kill him. Lying naked with her, kissing her, touching her, filling her, satisfying her, finding his own satisfaction inside her...

And it would be the sweetest death any man could ask for....

Dear Reader,

They say all good things must end someday, and this month we bid a reluctant farewell to Nora Roberts' STARS OF MITHRA trilogy. *Secret Star* is a fitting windup to one of this *New York Times* bestselling author's most captivating miniseries ever. I don't want to give anything away, but I will say this: You're in for the ride of your life—and that's after one of the best openings ever. Enjoy!

Marilyn Pappano also wraps up a trilogy this month. *Knight Errant* is the last of her SOUTHERN KNIGHTS miniseries, the story of Nick Carlucci and the bodyguard he reluctantly accepts, then falls for—hook, line and sinker. Then say goodbye to MAXIMILLIAN'S CHILDREN, as reader favorite Alicia Scott offers *Brandon's Bride,* the book in which secrets are revealed and the last of the Ferringers finds love. Award-winning Maggie Price is back with her second book, *The Man She Almost Married,* and Christa Conan checks in with *One Night at a Time,* a sequel to *All I Need.* Finally, welcome new author Lauren Nichols, whose *Accidental Heiress* is a wonderful debut.

And then come back next month for more of the best romantic reading around—right here at Silhouette Intimate Moments.

Yours,

Leslie Wainger
Senior Editor and Editorial Coordinator

Please address questions and book requests to:
Silhouette Reader Service
U.S.: 3010 Walden Ave., P.O. Box 1325, Buffalo, NY 14269
Canadian: P.O. Box 609, Fort Erie, Ont. L2A 5X3

Marilyn Pappano

KNIGHT ERRANT

Published by Silhouette Books

America's Publisher of Contemporary Romance

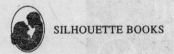

SILHOUETTE BOOKS

ISBN 0-373-07836-6

KNIGHT ERRANT

Printed in U.S.A.

Books by Marilyn Pappano

Silhouette Intimate Moments

Within Reach #182
The Lights of Home #214
Guilt by Association #233
Cody Daniels' Return #258
Room at the Inn #268
Something of Heaven #294
Somebody's Baby #310
Not Without Honor #338
Safe Haven #363
A Dangerous Man #381
Probable Cause #405
Operation Homefront #424
Somebody's Lady #437
No Retreat #469
Memories of Laura #486
Sweet Annie's Pass #512
Finally a Father #542
*Michael's Gift #583
*Regarding Remy #609
*A Man Like Smith #626
Survive the Night #703
†Discovered: Daddy #746
*Convincing Jamey #812
*The Taming of Reid Donovan #824
*Knight Errant #836

Silhouette Books

Silhouette Christmas Stories 1989
"The Greatest Gift"

Silhouette Summer Sizzlers 1991
"Loving Abby"

*Southern Knights
†Daddy Knows Last

MARILYN PAPPANO

After following her career navy husband around the country for sixteen years, Marilyn Pappano now makes her home high on a hill overlooking her hometown. With acreage, an orchard and the best view in the state, she's not planning on pulling out the moving boxes ever again. When not writing, she makes apple butter from their own apples (when the thieves don't get to them first), putts around the pond in the boat and tends a yard that she thinks would look better as a wildflower field, if the darn things would just grow there.

You can write to Marilyn via snail mail at P.O. Box 643, Sapulpa, OK 74067-0643.

Prologue

Nicholas Carlucci had risked his life on a regular basis for ten years without feeling the slightest fear or hesitance. Every time he'd gone to work, every time he'd gotten into a car with his boss, every time he'd picked up the phone to carry out one order or another, there had always been some danger. It came with the territory working as the personal attorney for the top organized crime figure in Louisiana. It was part of the job, and it had never bothered him. He had never been afraid.

Today he was.

It was a damp New Orleans morning, and he was dressed in a jumpsuit, awaiting transfer from the correctional center that had been his home the last two weeks to the federal correctional institute in northern Alabama. His hands were cuffed in front of him, his ankles shackled with leg irons, as he shuffled along, last in the line of four prisoners bound for the U.S. Marshal's Service van that would take them east.

He had known from the beginning that this day would

come. Still, he dreaded it. The thought of prison, of bars, electronic gates and armed guards, made his stomach queasy. Until the last two weeks, he had never been confined, had never spent even one night in jail. He didn't know how he would handle night after night in an eight-by-twelve-foot cell, with no freedom, no privacy, no dignity, being treated as something less than human, locked behind bars, too dangerous to unleash on the world. He didn't know if he could survive.

But it had been his choice. Smith Kendricks, the assistant U.S. attorney who was prosecuting Jimmy Falcone, had offered Nicholas a deal. He had been willing to keep Nicholas out of jail in exchange for his testimony. Nicholas had refused. He hadn't wanted Jimmy's lawyers to be able to accuse him of trading testimony for leniency. He hadn't wanted his accusations against his boss to be tainted in any way in the jury's mind, and so he had pleaded guilty to his own charges before ever setting foot in Kendricks's courtroom. He had chosen to go to prison because he'd had no other option. It was the only way to stop Falcone. It was the only way to fulfill his need for vengeance.

Awkwardly he climbed into the van and settled on the worn seat. It was a long drive to Talladega, and the marshals didn't offer to loosen the handcuffs or remove the leg irons for the duration. He clasped his hands, trying unsuccessfully to relieve the pressure on his wrists, and stared out the window as the doors slammed and the driver pulled away. It was barely five o'clock on October 15, too early for the sun to burn away the wispy fog that obscured everything around them. It wasn't fair that his last view of the city where he'd lived most of his life should be like this—dark, shrouded, mysterious. He needed something to remember, some image to keep him company for the next five years, some memory to keep him sane.

The van drove through the quiet city and eased onto the nearly deserted interstate, traveling through a ghostly haze that cloaked all signs of life around them. It was eerie, ethereal, almost like being dead. Sometimes it felt as if he were dead. Sometimes he was convinced he had died fifteen years ago on a rainy Baton Rouge street—his soul, at least, if not his body.

That was why, in all those years working for Falcone, he had never been afraid. He'd had nothing to lose. The worst anyone could do was kill him, and most of the time that would have been a relief, a welcome release from a life he couldn't bear.

That was why he shouldn't be afraid now. He had accomplished his goals. A conviction in Jimmy's case was inevitable. The old man was going to spend the rest of his life behind bars. He was finally going to pay for his sins.

The sound of the road under the wheels changed. Though gray mist still surrounded them, Nicholas knew they were crossing the Lake Pontchartrain bridge. Soon they would be passing through Slidell, then across the state line into Mississippi. In thirty-eight years he had rarely traveled outside the state, had never felt any desire to. Everything he needed could be found right here in Louisiana. The only things he wanted couldn't be found anywhere.

Forgiveness. Peace. Rena.

He raised both hands to rub his eyes. He didn't want to leave Louisiana. The only places important to him were there—the shabby French Quarter neighborhood where he'd grown up, the New Orleans mansion where he'd grown old and Baton Rouge, home to his greatest joys and his greatest sorrows. The state was too much a part of him to leave it behind.

But he *was* leaving it. He was being taken, manacled and shackled, four hundred miles and a world away from his home. So far that he might never find his way back, and for so long that he might be forgotten before he returned.

His thin smile was bitter. Then again, he might not live to come back. There were more than a few residents at the correctional institute who owed a favor or two to Jimmy. If his former boss wanted him to die in prison, he would.

But at least he would know he had won. He would know that Jimmy had been punished. He would die a satisfied man.

Chapter 1

The cab pulled to the curb behind a long line of parked cars, across the street and a block away from Kathy's House, and the driver looked in the rearview mirror. "Looks like they're having some sort of celebration today."

"Their first anniversary," Lainie Farrell murmured from the back seat. The women's center serving the New Orleans' neighborhood known as Serenity, named for its main street, had opened a year ago to great cynicism. Not many people besides its director, Karen O'Shea, had thought it would last through the first year, but not only had they survived, they had expanded. Last spring Karen had opened the Serenity Street Alternative School in the carriage house out back, and in early summer the neighborhood's first grocery store had opened, funded by a grant Karen had pursued. According to rumor, now she was working on tending both the residents' spiritual needs as well as the physical, trying to entice a nondenominational church and a doctor to open their doors down here. Major accomplishments for a neighborhood that everyone had once agreed should be dozed to the ground and turned into a garbage dump.

Lainie shifted on the seat, feeling the broken springs give underneath her. She'd been working at Kathy's House for three weeks now. They had no use for her particular skills—actually, they remained ignorant of her particular skills—but they always needed a pair of helping hands, and she provided them as their jack of all trades. One day she might fill in for the absent receptionist, and the next she would assist the nursing staff with inoculations. Yesterday she had mowed the large yard, watered the flowers and weeded the beds, and Monday she was scheduled to chauffeur a couple of residents to various offices downtown. Although the work was occasionally more physically demanding than she was accustomed to, she enjoyed it. Her mother had always told her that helping others was good for the soul, and the past three weeks had proved it to be true, at least to some extent.

Helping others when she wasn't lying to them through her teeth might prove a little more soul-enriching, but she wouldn't have the opportunity to find out. When her job here was done, she would leave Kathy's House, Serenity and New Orleans behind.

"They know how to party."

She glanced at the driver, seeing only the back of his head. Sam had done a fair imitation of a cabbie, driving like a bat out of hell while keeping up a steady stream of conversation. His mama would be proud, he'd joked, when he slid behind the wheel. All those years of college, law school and government service, and look where he'd ended up.

She would have taken a real cab, if it'd been possible to convince a real cabbie to come here. In the last ten years, the crime spiraling out of control had turned Serenity into an armed no-man's land. Until a year ago, even the New Orleans Police Department had drawn the line at Decatur

Street, where Serenity ended a few blocks back, refusing to actually enter the neighborhood itself. Then Karen had moved in and run into trouble with the punks and the gangs. Because she was the widow of a highly respected NOPD detective who'd been best of friends with another detective, an FBI agent and the U.S. Attorney himself, that policy had soon changed. The cops made routine patrols through the neighborhood now, but the cabs still stayed away.

"Do you think he's there?"

She didn't need to ask who *he* was. *He* was her only reason for being here. *He* was of great interest to the NOPD, the FBI and the U.S. Attorney. Especially the U.S. Attorney. Nicholas Carlucci had single-handedly made Smith Kendricks's case against Jimmy Falcone. Carlucci's testimony and the evidence he'd provided against his former boss and associates were in part responsible for Kendricks's move from an assistant's slot into the big boss's office over a year ago. There was a personal connection, too, some past relationship between Carlucci and Jolie Wade, an outstanding reporter who was the media expert on Jimmy Falcone and all his dirty dealings and who just happened to be Mrs. Smith Kendricks.

"I doubt it," she replied at last. A week after she'd started working down here, Nicholas Carlucci had come home, fresh from the federal prison system. She had been working in the yard that day, had seen him walk up the street, a duffel bag over one shoulder, and turn into O'Shea's, the bar across the street from Kathy's House that was owned by Karen's husband. Jamey O'Shea and Carlucci had been best friends when they were kids. Jamey had remained his only friend through the years he'd worked for Falcone.

Jamey had made available one of the two empty apartments above the bar, and Carlucci had moved in. According to Karen, he rarely came out. He just holed up in there and brooded—and he had plenty to brood about. The private vendetta that had led him to betray his long-time boss and everyone he'd ever worked with had failed. For ten years he had gathered evidence, meticulously building a case against Jimmy Falcone. He had put his own life in danger, had survived at least one attempt on it and had voluntarily accepted a prison sentence of his own, all so he could see Falcone punished—though why, no one knew. Carlucci had already been locked in a cell in Talladega when the guilty verdicts came back on the old man. Carlucci had been finishing the first year of his sentence when the appeals court had overturned Falcone's convictions.

Though Kendricks's case against him had been airtight, the appeals ruling hadn't really surprised anyone. Corruption ran rampant around Jimmy Falcone. So did fear. A half-dozen other times he'd gone to trial, and a half-dozen times the same things had happened. Witnesses had disappeared or developed amnesia. Judges were coerced or bribed. Jurors were blackmailed, threats made against their families. Always, the final result was that Jimmy had gone free. Nicholas Carlucci had risked his life and spent five years in prison, and Jimmy Falcone had walked free. Good reasons for brooding.

She had met Carlucci only once. She and Karen had gone to O'Shea's for cold sodas after work a few days ago, and he'd been sitting in a dark corner, nursing a beer. Jamey had introduced them, and he'd given her a look, a slight nod, then turned inward again. He hadn't looked like the dangerous man he was reputed to be. He had looked lost.

"You'd better go before people start wondering why I'm here." Sam turned in the seat to grin at her. "If they ask how you convinced a cabbie to come down here, tell 'em you used your considerable charms to persuade me."

She gave him a dry look as she picked up the bags on the seat beside her. "I'm not supposed to be charming. I'm supposed to be down on my luck."

"You certainly look the part." His teasing faded. "If you need anything…"

She nodded, then climbed out. She was standing on the sidewalk, shifting the two nylon duffels and the scuffed leather backpack when Sam leaned over to see her through the open window.

"Hey, what about my tip?"

She bent down, resting one arm on the door. "Here's a tip—get out of here before someone comes along and decides to rob you."

"Let 'em try. I've got a gun."

"So do most of the punks down here. Trust me, their guns are probably bigger than yours." She stepped back and, with a wave, he pulled away from the curb, making a tight turn in the street and heading for Decatur. Sighing heavily, she started toward the next block, Kathy's House and O'Shea's.

The anniversary party looked like a big success. The yard and the big, wraparound veranda were crowded with people, and the smell of burgers charcoaling filled the air. Several dozen cars were parked all along this block and into the next, and balloons, streamers and kid-produced posters decorated the length of the wrought-iron fence out front.

A thorough look identified a fair number of the guests for her. There were Smith and Jolie Kendricks, talking to Cassie and Reid Donovan. Cassie was one of the two teachers at the alternative school and Jolie's younger sister. Reid was Jamey's son from an ill-fated teenage marriage and a former member of one of Serenity's toughest gangs. Looking at him now, no one would ever guess that he'd once been as troubled as any kid Lainie had ever seen. Oh, the things the love of a good woman—and father and stepmother—could do for a man.

Farther down the veranda she saw Remy Sinclair and Michael Bennett talking with the minister Karen was trying to woo. The FBI agent and the cop were the other half of the friendship shared by Kendricks and Karen's first husband. Sinclair's wife Susannah was one of the center's two nurses, and Bennett's wife Valery had begun showing up to help out whenever she had a few free hours.

Her gaze lingered for a moment on Karen and Jamey—petite, red-haired with electrified curls, and tall, blond and handsome. Chubby one-year-old Sean sat on his father's shoulders, gazing around with that serious look only small children and men like Carlucci managed to pull off. Come to think of it, with his dark coloring, Sean looked much more like Carlucci than he did either parent. Of course, neither O'Shea was actually related to the baby. Karen had explained matter-of-factly in their first meeting that Sean was the son of a beautiful, dark-haired angel named Alicia and a sad young man named Ryan, who had died the day Sean was born.

She was much more generous toward Ryan Morgan than Lainie could have been. That sad young man had worked for Jimmy Falcone, and he had spent the last ten years of his life terrorizing the people of Serenity. He had made getting rid of Karen his personal mission—had vandalized her property, made threats and had even, one night, dragged her into the alley and beaten her. Only Reid's intervention had saved her that night. Only Falcone's decision to eliminate a problem out of control had removed the danger.

Just as she'd expected, she found no sign of Carlucci. He was probably in his apartment, as she'd told Sam, probably brooding. She wondered if Jamey had told him yet that he'd offered the empty apartment to one of Karen's staff, wondered how he felt about having a neighbor intruding on his solitude. If he didn't like it, he could always move—which, of course, would solve the problem, because then she, too, would leave. He certainly had the money to live someplace else. All those years Falcone had paid him well for his services and his loyalty, and most of it had gone into investments. Some of those years had been very good ones for market funds. He had come out of prison much more financially secure than he'd gone in and much less emotionally so.

Turning away from the festivities across the street, she found the multiple sets of French doors that stretched across the front of the bar open, the shutters folded back. There were no lights on inside, no customers at the tables, no one tending bar. The ceiling fans were on, making soft whooshing sounds and cooling the warm afternoon air, but everything else was quiet and still. There wasn't so much as a creak from the apartment upstairs where Carlucci lived.

Digging in her jeans pocket as she started across the room, she pulled out the key to the second apartment and folded her fingers around it. She had felt guilty three days ago when she'd given Karen her sad story—how she was having trouble making ends meet, how transportation was a problem, living so far away and with no money to spare for cab or bus fare. Karen knew better than anyone that Kathy's House didn't pay competitive wages. The majority of her staff was financially comfortable, either with money of their own or husbands who earned good salaries, which allowed them to work for her without worrying about money and bills.

Her boss had suggested the apartment upstairs as a solution with equal measures of optimism and caution. The place was nothing fancy, she'd warned. It was on Serenity, far and away from the safest area in New Orleans to live. There was no air-conditioning to combat the hot, humid days that plagued the city off and on through fall and winter. And—what she clearly perceived to be the biggest negative of all—Nicholas Carlucci was living across the hall.

On the plus side, the place was free. Lainie could consider it part of her wages.

The true plus side was Carlucci, she thought with a grim smile. The rest of it didn't matter.

Turning the corner at the end of the bar, she came to an

abrupt stop. Speak of the devil... Seated at the private table there, out of sight of the rest of the bar, was her new neighbor. His back was to the hallway behind him, and three empty beer bottles stood in a row in front of him. He held a fourth by its neck and fixed his gaze on her.

For a time they both simply looked, neither speaking, neither moving. Other than her two previous brief, in-the-flesh sightings, she had seen only photographs of him, grainy, scowling shots from the newspapers and a clear black-and-white mug shot taken when he was arrested. The printed image didn't do him justice. He was handsome in a dark, deadly, dangerous sort of way. His hair was black, longer than her own. His eyes were deep brown, his skin dark olive. He hadn't shaved recently, giving him a decidedly disreputable look that his cigarette and well-worn scowl intensified.

After a moment that seemed to last forever, he moved, knocking ash into an ashtray, taking a long swig from the bottle he held. "You must be the new neighbor."

She nodded. "I'm Lainie—"

He interrupted with a gesture of the bottle. "I remember. You work at the women's center. Why aren't you over there at the party?"

"I don't know anyone, and I'd rather get unpacked." At least the second excuse was accurate, even if the first wasn't. Truth was, she knew too many of the wrong people over there. Kendricks, Sinclair and Bennett were people poor, down-on-her-luck, in-need-of-her-boss's-charity Lainie Farrell shouldn't know. Of course, she could pretend they were strangers, but she wasn't up to it, not yet. "Why aren't you over there?"

"No booze allowed. Besides, I wouldn't exactly be a welcome guest. Don't you know I'm the sort of person they're hoping to rid Serenity of?"

"Friends of Jamey are always welcome." The community had a great deal of respect for Jamey O'Shea. For years before Karen had come, Jamey had been their caretaker, their guardian, their only hope in a place that had lost hope. Now he shared that role with his wife, his son and his daughter-in-law.

"Not this one." He drained the last drink, then, with one foot under the table, nudged the opposite chair back. "Sit down. Have a drink."

She didn't want to. She wanted to go upstairs, unpack and spend the rest of the day settling in. She wanted a little rest and a few hours to prepare herself before dealing with work. But, knowing it was best, she tugged the straps from her shoulders, laid the three bags on the floor against the far wall and slid into the ladder-back chair.

He placed the empty bottle in the row of other empties, then rose easily to his feet. "Beer?"

"Sure." He disappeared behind her, then returned with two more bottles, icy cold from the cooler. Just holding the bottle seemed to lower her body temperature by a few degrees. "Is this how you spent your first two weeks of freedom?"

"You don't get cold beer in prison, you know. You don't get a lot of stuff in prison. Beer. Decent food. Privacy." Once again he fixed his deep, dark gaze on her. "Sex."

She took a small sip to ease the sudden dryness of her mouth. Sex. That was the prime topic of conversation among the all-female staff at the center. He was too handsome, too wickedly sexy, too darkly sensual, and for five years he had been locked up far from the nearest willing woman. How had he coped with his enforced celibacy? Had ending it been the first thing on his mind when he'd been released? Was that the reason he'd spent his first night of freedom in Montgomery instead of coming straight home?

She hadn't wondered—hadn't allowed herself to—but now she couldn't help it. Her thoughts were straying that way whether she wanted them to or not. Never one to dodge a logical, if unexpected response, she forced her voice to steady itself as she nonchalantly asked, "And have you gotten them now that you're out of prison?"

With a cynical smile, he opened his arms wide to encompass the building around them. "I'm living above a bar where there's more booze than a thirsty man could ask for. I have enough privacy to make a hermit jealous, and while the food's not great, since I'm the one cooking it, I have no one to blame but myself."

He forgot one. Forgot or deliberately left it for her to ask? Maybe he thought she wouldn't. After all, the status of a stranger's sex life was hardly proper conversation. Maybe that was why she asked. "And the sex?"

"In good time." His smile lost its cynicism and was replaced with a hint of wicked promise that sent a small shiver down her spine. "All in good time."

The sun was setting and O'Shea's was filling with customers when Nicholas cleared his table and headed upstairs. In the hours of quiet before the party across the street had broken up, he'd smoked a half-dozen more cigarettes, finished off one more beer and a sandwich and listened to the soft sounds of his new neighbor as she unpacked.

She hadn't been very sociable, this Lainie Farrell. Maybe she just wasn't a talkative person. Or maybe she figured an ex-con didn't warrant expending much effort at friendliness. That was okay. He didn't have much use for sociability, either, and he had no use at all for neighbors.

Jamey had asked if he objected to one of the center's employees moving in, and Nicholas had said no. Truth was, he objected a lot. He had come to Serenity looking for privacy, for solitude of the kind that had been denied him the past five years by the Bureau of Prisons and for ten years before that by Jimmy Falcone. He didn't want to know that someone else was sharing his space or to be aware of anyone else's presence. He didn't want a neighborly neighbor.

If their brief exchange was anything to judge by, he had no reason to worry. Lainie Farrell seemed a number of things, but neighborly wasn't one of them. She might be no trouble at all.

Almost immediately he scoffed at that conclusion. She was a woman, pretty, with eyes of the color that had long been his one weakness, and he was a man whose life had lacked intimacy of the physical variety for more than five years, of the emotional sort for three times longer. She was going to be trouble.

Inside his apartment he went to one of the two windows that overlooked Serenity. All the cars were gone from the street, all the guests gone from Kathy's House. Except for the inexpensive lawn chairs stacked on the porch and the trash bags near the driveway, there was no sign that a party had taken place. It was just a quiet evening for the family, sharing a quilt on the grass, while Jamey tended bar downstairs.

In a very real sense, both he and Jamey had been without family since they were born. Nicholas's mother had walked away not long after his sixth birthday, and he'd never seen her again. As for his father, if she had even known who he was, she'd never told. Jamey's parents had been alive, married and living together until he was grown, but they had required more parenting and support from him than they'd ever given *to* him.

Now he had a real, honest-to-God family—a pretty little wife who clearly adored him, an adopted son who had wrapped both parents around his finger, another son with whom he'd finally come to terms and a daughter-in-law.

And Nicholas was still alone. Always alone.

There had been a time when he had wanted marriage, children, a home—all the things he'd never had. A time when he had believed that he was going to get it. Now he knew better. Now all he wanted was to be left alone.

Right on cue a knock sounded at the door. He didn't turn

away from the window but called loud enough to be heard.
"Yeah?"

The door swung open with a creak, but his visitor didn't
speak right away. He knew who it was—felt it in the atmo-
sphere that suddenly seemed charged with a tension that
hadn't been there two seconds ago. She had brought it with
her—this awareness, this edginess.

"What do you want?" he asked, not caring that the question was blunt, the tone less than friendly.

There was the soft whisper of footsteps coming closer,
but not too close, then a response. "Nice place."

He didn't mean to grin. The comment was just too ridiculous to do otherwise. "Thanks. I like it." Finally he
turned from the window, leaned against the sill and subjected the apartment to the same study she was giving it.
The room was about twelve by twelve, spacious by Serenity
standards, with a nine-foot ceiling that was water-stained
and sagging. The walls were institution green and hadn't
seen fresh paint in at least thirty-five years, and the drapes
at the windows were gold, at least as old as the paint and
in just as sorry shape. As for furniture, there wasn't any.
Except for the bed and one wobbly night table, the apartment was empty.

Jamey had offered him the place across the hall when
he'd arrived nearly two weeks ago. The layout was identical to this one, but Cassie, who'd lived there before her
marriage to Reid, had invested a lot of hard work in making
it livable. It compared favorably to most apartments in the
city. For Serenity, it was downright luxurious.

Nicholas wasn't sure why he'd chosen this one instead.
Maybe because, drab as it was, it was a definite improvement over the eight-by-twelve-foot cell where he'd spent
the last five years. Or because the other apartment, with its
vivid yellow and salmon walls, reminded him too much of
the house he'd left behind. Maybe he'd felt he hadn't deserved someplace pretty and nice to live, not after every-

thing he'd done. Whatever the reason, he was comfortable with the ugly green walls and the rotting drapes.

At last his gaze settled on the woman. He had already noticed that she was pretty, but he'd based that on vague impressions—pleasant features, brown hair, hazel eyes. Now he noted the specifics, like the fact that her hair was about as short as he'd ever seen on a woman, sleek and a deep, rich brown. Her nose was just the slightest bit crooked, and her cheekbones were high. A cupid's bow shaped her mouth, and her eyes were hazel.

He had been known to go to bed with a woman for no reason other than her eyes were hazel.

Definite trouble.

"Jamey asked me to tell you that there are leftovers from the party in the refrigerator," she said at last.

He nodded once in acknowledgment and waited to see what else she had to say. Jamey could have delivered the message himself, or he could have said nothing at all, knowing that sooner or later Nicholas would head down to the kitchen to find something for dinner.

She gave the room another long look, then said, "This place could use some work. Karen keeps a supply of paints and supplies across the street for people who want to do a little remodeling."

"It suits me the way it is."

Now he was the recipient of one of those long looks. "I don't think so," she murmured.

"And what, in your opinion, does suit me?"

"Antiques. Persian rugs. Exotic woods."

She had just summed up his quarters on Jimmy's estate in five neat words. Antiques worth hundreds of thousands of dollars, one-of-a-kind Southern originals coveted by every serious collector in the country. Imported rugs, also antique, also worth thousands. Furniture, cabinetry and trim of teak, ebony, rosewood and mahogany. It had been the most beautiful, most elegant place he'd ever seen. He had lived there six years, and he had hated it.

"That was Jimmy's house, not mine," he said, hearing the odd emptiness in his voice. For years he had never spoken the man's name without the proper respect and deference expected from a loyal employee, with his hatred and obsessive need for revenge carefully hidden. The first year in prison, when he had thought he'd won, he had taken a great deal of pleasure in speaking the name and knowing that he had accomplished what no one else—not Falcone's enemies, not the local police, not even the United States government—could do. Now he felt nothing. Jimmy had won. Nicholas had lost. Again. For the last time.

"Jimmy Falcone, the gangster."

His gaze narrowed just slightly. "For someone new to New Orleans, you certainly seem to know a lot about ancient history."

"What makes you think I'm new to New Orleans?"

"Because I've never met a native or even anyone who's been here a while who talks the way you do." Her accent was definitely of the South, just as definitely not of Louisiana. It was pleasant, though—soft, sweet, like honey on a warm day. Rounded sounds in a voice too feminine for his own good.

With a faint smile and a nod, she acknowledged that he was correct. "I came here about a month ago."

"Why?"

A hint of uneasiness crept into her shrug. "I was looking for someplace different."

"Different from what?"

"From where I used to be. I thought…" Another shrug, more uneasiness. "I thought things would be better here."

Better than what? he wanted to ask, but he already knew her answer. *Than the way they used to be.* How bad could things have been that moving to a new city and taking a job that, according to Jamey, couldn't pay a living wage was better?

Stupid question. He knew from his own experience just how bad things could be. He knew how it felt to be abandoned, alone, unwanted and unloved. He'd been hungry, homeless and utterly hopeless. He'd lived half his life with the sort of grief that ate into a man's soul. Lainie Farrell could have been trying to escape grief, poverty, loneliness or emptiness, trouble with the law, with her family, with a man. Working on Serenity for poverty-level wages wasn't much, but it was an improvement over being homeless and on the hand-out lines or playing punching bag to some drunken bastard's temper. It was better than a great many situations.

Whatever her particular situation was, he didn't want to know. He didn't have the energy to care. "You've learned a lot in a month."

"When someone's the subject of as much gossip as you are, it's easy to learn."

"People talk about me a lot?" He wasn't comfortable with the idea, although he'd expected it. For a time he'd been Serenity's biggest success story. He'd lived in a beautiful house on one of the area's most impressive estates. He'd earned a six-figure income, worn custom-tailored suits and driven cars that cost enough to support two or three families down here for a year. Almost as important, he'd had power. People on Serenity lived their lives knowing they didn't matter. Poverty had left them with no voice. No politician or city official cared about their needs. The people here didn't pay enough in taxes to make their complaints worth listening to. They didn't contribute money to election campaigns or even exercise their right to vote. They were invisible to the government that was supposed to help them.

In the ten years he'd worked for Falcone, Nicholas had never been invisible. Wherever he'd gone, he'd been treated like a man with money and power. Few people, if any, had cared that the money came from criminal enterprises, that the power extended from a major crime boss.

He wished he could be invisible now.

Across the room Lainie shrugged. "You're the most interesting thing that's happened in the neighborhood in months."

He wondered if *she* found him interesting. Her behavior downstairs this afternoon would suggest no, but here she was. She could have delivered Jamey's message and left again, but she seemed comfortable leaning against the door-jamb and talking—as long as they weren't talking about her.

"Where did you live before you came here?" he asked, testing the theory. The shadows that crossed her face proved him right.

She shifted her body so that her hands were tucked between the wood and her back and moved her gaze to a stained spot on the floor. "Georgia."

"What city?"

Another shift, an uneasy look, an unsteady voice. "I grew up in Savannah," she said at last, "but I've lived the last five years in Atlanta."

So awkward. Did she have something to hide, or was he simply stirring up memories that she didn't want to face? He'd had plenty of those of his own. For ten years he'd kept the most important ones locked tightly away, unable to live with the guilt and the sorrow, taking them out only when necessary to shore up the hatred that had kept him going. In prison, once he'd been locked away, he had found it impossible to keep the memories at bay. They had haunted him, tormented him and, eventually, come to comfort him.

"So what do you do over there?" With a backward jerk of his head, he gestured to the house across the street. When Jamey had written a year ago about his marriage, he had mentioned the women's center. Nicholas had figured it was doomed to fail. The residents' resistance to outside interference, combined with the usual vandalism and threats, would surely leave the place boarded up or burned down before it even got open and running, he had thought. Obviously he had been wrong.

"A little bit of everything. I fill in wherever they need help." The edginess gone, she gave him another of those long looks. "If you don't have any plans for the immediate future, they could use a little help from you."

Nicholas Carlucci doing volunteer work at a women's center in his old neighborhood, like some sort of do-gooder, someone with a conscience. Now there was an unlikely image. "I'm no gardener or handyman."

"Good, because those are my jobs. But you *are* a lawyer."

"A lawyer convicted of multiple felonies. A disbarred lawyer."

"They disbarred you. They didn't magically erase your knowledge and understanding of the law. They can't stop you from offering advice for free."

His smile was cynical. "Look at my life. Look at the mess I've made. Would you take advice from me?"

"They say you were one of the best lawyers in the state. There are clients at the center who need better help than they can get through legal aid but don't have the money to pay for it."

He shook his head. "Sorry."

The signs of her annoyance were subtle, but he recognized them—the thinning of her lips, the narrowing of her eyes, the slight cooling of her voice. "Think about it. Maybe you'll change your mind." With that she pushed away from the door, walked out and closed it quietly behind her. A moment later he heard her own door across the hall close.

Change his mind? He didn't think so. He had known

from the moment he'd accepted the first case Jimmy Falcone had brought to him that his legal career would be short. Even if he got his license to practice law reinstated, who would want a lawyer who'd gone from representing the bad guys to being one himself and then betraying them? Decent people wouldn't want his help, and he had no desire to help guilty people. He'd done enough of that with Falcone.

Leaving the window, he went into the bedroom, where he'd spent the better part of the past two weeks, like the past five years, day after day lying on his back, staring at nothing. By now he recognized every water stain above and every lump in the mattress underneath. Thanks to the open windows, he knew the routines of the street by sound alone. He heard the voices of kids going to school, the footsteps of parents going to work, the sound of running water as the flowers in front of O'Shea's were watered, the doors opening downstairs and the slow scrape of the chair as the first customer seated himself.

Now he would have new sounds to listen for. The water running in the bathroom next door. The light tread of footsteps on the stairs. The opening and closing of her door. The sounds of living of Lainie Farrell, with her sleek hair, pouty mouth, nice body and pretty hazel eyes. Right now she was just an intrusion, but she held the potential to become so much more. An annoyance, a threat, a temptation, a danger, a regret.

He sat down on the bed near the night table, and the springs squeaked. The table that wobbled on uneven legs held only two items: an alarm clock that had been flashing the wrong time—*12:00*—since he'd moved in and a photograph of his first temptation, his first regret. It had been taken on the LSU campus in Baton Rouge on a sunny fall day. The color was faded, the clothing dated, but it was his most prized possession. It was the only photograph he had, dated and signed on the back. *Love, Rena.* It had gone with him everywhere, from one apartment to the next in Baton Rouge, from the third-floor walk-up above his first storefront office to a fancier place on the edge of the Garden District to Jimmy's bona fide Southern mansion across the river. To the prison in Alabama and now here, only a few blocks from where he'd started out forty-three long, hard years ago.

Looking at her now with the distance of age, he could admit that she wasn't a great beauty, though he'd thought so at the time. Her hair was brown, long and straight, her nose freckled, her mouth always smiling, her hazel eyes always laughing. She had saved his life the day she had walked up to him on campus and introduced herself. He'd been one frustration away from taking the next bus back to Serenity and living out his life as a failure, but Rena had stopped him. Within a month they were living together. After another month he had asked her to marry him. When he finished law school, she had promised, and she had dropped out of her own classes to make it an easier goal. She had worked two jobs and paid the bills, and he had taken the heaviest class loads the school allowed and studied every spare minute of the day.

But it had been for nothing. He had finished law school, but there'd been no marriage, no kids, no home, no future. By then Rena had been dead for three years, and it had been Nicholas's fault. His and Jimmy Falcone's.

He picked up the picture, holding it as if it were a fragile object that might disintegrate at his touch. In the intervening years he had aged, of course, from time to time noticing another gray hair popping up where before there'd been only black. He was more than twice her age now, old enough to have a daughter her age, but she had been captured in time, forever young, forever beautiful, forever and always the only person who had ever mattered.

Everything he'd done in the last half of his life had been for her. All of it before her death had pleased her. Everything after would have shamed her. In losing her, he had become a man who no longer deserved her. He had dishonored her memory. He had dishonored himself.

And he would do it all over again given the chance.

Lainie slept in late Sunday morning, making up for the long hours she'd stood in darkness at the window last night and stared out over the street. She had watched lights go off in houses and apartment buildings down the block and had seen the kids come out like cockroaches in the night—the teenagers and the young adults whose age qualified them for that description if their actions didn't. A year ago they had congregated in the park, trashing it every night for Karen and her converts to put right every morning, but finally they'd admitted defeat. Now they gathered in the street or on the sidewalks. They had been quiet last night, with none of the loud music, raucous laughter or outbreaks of trouble that had once disturbed everyone's sleep, but they had bothered her all the same.

Working on Serenity had been one thing. She'd been like most of the staff at the center—a nine-to-five soldier. They did their good during daylight hours, coming after the sun was well above the horizon and leaving again before it set, going to their safe homes in their safe neighborhoods and putting Serenity and its problems out of their minds until their next daylight foray.

Living here was totally different. Though circumstances had improved since Ryan Morgan's death last year, there was little safety to be found on Serenity. Those punks on the street last night had chosen to drink beer and talk. They could just as easily have decided to open fire on the darkened apartments around them. They'd done it in the past. There wasn't a person on Serenity who didn't know someone who had died an early and violent death.

Of course, she knew someone, too, and she'd lived in a neighborhood that shared much more in common with New

Orleans' prestigious Garden District than Serenity. But violent death in that neighborhood had been an aberrancy. Here it was a common occurrence.

She sat cross-legged on the bed, a cup of tepid coffee in one hand. Rather than get dressed and go downstairs to make real coffee, she'd settled on hot water from the bathroom and a spoonful of instant crystals. Soon, though, she would dress and venture out. She was going shopping today. She didn't intend to spend a lot of money on the apartment, even if the money wasn't coming out of her own pocket, but, unlike her neighbor, if she was expected to live here for an unspecified period of time, she required a minimum of comfort. That included, at the very least, someplace to sit besides the bed and someplace for her clothes besides the floor. Cassie Donovan had given her directions to a nearby shop that ambitiously called itself Vieux Carré Antiques. What they sold was mostly junk, but the owner was brave enough to deliver, and there were usually decent bargains to be had on furniture, provided a person wasn't too picky.

If Lainie were picky, she wouldn't be living here, job or no job.

After swallowing the last of the coffee, she gathered a complete set of clothes and left the apartment, locking the door behind her. It was a silly gesture, really. The bar downstairs was closed, so there was no one else in the building but Nicholas Carlucci. The chances that he might slip into her apartment while she was in the shower were somewhere between slim and none. Such an act would require interest of a degree that he certainly hadn't displayed. Still, while she'd brought little enough with her yesterday, there was an item or two in her bedroom that she would prefer escaped everyone's attention, especially his.

The bathroom at the end of the brightly painted hallway was long and narrow, with a big, old tub filling more than half the space. The tub was probably original to the room, the shower a later addition. The entire room, also on the receiving end of Cassie's creative attention, was done in white—walls, built-in shelves, trim, floor, everything except the ceiling, which had been painted a lovely sky blue.

She closed and locked the door, then stripped off the white V-necked T that served as a nightshirt. While the water in the tub heated, she inventoried the contents of the shelves that were the only personal items in the room. There was her own makeup, perfume, toiletries and towels—nothing too personal, everything generic or bargain-basement priced. The contents of the higher shelves were no more personal or revealing: Carlucci's toothbrush, toothpaste, shaving cream and a six-pack of bath soap, minus one bar. Shampoo, conditioner, a razor and blades, four neatly folded towels, matching washcloths and a half-empty bottle of aspirin.

Carlucci didn't strike her as a man who got headaches but rather gave them to everyone else.

With a shrug, she pulled the twin white shower curtains around the tub, turned on the shower and stepped inside. On a shelf she found the missing bar of soap and used it to lather her washcloth and her body, trying seriously not to think about whose hands had touched it last, not to acknowledge the odd intimacy in using the same bathroom, the same tub, the same soap.

Showered and shampooed, dried, powdered and dressed, she left the bathroom with the T-shirt in hand and made it less than five feet before realizing that she was being watched. Carlucci's door was open, as if he'd just come upstairs, and he was standing in front of it. As she watched, he slowly shifted, turning to lean one shoulder against the frame. He was dressed in what seemed to be the unofficial uniform of the men of Serenity. While the punks on the street last night had shown a decided preference for trendier styles and colors, the men wore jeans and T-shirts.

And no one did more for snug, faded jeans and close-fitting white T-shirts than Nicholas Carlucci. This wasn't the lawyer of silk suits and leather shoes, of elegant homes, imported cars and high bank balances. This was the rebel. The renegade. The bad boy.

Oh, but he was no boy.

And that was the last thing in the world she needed to notice.

Her feet stopped moving of their own will, and her hand knotted into a fist inside the folds of the T-shirt she carried. She took a deep breath, but it didn't go far. There was a familiar tightness to her chest that kept it from expanding—fear, nerves, self-protection, arousal. Any combination or all of the above.

She reached blindly and found the stair rail, grateful for its support. "Good morning."

He raised one brow slightly. "It's afternoon."

"Then good afternoon." He moved as if to go inside, and she hurriedly spoke again. "I didn't hear you downstairs when I got up."

"Maybe because I wasn't downstairs."

This time it was her turn to lift one brow. "I was under the impression that you never went out."

"You were wrong."

"Maybe. There's a first time for everything." She shrugged. "I was going to stop by before I left. I'm going furniture shopping. I thought you might like..." Almost losing her nerve, she blurted out the rest. "To come along."

For a long moment, his gaze didn't waver from her face. Then, with a semblance of a smile, he looked away. "There you go insulting my apartment again. What's wrong with having just a bed and a table?"

"I guess you got used to the minimalist look in prison."

"There I had a dresser the size of a nightstand, a steel shelf bolted to the wall and a thin, lumpy mattress.

It was about as comfortable as I imagine a slab at the morgue would be. I'm satisfied with what I have now."

There were people out there who wouldn't mind seeing him on a slab at the morgue. That was why she was here—to keep an eye on him. To protect him.

And who was going to protect *her?*

"So you don't mind spending all your time in bed."

There was that odd little gesture again, almost a smile but not quite. "I've spent some damned satisfying hours in bed."

Wrong conversation, she warned herself. This was definitely the wrong tack to take. But she responded anyway. "Alone?"

It was more like a smile this time. "No, not alone. But the current situation is temporary. Like I said yesterday, it'll change in time."

All in good time. That was exactly what he'd said. Four innocent words that had nothing to do with her, and yet they had made her hot, shivery and uneasy.

"Where is this place?"

For a moment she looked blankly at him, the question not registering. With a slow blink, she gave him the name and general location of the store.

"Let me know when you're ready. It can't hurt to look." Without waiting for a response, he went inside the apartment and closed the door.

Lainie stood there, taking short, shallow breaths until the tightness in her chest eased, then forced herself to move one step at a time into her own apartment. Before she'd ever set foot outside Atlanta, she had been warned that Carlucci was handsome as sin, devilishly sexy and hard to resist. It hadn't taken ten seconds the day he'd come walking down the street with his bag to know the warning was based in fact. She had just somehow expected to be immune. After all, this was business, and she never let pleasure interfere. Besides, she wasn't some giddy, eager, easily impressed young woman. She'd had her share of exciting, reckless and hopelessly doomed relationships, but those days were long behind her, and the days for an affair with an ex-con mob lawyer who had stood for everything she stood against would never come.

She had no cause for worry. Every woman at Kathy's House, happily married or not, had entertained at least one lustful thought since he'd come, and not one of them besides Karen had even gotten close enough to speak to him. Not one of them was living across the hall from him in what was turning out to be more intimate circumstances than she'd expected.

Besides, she was hardly the sort of woman a man like him would turn to to break a five-year sentence of celibacy. No doubt he had a little black book overflowing with the numbers of women who were his type—wild, wicked and reckless. She, on the other hand, was settled, far from daring and too much effort for the results. And then there was her job. Behavior that was the least bit inappropriate would earn her a reprimand. Something so outrageous as an affair would mean the end of the career she had worked so hard for. She was mature enough to know that the best sex in the world wasn't worth losing her job.

Once again in control of her wayward emotions, she put on shoes and socks, then tucked a wad of cash into her pocket. Kneeling on the floor, she reached inside the hidden compartment in the bottom of her backpack and pulled out a compact .22 Beretta. It was smaller than what she was used to, but a good little gun, especially easy to conceal. She tucked the clip-on holster inside her jeans at the small of her back, then pulled her shirt down to cover it as she left the apartment.

Across the hall, she knocked at Carlucci's door. He was waiting. They left the apartment and covered half the distance to Decatur before he broke the silence. His question picked up the conversation they'd begun in his apartment yesterday afternoon as naturally as if eighteen hours hadn't passed since then.

"Who did you leave behind in Atlanta?"

"Nobody." She had plenty of friends in the city—co-workers, neighbors, people she'd met here or there over the years. She never spent an evening alone unless she wanted to, never ate a meal alone unless it was her choice. Whatever she might want, all she had to do was pick up the phone and call, and someone would be waiting. But none of them would really miss her while she was gone, and when she left the city permanently, as was bound to happen with the job, she wouldn't keep in touch with any of them.

"Nobody, huh? Have you ever been married?"

"Once. You can't imagine how depressing it was to wake up the morning after and realize what a tremendous mistake I'd made."

"I don't imagine it was much different from waking up my first morning in prison."

He was being polite—a quality she somehow hadn't expected. There was no way she could compare her unhappiness with her marriage to his prison term. She had given up only a small part of her freedom—the rights to see other men and think only of herself—while he'd been locked up for five years in a cage that most people wouldn't consider adequate for a dog. She'd been free to go where she wanted, to do what she wanted, to seek a divorce or try to make the marriage work, and she'd still had her job. Her work had gotten her through the tough parts—the realization that the marriage *couldn't* work, the recriminations, the divorce.

Five years later she had come close to repeating the same mistake, as close as two weeks before the scheduled ceremony. Maybe she'd just had two bouts of bad luck, or maybe it was some flaw in her character. Maybe she was one of those women that were often the subjects of psychobabble self-help books. *Women Who Can't Recognize a Loser Until It's Too Late.*

Or maybe she'd just inherited the problem from her mother.

"How long did it last?"

"Four years."

"No kids?"

"We were spared that," she said, making her voice extra dry to hide the fact that she had wanted children. Her chances of having them were getting slimmer every day. At the end of this year she would turn forty. Her biological clock would turn into a high-speed countdown timer, and there wasn't a likely candidate for fatherhood anywhere in sight.

"Where's the ex-husband?"

"Last I heard, in Florida."

"What about friends?"

Her shrug was careless. "I had some."

"Family?"

"I had one of those, too." They reached the end of Serenity and turned onto Decatur and toward the more recognizable, tourist-oriented part of the French Quarter. Tucking her hands into her pockets, she answered the questions he was sure to ask. "My father still lives in Savannah. I haven't seen him in more than twenty years. I have an older brother whom I haven't seen in twenty-five years. As for my mother..." She paused for a fortifying breath. "She's dead. She died when I was fourteen."

"I'm sorry." It was a perfunctory response, neither sincere nor insincere.

"What about your family?" She already knew the bare bones of his background—that his mother hadn't been married, that his father was listed as unknown on his birth certificate, that she'd abandoned him to the charity of the Catholic church that still stood, long empty and crumbling, on Divinity, one of the three main streets that made up the neighborhood of Serenity.

"You mean there's something the gossips actually left out?"

"Maybe I just didn't get to listen long enough. I do have to work, you know."

He remained silent so long that she'd decided he wasn't going to answer. Now there was a response that hadn't occurred to her when she'd been on the receiving end of his questions. Maybe it was because she knew he'd been a lawyer, and lawyers naturally expected answers. Maybe it had more to do with her own job. Like a lawyer, she was accustomed to asking questions, not answering them. Maybe the novelty of the turnaround had prompted her to answer. Or maybe—

"When I was in first grade, my mother got me up every morning, fixed oatmeal with brown sugar and orange juice for breakfast and walked me to school before she went to work. She was a maid at a hotel over on Bienville Street. She worked long hours for very little money." Another silence. "One Wednesday morning, the second week of November, she got me up, fed me and told me to go to St. Jude's after school. She kissed me and went off to work, and I never saw her again."

"What happened then?"

"I lived at St. Jude's off and on until I was eighteen."

"What about your mother's family?"

"Her mother died years before I was born. I never met her father." His smile was cynical and dark. "Tomaso Carlucci was a God-fearing man who condemned sinners wherever he found them. He threw my mother out when he found out that she was pregnant, and he had nothing to do with her again."

"So she came here from… Where did they live?"

"Here. New Orleans. About six miles across town."

They stopped to wait for a green light to cross a busy

street, and she looked wide-eyed at him. "You lived six miles from your grandfather and never met him? They never asked him to take custody of you? You never confronted him when you were older?"

"Why would I want to meet him? He turned his pregnant, eighteen-year-old daughter out on the street with no money, no place to go and no skills for a job. Why would I want to know someone like that?" He gave her an up-and-down look that was cynical, at best. "Why the shock that I never wanted to meet a man who, blood ties aside, is a stranger who means nothing to me? You just admitted that you haven't seen your father in twenty years. Did you live with him?"

"Until I was eighteen."

"Did he support you?"

Her only answer was a raising of one brow.

"He's not a stranger. You *know* him. But you don't have anything to do with him. Why?"

The light had changed, and people were pushing around them to cross the street. Neither of them moved, though. They continued to stare at each other. His eyes were dark, his mouth thinned, and her nerves were taut. "I avoid him *because* I know him."

"Oh, come on, he's your father," he mocked. "What could he have done to deserve the cold shoulder from his only daughter?"

She looked away to see the light turn yellow and the crosswalk sign flashing Don't Walk. She stepped off the curb anyway, looking back to answer before she darted across the street. "He killed my mother."

Chapter 2

By the time Nicholas caught up with her, she was passing their destination. He dodged a tourist, caught Lainie's arm and turned her to face him. There were a half-dozen questions he was about to ask, but the stubborn, defensive look on her face indicated that she expected as much. Instead he immediately released her. "You missed the store."

He saw the surprise in her eyes that he'd let the subject drop. Then her gaze shifted past him to the business one door back and, without a word, she walked back, pulled the door open and went inside.

There was a very good reason he hadn't pressed for more information regarding her mother's death, and it had nothing to do with the fact that she obviously didn't want to discuss it. The simple truth was he didn't care. As one child who'd grown up motherless to another, he could say he was sorry, but on a personal level, he just didn't care. It meant nothing to him. *She* meant nothing to him. Hell, he didn't know anything about her except that she was a problem he didn't need…and she had those eyes. Pretty hazel eyes.

Scowling, he retraced his steps to the entrance of Vieux Carré Antiques. It was in the middle of the block, a narrow storefront that extended all the way to the street behind, and every inch of its interior was packed. It smelled of dust, must and strong solvents and reminded him too strongly of St. Jude's. In his time there, he had thoroughly explored the church and rectory, sometimes with Jamey, usually alone, and he had discovered all kinds of dusty, unused, unwelcoming places. Of course, the whole church had been unwelcoming to him. Father Francis hadn't been much different from Tomaso. He had judged the sinner as well as the sin—and, in Nicholas's case, the result of the sin. He had demanded retribution and penance and had offered precious little forgiveness in return.

Although he saw Lainie one aisle over and forty feet down, he didn't head in that direction. He wandered instead around the perimeter of the store, skimming over the merchandise stacked ceiling high. One man's trash was another man's treasure…rather, another woman's treasure, he amended as he rounded a corner and nearly bumped into a shapely blonde kneeling there. Working on papers spread over the wood floor, she was applying stripper to a small table. She glanced up and smiled when she became aware of him. "Hi. Find anything you like?"

Though he doubted that she intended her simple question to come off as a come-on, it did. Her smile was sultry, her gaze beckoning, her voice low and smooth, like the rustle of bedsheets against skin. He was tempted to offer his own come-on, bluntly phrased and straight to the point. *I think I like you. Show me to a bed and let's find out.* That was one sure way to find out if the invitation was deliberate. If sexy and sensual were just normal for her, she wouldn't hesitate to set him straight. But if that was interest in her eyes… Hell, she wasn't his type—if he even knew after so many years alone what his type was—but she was pretty, and if she were willing, he would certainly be able.

With a faint smile and a shake of his head, he moved on. He'd been *able* for a little over two weeks now. For five years he had thought that was the first thing he would do when he walked through those doors: find a woman, any woman, and not come up for air for, oh, a month or so. In fact, he had spent his first evening of freedom in an Alabama bar with just that in mind. The place had been full of women pretty enough to make him notice and willing enough to tempt him, but when he'd gone to his room at the motel next door, he had gone alone. Back here in New Orleans, where he could pick up the phone and have his pick of women in a matter of minutes, he was still alone. He wasn't sure what he was waiting for. He wanted sex, not a relationship, not even a meaningful experience. Just sex. All he needed was a warm body, and there were plenty of those around.

But he was still waiting, and damned if he knew why.

Turning another corner, he saw Lainie a few yards ahead, standing in front of a dresser, a thoughtful look on her face. He stopped a foot or so behind her and repeated the blonde's question. "Find something you like?" He asked it without the same risk. It wasn't likely she would offer a suggestive answer, wasn't likely the thought of sharing a bed with him had ever entered her mind.

Although now, damn his own thoughts, he might never get it *out* of his mind.

"Yeah." Her tone was absentminded as she studied the piece. "It looks kind of awful, but... I like marble."

The dresser was old, much abused but well made. It had four drawers, two on each side, a low shelf that joined them, an intricately shaped mirror and serpentine marble tops. The piece did look awful. It had been painted so many times that the cheval mirror was locked in place and the drawers no longer closed completely. The top layer of paint was white, and where it had flaked off, shades of green, brown and electric blue showed.

Stepping around her, he flipped the price tag over. "Not a bad price if you don't mind the paint or a lot of work."

She didn't interrupt her inspection to reply. As long as she was preoccupied, he took the opportunity for a look of his own. She was dressed in jeans that fitted comfortably but not too snug and a heavy cotton polo shirt in bright yellow, and her hair... Well, hell, there was nothing different she could do with it. As short as it was, it lay one way, and that was it. Not many women had the bone structure to carry off such a severe cut—the pretty blonde back there didn't—but the style flattered Lainie. It gave her a wide-eyed innocent look...but she was no innocent.

She was tall, five-eight, maybe five-nine, and all curves—full breasts, narrow waist, rounded hips. Hers was the sort of body that enticed a man, that promised every pleasure known to man and delivered every wicked one.

Damn, but it'd been a long time since he'd experienced that kind of wicked.

Maybe that was what he wanted: not just sex, but *great* sex. Maybe he wanted that first time of breaking his abstinence streak to be truly memorable—wild, wicked, reckless, dangerous, damn-near-die-before-it-was-over sex. If so, he knew exactly who to call.

And it wasn't Lainie Farrell.

Why did that knowledge disappoint him just a little?

"All right," she said, pulling him back from a thought he didn't want to explore. "I'll take it. Now I need a sofa."

She wandered away, and he followed her. By the time she finished, she'd bought the dresser, a sofa, a chair and a couple of small tables, all for under seventy-five dollars. After giving her address to the blonde, she led the way outside and they headed back toward Serenity. At the first stoplight—the same intersection where she'd dropped her bombshell about her mother, then slipped off—she turned an even gaze on him and dropped another. "Can I ask you something?"

"Nothing's stopped you yet."

"Is it true that Jimmy Falcone threatened to kill you if you came back to New Orleans?"

Stiffening uncomfortably, he turned to watch the Sunday afternoon traffic. By rights, only three people should know about the threat: the man who'd made it, Jimmy; the man who'd delivered it to Nicholas while he was still in prison, Vince Cortese; and Nicholas himself. Nicholas hadn't told anyone, but the U.S. Attorney knew. The FBI knew. People on Serenity knew. That meant Jimmy was talking, and if he was talking, it meant he was serious about the threat. Nicholas's five years in prison wasn't enough to satisfy him. He intended to make an example of Nicholas, to use him to show everyone else what happened when you crossed Jimmy Falcone.

Smith Kendricks and Remy Sinclair had come to Alabama two days after Nicholas's visit from Vince. They had advised him not to return to the city, and when he had insisted, they had offered him protection. All these years they'd been after Jimmy, and they still didn't understand his one rule of business: nothing kept the old man from his goals. If he wanted Nicholas dead, it would happen. Maybe not right away, maybe not in six months or even six years. Hell, as warped as Falcone was, he would enjoy dragging it out. He would take great pleasure in keeping Nicholas wondering day after day, month after month, if this was the time he would die. It would double his enjoyment to give Nicholas time to adjust to life on the outside, to maybe find a job and a place to belong, maybe even someone to belong to, to lull him into thinking that the old man had forgotten him, to wait until he was in a position where he had something to lose and then strike.

Would it disappoint Jimmy if he knew that Nicholas wasn't anticipating the worst, that he didn't look over his shoulder every time he went out for a familiar face or an unfamiliar threat? If he knew that Nicholas was never going to have anything more to lose than he had right now? If he knew that his target didn't much care whether they killed him? If they killed him, they killed him. And if they didn't...

Sometimes he thought that would be the crueler of Jimmy's choices.

"Yeah," he said at last, settling his gaze on her. "He said something to that effect."

"So why did you come back?"

"I didn't have anyplace else to go."

"There's a whole country out there."

"Not for me. This is my home."

"What if your presence here puts other people in danger—Jamey and Karen, Reid and Cassie?"

You, he wanted to add. If anyone was in danger because of him, it was the neighbor five feet across the hall, the woman standing right beside him on a public street corner. Some of Jimmy's best work had been done on public streets. But that was a big *if.* "This thing with Jimmy is personal. He's not going to do something reckless like have his men open fire on a crowd of people hoping to get me. He'll want to do the job himself. He usually does when it's personal."

"You know his preferred methods of killing." Her voice trembled just a bit, and there was a shade less color in her face than before. He regretted reminding her of exactly what he was.

"I worked for him for ten years." His words were clipped, his manner deliberately distancing. "I know."

"You helped him get away with murder, and then you betrayed him. Why?"

Jolie Wade had asked that question. So had Smith Kendricks, Remy Sinclair and Vince Cortese. Nicholas had had only one answer, and he'd given it—part of it—five years

ago to Jolie and Smith: because Falcone had killed someone. That was all he'd told them, but he suspected that they
had guessed it was a woman. Jolie had known him so
well—more intimately than any other woman but one—and
Kendricks had just started looking at her exactly the way
Nicholas used to look at Rena.

Why? He could tell Lainie Farrell what he had never told
anyone else. That he had decided one rainy night in Baton
Rouge that he would bring down Jimmy Falcone or die
trying. That he had deliberately cultivated clients in his
practice that would catch Falcone's attention. That the job
with Falcone had been a vital part of his plan. That he had
made a conscious decision to temporarily become everything he despised in order to destroy it. That he'd done
things he wasn't proud of, but in his mind, the end had
justified the means. That, in effect, he had been undercover,
pretending to be something he wasn't in order to gather
evidence to punish a major criminal.

His smile was thin and mocking. Right. Like she would
really accept that.

He didn't need to tell Lainie Farrell anything. He didn't
make excuses. He didn't try to justify what he'd done or
to win sympathy. He had committed crimes, had bribed and
threatened witnesses. He had fabricated alibis and testimony, had dug up dirt used to blackmail judges and cops,
had lived a life of lavish comfort paid for by Jimmy's trade
in drugs, prostitution, protection and gambling. For ten
years he had been just as dirty as everyone believed. The
circumstances of Rena's death didn't change any of that.

"It was the best job offer I had. Good pay, good hours,
good benefits."

"If it was such a great offer, why did you turn on him?"

Tired of the conversation, he gave her a weary look.
"Maybe I just got tired of the games. Maybe I got tired of
looking at myself in the mirror every morning. Maybe I

wanted to give the government a fighting chance. Maybe—''

"Maybe you got tired of living."

He looked at her, so serious and still. "Maybe I'm tired of talking about it. If you're worried about your safety, don't be. Jimmy tries to avoid killing innocent bystanders whenever possible." Though sometimes it happened anyway. "If I thought I was putting anyone else in danger, I would leave Serenity. But I honestly don't believe that's true." Before she could start to relax, he added one last warning. "A word of advice, though. If you ever see me leaving O'Shea's with a couple of guys bigger than me, try not to look too closely at their faces. You wouldn't want to be a witness against Jimmy. Trust me."

"How's it going with Nick?"

Lainie looked up as Karen O'Shea slid onto the picnic bench beside her. She and Nicholas had been almost home when Jamey had called to them from across the street, inviting them both to join the family in the backyard. She would have preferred going straight upstairs to the apartment, but she had followed Nicholas across the street and around to the back. Sunday dinners were an O'Shea tradition, cookouts when the weather permitted. Today's had included Luke Russell, the minister, and now them.

She didn't answer Karen's question immediately, but instead focused on the name she'd used. "Everyone calls him something different, don't they?"

"Jamey calls him Nicky—but what can you expect from a grown man who goes by Jamey?" Karen grinned. "I picked up Nick from Reid, I guess. I'm certainly not about to call him Nicky, and calling him Carlucci seems just a little unsociable. What about you?"

"Nicholas," Lainie replied absently as her gaze slipped across the yard to where the men were gathered in the shade of a giant live oak. "It suits him."

"So answer my question. How are you two getting along?"

"Fine."

Her boss gave her a pouting look. "You're living across the hall from Mr. Tall, Dark and Dangerously Sexy, and that's all you have to say?"

On the other side of the table, Cassie Donovan stepped over the bench and sat down, settling Sean on the table in front of her. "You're a married woman and a mother now, Karen. You're not supposed to even notice tall, dark and dangerously sexy."

"I'm married, not dead," the redhead retorted. "Can you honestly tell me that you haven't looked, too?"

Cassie's smile was serene and sweet. "I outgrew dark and dangerous when I was a child. Frankly I don't see what the fuss is. Yes, he's handsome, but so is Jamey." The smile grew sweeter. "So is Reid."

Karen dismissed her opinion with a wave of one hand. "Newlyweds. So, Lainie, where did you guys go this afternoon?"

"To the antique store Cassie recommended." Lainie scraped a bit of fudge frosting from the plate that had held her walnut brownie and licked it from her finger. She and Nicholas had been too late for the burgers, but there had been enough leftover potato salad, baked beans and brownies to make a meal. "I found this great old dresser. It needs a ton of work, but it's got serpentine marble that's in excellent condition. I got some other stuff, too. It's supposed to be delivered tomorrow, so I guess I'll turn my living room into a workshop for a while."

"And live with those fumes?" Karen wrinkled her nose. "Maybe you should wait until you're better friends with your neighbor so you'll have a place to escape to."

Cassie mimicked her mother-in-law's earlier dismissive tone and wave. "Matchmakers."

Lainie's gaze drifted across the yard to the live oak once

again. There was no match to be made between her and Nicholas. If she ever married again, which she doubted, it would be to someone very much like her. Someone respectable and law-abiding. Someone she could introduce to her co-workers, whose mere presence in her life wouldn't mean the loss of her job. Someone who lacked even a passing familiarity with violence. It would be to someone she could reasonably count on growing old with, who would give a damn if his life was threatened, who would never stubbornly tempt fate—and Jimmy Falcone.

On the other hand, if she was looking for an affair, she would have to vote with Karen. Nicholas was dark, handsome, dangerous and sexy. Even in a group of gorgeous men, he stood out as the handsomest, the darkest, the most sensual. The way he moved, the way he talked, the way he listened, the way his eyes got so intense... If she weren't such a sensible woman, if her job weren't too important to lose, she would be no different than every other woman whose fantasies he inspired.

But she was sensible and her career was important, and she seriously needed a little of Cassie's he's-handsome-so-what? attitude.

Still, not just yet, a wicked voice pleaded as he looked up and met her gaze. For a long moment he simply looked at her, his expression enigmatic. He didn't smile, nod or acknowledge her in any way. He simply looked, and under the weight of his gaze, she grew warm. Her mouth turned dry, and she reached blindly for the soda in front of her, knocking it over. Finally, as Cassie lifted the baby away from the encroaching pool of cola and Karen grabbed for napkins to blot it, Nicholas responded—not with a real smile, just the suggestion of one, barely lifting the corners of his mouth, revealed more fully in his eyes—and then turned back to the men around him.

Lainie sat motionless, forcing deep breaths of air into her lungs, as Karen cleaned the mess she'd made and Cassie

talked softly with Sean. Sensible. She was sensible, right?
Thirty-nine going on forty. A career woman. Survivor of a
bad marriage, a worse divorce and an awful engagement.
Sensible, levelheaded, responsible and smart, not ruled by
hormones since she was twenty-four years old.

Now she was remembering how it had felt.

Belatedly reaching for napkins, she forced her attention
away from Nicholas and helped soak up the last of the soda.
After piling the soggy napkins high on her plate, she accepted the replacement soda Karen offered with a sheepish
thanks and an apology.

"Forget it," Karen said breezily. "We're used to spills,
aren't we, Sean?"

At the mention of his name, the baby looked up from
the necklace he was trying to tug from Cassie's neck and
gave his mother a smile sweet enough to melt the coldest
heart. Maybe there was still a chance for her, Lainie
thought. If she couldn't have her own children, maybe she
could adopt. She made a good income. She was respectable,
well liked by her colleagues, depended on by her neighbors
and friends. She didn't have anything to offer in the way
of family, just a father she would never let near any child
of hers and a brother who'd left home only days after their
mother's funeral, but she could compensate.

It had been so long since she'd seen Scott that sometimes
she almost forgot his existence. He'd been only seventeen
when he'd taken off, troubled, angry and bitter. Occasionally she let herself wonder what kind of man he'd grown
into—if he had, in fact, lived long enough to become a
man. Had he turned out like their father? Did a troubled,
angry, bitter child on his own have much hope of anything
better?

Maybe. By all reports, Reid's early years had been much
more difficult than Scott's. Born into a marriage that never
should have been, he'd always been poor, always unwanted, always surrounded by the criminal element. His

mother had taken him off to Atlanta when he was just an infant, where she had neglected and abused him for years before abandoning him practically on the doorstep of the father she'd taught him to hate. By his sixteenth birthday, he had been homeless, left to fend for himself in a world that didn't give a damn. It was no wonder that he'd joined the toughest gang on Serenity. It was a great wonder that he hadn't ended up in prison or dead, and nothing short of a miracle that he was now a happily married, responsible, productive member of the community.

Maybe Scott had been as lucky. Maybe he was married, happy and raising children who adored him.

Or maybe he was in prison or dead.

She had tried to find him, had exhausted every resource open to her and learned nothing. He could have changed his name or left the country. Any one of the countless dangers that faced runaway kids could have befallen him. He could be a John Doe in a pauper's grave anywhere in the country. He could be a skeleton in an unmarked grave somewhere.

The night he'd left Savannah, she had begged him to write to her. Losing both him and their mother had been too much to bear. She'd needed contact with him, even if it was only a card from time to time. But he had refused. She'd had no privacy from their father. The risk of his learning Scott's whereabouts was too great, her brother had insisted before he'd kissed her, told her he loved her, then slipped out of her life.

One more reason to hate Frank Ravenel.

"You look like you're a million miles away."

Lainie blinked and found Karen and Cassie watching her. She gave them a wan smile. "Just a thousand or so." She stood, climbed over the bench, then rested her hand on Karen's shoulder. "Thanks for the lunch. I think I'll head home now."

Her boss didn't ask her to stay longer, although she looked as if she wanted to. "See you tomorrow."

Cassie said goodbye, and Sean gave her a sloppy kiss on the cheek, but the men didn't notice her leaving. Not that she wanted them to, of course. Not that she wanted Nicholas to.

The front gate squeaked as she closed it behind her, then she stood for a moment on the sidewalk. She could go right, leave Serenity and take in the sights and sounds of the French Quarter, pretending to be just a tourist without a care in the world beyond squeezing all of New Orleans into one short vacation. She could go across the street to O'Shea's and spend the rest of the day alone in a bare apartment with no television to watch, no radio to play, nothing to read and less to do.

She turned to her left, toward the park, and walked with her hands in her pockets, her gaze shifting frequently from the broken, uneven sidewalk in front of her and the buildings on either side. She hadn't gotten more than a block when her steps slowed as three men came out of a house on the left and started down the sidewalk. They slowed, too, pacing themselves so that they would reach the car parked on the street an instant before she did. If she crossed the street to avoid them, they would move more quickly to cut her off. If she turned around and started for home, they would follow her.

She had been warned about them before she came to Serenity and again on her first day. Such warnings were a standard part of the welcome-to-Kathy's-House speech that Karen delivered. The one in the middle was Vinnie Marino. Big, ugly and more than a little sociopathic, he had taken over Falcone's business down here after Ryan Morgan had turned up dead of a gunshot to the head. It was rumored that Marino had been the one to carry out Ryan's execution, but no evidence supported the theory. Of course, when Falcone was involved, evidence was hard to find.

Beside him was Ryan's younger brother, Trevor. He was twenty-two, good-looking and proof of the adage that appearances could be deceiving. For all his youthful innocence, Trevor was nothing but a thug. Whatever decency the kid had possessed had been lost after his brother's murder. He was as coldhearted as they came.

Tommy Murphy walked a few paces behind them. As criminals went, he was strictly small-time—petty larceny, an occasional assault, an even less occasional auto theft. As people went, he was small-time, too, with no goals, no plans or aspirations. He was perfectly satisfied being nobody.

They stopped side by side, blocking the sidewalk and facing her. Lainie knew it would be a mistake to try to avoid them by going into the street, so, drawing a deep breath for courage, she continued walking, keeping her pace slow and steady, finally coming to a stop a few feet in front of Marino.

His blue gaze locked with hers, he grinned. "You're new around here, aren't you?"

"She's one of those do-gooders over at the women's place," Murphy announced.

"Oh, darlin', you could do me some good. Why don't we go someplace private and let Vinnie welcome you to the neighborhood?"

He raised his hand, and Lainie knew he was going to stroke her hair and probably a whole lot more. She thought of the gun tucked in her waistband and knew that each of them most likely had bigger, deadlier guns with more shots and hotter loads tucked in their holsters, along with whatever other weapons they liked. Morgan, it was known, was handy with a knife and usually had at least one within reach.

Moving quickly before he could touch her, she grabbed Marino's hand, pulled his arm out straight and bent his wrist back. Twisting his arm to put pressure on the elbow, she forced him to his knees, then bent closer. "Let me do you some good," she agreed, her voice soft and pleasant. "Let me warn you that the next time you try to touch me, I'll break your wrist *and* your arm *and* your elbow. You try it again after that, I might be forced to really hurt you." She gave his wrist one hard turn for good measure, making him yelp in pain, then let go, stepped over his legs and, with a shaky, silent breath, walked away.

Nicholas leaned against a dusty, empty storefront on the corner and watched Vinnie Marino struggle to his feet, turn to yell an obscenity at Lainie, who pretended not to notice, then give Tommy Murphy a shove that lifted him onto the hood of the car. For a moment, when he'd first seen the men block her way, he'd thought it was lucky for Lainie that he'd followed her from Jamey's. Serenity's streets were usually safe during daylight hours, according to Jamey, but there was always the odd incident. So much for luck, though. She hadn't needed his help.

Which made this incident odder than most.

Women didn't stand up to Vinnie Marino and walk away unscathed. If he had the brains, Marino would be another Jimmy Falcone in the making. He had no respect for human life and no concern for right or wrong. He took what he wanted, property or people, and damned if they didn't want to be taken. He was the coldest, meanest bastard around—sometimes too cold and mean even for Jimmy. Five years ago the old man had considered Vinnie a problem that would eventually have to be dealt with. It didn't seem the problem was any more under control now than it had been.

The car drove by slowly, Marino giving him a nod of acknowledgment, one ex-con to another. One soulless bastard to another. The simple gesture left a bad taste in Nicholas's mouth.

Once they were out of sight, he crossed the street and

followed Lainie to the park. He expected to find her sitting on one of the benches, but instead she was on her knees beside the flower beds that rimmed the mortared walls supporting the wrought-iron fence. She was pinching off dead blossoms and pulling weeds that had sprouted through the pine bark mulch.

"Nice move."

Her only response was a steady glance.

He walked through the gate and followed stepping stones to the nearest bench, sitting on the back, resting his feet on the seat. The position allowed him a clear view of her left profile. "It's a cop thing, you know. Called a wrist lock."

"It's a self-defense thing called doing whatever works."

Although he'd never known anyone who wasn't a cop to use it, she was probably right. It was an easy technique that required only speed. Size and strength were irrelevant. A slender woman could use it on a man twice her size with satisfying results, as Lainie had just demonstrated. "Why did you find it necessary to take a self-defense course?"

She pulled one last weed, then turned around to sit on the ground facing him. "I'm a woman."

And women were victims. It was a simple, sad fact of life, especially with people like Vinnie Marino. With people like her ex-husband? Maybe her father? "Next time he won't give you a chance to take him down."

"Then I'll pop his eyeball out. Or I'll give him a blast of pepper spray."

"Or you could just try to avoid him."

She drew her knees up and clasped her hands around her legs. "What are you doing here? I thought you were talking with Jamey and the others."

He *had* been talking to Jamey and his guests and thinking that it wasn't a half bad way to spend a Sunday afternoon. Then she had left, and it sounded sappy, but suddenly standing under the old tree discussing Serenity's woes and ways to alleviate them hadn't seemed so interesting anymore. He had wanted to know where she was going and why. So he had followed her—to her advantage, he'd thought when Marino had confronted her. To his own advantage, he knew now as he watched her sitting in the sun.

Instead of answering her question, he looked around the park. It was a large lot, with the brick walls of neighboring apartment houses forming two sides, a free-standing brick wall across the back and the iron fence in front. The back wall was painted with a mural of familiar places—the Serenity he had grown up on. The artwork had been provided by Reid, the images probably by Jamey.

"There used to be a house here. It burned down when I was a kid," he remarked, remembering not the house but its destruction. The fire had been spectacular, a better show by far than the fireworks displays his mother had once taken him to see. He'd stood on the porch of their apartment house down the street, listened to the sirens of the fire engines and watched the flames light up the night. "The owners walked away from the place, and the parents decided to claim it for a park."

"The owners took their insurance money and found a better life."

He gave her a curious look. "Maybe everyone has insurance where you come from, but not here. I guarantee you there's not a place in this neighborhood with insurance. No one can afford it."

Her face turned pink at his mild rebuke. Maybe she was having a run of bad luck now—unable to find a job with decent wages, living in a plain apartment in a shabby building in a low-income, high-crime neighborhood, her life reduced to whatever she could carry in two gym bags and a backpack—but she hadn't always been down. She was accustomed to better circumstances. Whatever she'd done in Atlanta, whoever she'd been, Serenity was a big step down.

"The adults did most of the work on this place, but the kids helped. We cleaned it up, planted grass, put in benches and the swings. It was the only place on the street that had grass. The littler kids had never seen it before. They had always played in the dirt and the street.'' He wondered if she had any idea how dismayed her expression was. ''Bet you had a lot of grass back in Savannah.''

''Savannah has its poor neighborhoods just like everywhere else.''

''But you didn't live in one of them.''

''No,'' she admitted. ''We had a big house on one of the squares. It had been in my mother's family for generations.''

And now her father had it. Her father who, she claimed, killed her mother. The knowledge couldn't be easy for her to live with.

''She never had a job outside the house. He wouldn't hear of it,'' she went on, derision underlying her voice. ''But I was glad, because she was always there when we came home from school. She was active in all the usual clubs and did volunteer work at the hospital, the museum and our schools, but first and foremost she was a wife. Her most important job was keeping my father happy, and with a man like him, that was never an easy job. Her favorite job, after being a mother, was gardening. We always had the prettiest yard on the square. To my father that was woman's work, which he was above, so he never bothered her there. I spent hundreds of hours working with her, digging, planting, weeding, talking.''

She fell silent, and Nicholas looked away. When she'd announced on the street corner this afternoon that her father had killed her mother, he had wanted to hear the details. He had followed her, intending to ask as many questions as were needed to get the answers. Now that she was talking willingly, he didn't want to listen. He didn't want to know even one of her sad stories. Hadn't that been his policy for fifteen years? *Don't get involved. Don't let anyone touch you. Don't give a damn.*

But he did want to know just this one too-personal story. Then no more.

"My father was very demanding. He had very rigid ideas of appropriate behavior, dress, interests, activities. My mother was an easy target for him. She'd been taught since she was a child that a woman's first priority was always her husband, that he was always right, that if she didn't please him, the failure was always hers. Of course, he was impossible to please. Nothing she did, nothing my brother did, was ever right. The only peace she ever found was in the garden. The only peace for my brother was away from the house."

She rolled onto her knees and went back to work weeding and deadheading the flowers, making two neat piles in the grass. Nicholas watched them grow, weeds in one pile, faded orange and gold flowers in the other, while he waited for her to go on. He didn't prompt her, didn't urge her to rush on with a story that was difficult to tell. He'd learned that in his early days as an attorney. There was a time to nudge, a time to ask questions, a time to draw the details out, and there was a time to keep your mouth shut and wait. This was one of those times.

When she reached the end of the bed, she got to her feet, dusted her hands and looked around. He expected her to head for the back corner and its L-shaped brick planter, but instead she came around behind the bench and leaned against it. "The spring I was fourteen, we spent every free hour working in the garden. My mother was pretty easygoing about most things, but with gardening, she believed in all or nothing. We dug up the beds, tested and amended the soil, drew up plans, laid out plots. We put in hundreds of bedding plants, plus roses, azaleas, wisterias, jasmines, honeysuckles and forsythias. When we finished one Sunday evening, we had this beautiful garden that filled the entire yard, front and back. It was our best effort ever. That night she had yet another run-in with my father, with lots of screaming, yelling and hitting. The next morning, while my brother and I were in school and our father was at work, she went into the garden with a cup of tea and an overdose of barbiturates. I found her slumped on the bench there when I got home."

So her father had made her mother's life so miserable that the only way she could cope was by ending it, leaving her children to live with the man she could no longer bear to live with. It had been a selfish solution, but maybe, for her, it had been the only solution. Just as leaving a six-year-old child in the care of a mean-spirited, coldhearted priest must have been the only solution Maria Carlucci could find to her problems.

Now he knew more about Lainie Farrell than he wanted to know.

Maybe.

"You said your father hit your mother. Did he hit you?"

She smiled, but there was nothing pleasant about it. "Oh, no. I was Daddy's little girl. Scott could do nothing right. I could do no wrong. Even when I did something wrong, I was never punished." She paused, then offered an example. "We were never allowed in our father's study, but one morning I went in there anyway. While playing, I broke a decanter of scotch on his desk. I panicked. I didn't tell anyone, didn't clean it up, just ran out and closed the door. When my father discovered the mess a few days later, he was livid. The decanter was antique crystal, the scotch old and expensive. The papers on his desk were soaked, the leather desk pad was ruined, and the desk... Mahogany. Two hundred years old. Worth a fortune." The smile grew tense, then faltered. "He blamed Scott. Even though I told him I did it, he didn't believe me. If my mother hadn't stopped him... I thought he was going to kill Scott."

And how had she stopped him? Nicholas wondered. By deflecting the brunt of his rage on herself? By letting him

beat her instead of her son? How hard had that been for
Lainie to live with?

Hard. Though it hadn't been her fault—she had admitted
the truth and hadn't tried to cast guilt elsewhere—she still
blamed herself all these years later.

"Is that why you haven't seen your brother in twenty-
five years?" No matter how innocent she'd been, Scott
must have resented her preferential treatment at least a little. He must have wondered why she was so special, why
her life was easy while his was so damn hard.

"He left home right after Mama's funeral. All his life
she had been the only thing standing between him and daily
beatings. With her gone..." She shrugged.

So she had lived the next four years of her life alone
with the man whom she blamed for her mother's death and
her brother's disappearance. He wondered what her father
had thought, felt, done. Had he ever accepted any responsibility for his wife's suicide? Had losing half the family
made him see the error of his ways? Had he ever felt even
the slightest remorse? Probably not. People like him didn't
see life the way everyone else did. He probably considered
himself the victim in the tragedy. He'd been a good husband, a good father and provider, and look how his family
had repaid him. His wife had died, his son had run off and
his daughter had disowned him. Ungrateful failures, every
one of them. He deserved better.

Jimmy Falcone shared the same kind of reasoning. In his
mind, he had been the injured party five years ago, not the
people he'd wronged, terrorized or killed. He was an innocent businessman, minding his own business, and Nicholas had betrayed him. He'd blamed the charges, the trial
and the convictions all on Nicholas, as if his extensive
criminal history had played no part.

At least Lainie's father had let his victims go. Jimmy
rarely let one of his escape. Nicholas wasn't expecting to
be the first.

Turning away from the thought, he stood up and stepped down to the ground. When he started around the park, she trailed along. "You weren't here when they replanted this, were you?"

She shook her head.

"There used to be a lot more trees and bushes. A lot more private spots. Just about all of the kids in the neighborhood lost their virginity here." He grinned. "That's probably why there aren't any private spots here now."

"Does that include you?"

"It does." It had been a warm fall Saturday night. He'd just turned eighteen—old age on Serenity for giving it up—and had needed a couple of beers to overcome his nerves. All she had needed was his kisses and his promises of love. He had loved her, in the only way he could at that time, but it had taken Rena to show him what real love was about. "Her name was Jolie. She was a pretty little green-eyed blonde who had no idea that it was my first time, too."

"Ah, the male ego."

He couldn't deny it. "She's married to the U.S. Attorney now."

"A big step up."

"She deserved it. She's the best damn reporter I've ever seen. She's probably the person Falcone hates most."

"After you."

He stopped in front of Reid's mural and studied it for a moment. Forty years ago, Serenity had been poor but livable. It had begun changing for the worst about the time Nicholas had entered his teens. By the time he'd left for Baton Rouge, everyone with a hope in hell had been dreaming and scheming to escape. They'd gone from poor to dirt poor, from grim to hopeless. The crime rate had shot up, the hookers and the drug dealers had started moving in, and the gangs had begun taking over.

Fifteen years after that, it had been a war zone. He had

used Jolie to pass along his evidence on Falcone to the feds, and they had made the exchanges right here in this park. His reputation and his association with Falcone had allowed him to come and go without risk, but Jolie had taken her life in her hands every time she'd driven down the midnight-darkened streets. He had been a selfish bastard to make her come here, but at the time he'd been incapable of thinking about anyone or anything but vengeance.

He located a few significant places on the mural—the house where he and Marie had lived one floor below the Wades, white then, gray now; St. Jude's, once the heart of the community, closed now for ten years or more; the tiny camelback house, divided into three tinier apartments, where the O'Sheas had lived; and this park, a bright patch of green with flowers and laughing children. Then, finally, he met Lainie's gaze. "Jimmy doesn't hate me."

"He wants you dead."

"True. But he's always liked me. He said I was the son he never had. He trusted me with the most intimate details of both his business and his life."

"He considers you a son, and yet, given the chance, he would kill you."

It must sound strange to her, but it seemed perfectly logical to him. Maybe he'd worked for Falcone too long. Maybe he'd been dead emotionally too many years to have the same appreciation of life and love that she did. "Killing me wouldn't diminish the affection he felt for me. It would be business, and Jimmy is first and foremost a businessman."

"He can separate business and emotion that completely." She sounded skeptical.

"Darlin'…" The endearment slipped out as he turned to face her, moving to stand directly in front of her. He tried not to notice it. "If you betrayed him, he could kiss you, look you in the eye and tell you he loves you and mean it with all his heart, then put a bullet in your brain. He would regret it when it was done, but he would do it. *Nothing* interferes with business.''

For a long moment they both remained motionless, too close, gazes locked. She appeared just a little troubled. Surely not on his behalf. She didn't even know him. Then again, the person most likely to regret his impending death was the one who didn't know him. Those who knew him, with the exception of Jamey and Jolie and Smith Kendricks, thought death was no more than he deserved.

She was about to speak when, next door, a door slammed and children's voices filled the air. They came running past the fence and into the park, one black, one white, one Hispanic. Serenity's own Rainbow Coalition. As one, they skidded to a stop just short of the swing set and watched them. It was unfortunate that kids had to be so wary in their own neighborhood park, but only a year ago, these kids never would have been allowed outside to play at all. Wariness was a small price to pay for fresh air, green grass and sunshine.

Lainie broke the stillness that extended from them to the kids thirty feet away. ''Hey, J.T., Javier, Adam.''

''Hey, Miss Lainie.'' It was the black boy who'd been in the lead who answered. ''Who's that?''

''This is Nicholas.''

''He's the one that just got out of prison,'' Adam said, his whisper carrying easily across the distance.

In another neighborhood, that remark could be construed as a warning or a criticism, Nicholas acknowledged. Here, it was just a fact of life. Someone from Serenity was always in prison, going to prison or just getting out.

''Where's your mama?'' Lainie moved away from him and toward the boys. He felt the precise moment she stepped beyond arm's length and into the vast space that was acceptable distance between two people who barely knew each other. It wasn't so acceptable to him.

Neither was the knowledge that he wanted her closer.

"She's coming." J.T. climbed onto a swing, standing on the seat and gripping the chains with both hands. "She said she was going to do some weedin'. She said if we helped her, we could go to the store for ice cream when we're done."

"Good. It'll save me from having to finish it tomorrow." She helped Javier into a swing, pulled it back a few feet and let go, then gave Adam a couple of pushes as she passed him. After tossing the weeds she'd pulled into the trash and scooping the dead flowers into one hand, she waited at the gate. For him or J.T.'s mother? The latter, he suspected, but it didn't stop him from joining her.

He leaned against the warm iron of the fence, shoving his hands into his pockets. From the other side of the gate, she turned toward him and smiled, a warm, friendly, welcoming smile. The sort of smile that could tie a man's stomach in knots. The sort of smile that a person who had never received many such smiles needed to grab and hold on to with both hands.

It was the sort of smile that was rarely directed at *him*.

"Hey, Shawntae. J.T. tells me you've enlisted them in the weed brigade. My knees and fingers are grateful."

"It's their park, too. They can't expect you and Karen to do all the work."

While they talked, Nicholas slipped past the young woman and onto the sidewalk. It hadn't been a bad way to spend an afternoon, he'd thought earlier, and he still agreed with the assessment. He didn't need another day like it, though. He didn't need confidences from unhappy pasts, didn't need talk about sex when his body was starting to crave it. He didn't want to know private things about her, didn't want to think intimate thoughts about her. He didn't need to stir up desires that she couldn't fulfill, didn't need to want things that she wouldn't give.

All he needed was to be left alone, and right now, right this minute, he was. Lainie was still occupied with J.T.'s mother. All he had to do was walk away. By the time she noticed he was gone, he would be halfway to O'Shea's. By the time she got there, he would be in his apartment with the door locked—though he didn't know whether for her protection or his.

Better yet, he could bypass O'Shea's and head for Bourbon Street. He'd known a dancer down there, a pretty little redhead who'd been too good for him, but she hadn't cared. Chances that she was still there were slim, but if she wasn't, someone would have taken her place. Someone who would be eager, willing and far more attainable than Lainie Farrell.

All he had to do was walk away.

But he didn't. He waited. For Lainie.

Chapter 3

It had taken Lainie a week or so to become accustomed to the sort of work she normally did at Kathy's House. Between yard work, making minor repairs and doing a little painting, she spent much of her time on her feet, bending, lifting, stretching.

It took less than eight hours Monday to miss the physical labor.

She'd been playing chauffeur all day, taking one young mother and her baby to a local hospital for a consultation and driving another client to her lawyer's office to discuss her pending divorce. Now she was sitting in the waiting room at the Social Security office while elderly Mrs. Montoya tried to straighten out some problem with her monthly check. Driving and waiting were *not* her favorite ways to spend an entire day.

"Hello, darlin'."

Lowering the newspaper she was reading, she was all set to intimidate away whichever male had made the mistake of thinking that she might be interested in anything he might say. Instead she found Sam, looking as disreputable as anyone in the city and grinning from ear to ear. "Don't call me darlin'," she said automatically. "I don't like it."

But that wasn't exactly true. She hadn't minded it yesterday in the park. Even though Nicholas's use had been totally casual, totally meaningless, some unruly part of her deep inside had liked the way it sounded, had liked the way it felt.

As she folded the paper, Sam took the seat next to her. "How's it going?"

Karen had asked the same question yesterday. Lainie offered the same answer today. "Fine."

"Seen much of Carlucci?"

"Some." *Not enough.* After they'd returned to O'Shea's from the park, he had gone to his apartment, then left again soon after. She hadn't heard his door close or his footsteps on the stairs. If she hadn't decided to eat her dinner in the closed bar with the television for company, she never would have known he was gone. But she'd gotten interested in a cable movie and had still been down there when he'd finally wandered in after eleven. His key in the lock had startled her into pulling the pistol from its holster. Luckily she had recognized him in time to hide it under the table.

Not that it'd been necessary. For all the attention he'd paid her, she could have had an antitank assault weapon on the table and he wouldn't have noticed. He had locked up behind him, muttered something that might have been good-night—or maybe not—and gone upstairs. She had sat at the table another hour, wondering where he'd gone, who he'd seen, what they'd done, before finally dragging herself off to bed. She hadn't slept well.

"Have you talked to him?"

"Some."

Frowning, he turned in the chair to face her. "You work alone a lot, don't you?"

"Some. Why?"

"It shows. This is how it goes when you have a real live human partner. He asks questions, and you answer them in real sentences with information and nouns and verbs and everything so he can go back to the office and fill out a report. Now let's try it. Have you learned anything interesting?"

Plenty. "He's not the slightest bit concerned that his former boss wants him dead."

"We already knew that. You're here because he turned down our offer of protection, remember? Has he heard from anyone in Falcone's organization since he got back?"

"I don't think so. I didn't get that impression." She mentally rewound to Saturday afternoon in the bar and filled Sam in on everything that had happened since. Well, not quite everything. She didn't tell him that, as of Saturday afternoon, Nicholas hadn't had sex in five years and counting—though she wondered if his late return Sunday had meant an end to the wait. She didn't mention that he'd lost his virginity in the local park with the girl who had grown up to marry the U.S. Attorney for this district. She left out the fact that she had confided in him the story of her mother's death, something even her ex-husband had never heard. She certainly didn't mention that he'd called her *darlin'.*

"Try to stay as close to him as you can," Sam advised when she was finished.

"I'll do what I can, but he's not exactly eager for company."

He gave her an appreciative look. "Darlin'... Oh, excuse me, you don't like that. Sweetheart, he's been in prison for five long, solitary years—years without women. Maybe it's not the same for a woman, but for a man, that's a lifetime. If I were in his place, I'd spend time with you even if all I got to do was look."

"If I were in his place, I'd be going where I could do a whole lot more than just look," she retorted. As maybe he had last night. Why did she dislike that idea so much? Unwilling to acknowledge the obvious answer, she got to her feet as Mrs. Montoya came out of the inner offices and started toward her. "There's my lady. I've got to go."

He glanced lazily toward the old woman, waited until she was close enough to hear, then caught Lainie's hand. "You sure I can't change your mind, sugar? I know a great place across the river. They serve the best Cajun food you'll find anywhere."

She couldn't help but smile at him. He wasn't particularly handsome, but he did have the most engaging grin, and the *sugar* was a nice touch. "No, really, I can't. Sorry." Pulling free, she steered Mrs. Montoya toward the door.

"There was a time when I used to attract all the young charmers wherever I went," the old lady said with a wistful sigh. "It's hard to believe now, but I was quite a pretty girl when I was young."

"I don't find it at all hard to believe. I hear old Thomas is smitten with you." Thomas Campbell lived on Trinity Street, where he and his wife had raised four children and had been enjoying their retirement until a drive-by shooting took her life. Soon after, he'd become a regular at O'Shea's. Lately, according to talk, he'd been coming for companionship more than the booze, and Karen said he'd been paying more than the usual attention to Mrs. Montoya at the neighborhood cookouts. It was nice to know romance was alive and well at their age. Just in case she was still looking then herself.

Mrs. Montoya's face turned a delicate pink, and her laugh was a self-conscious giggle. "Old Thomas is just that—old." Then the look in her eyes turned devilish. "But he's not dead, and neither am I."

The comment brought to mind Karen's remark yesterday when she'd responded to Cassie's teasing about noticing Nicholas. *I'm married, not dead.* Lainie didn't have that much protection. She wasn't married. For all practical purposes, there was no reason why the Lainie Farrell everyone on Serenity knew shouldn't notice Nicholas—and respond. No reason except that she was deceiving everyone, including him. No reason except that she wouldn't be around long, that she would like to return home with her heart as intact and untouched as when she'd left.

Plus the small matter of professional misconduct. If Nicholas Carlucci wasn't her job, she would be prohibited from any contact with him at all. Because he *was* her job, she was prohibited from any intimate contact. Everything between them was business. She had to remember that.

After negotiating evening traffic, Lainie took Mrs. Montoya home, returned Karen's car and keys to her, then headed home herself. One job was finished for the day, but the other was about to start. It would be easy work if Nicholas stuck to his usual routine and stayed locked inside his apartment, but if he chose to go out again, like last night... She would much rather accompany him than try to follow him, but how much luck would she have inviting herself along if his reason for going involved a woman?

Maybe she shouldn't wait to hear his plans, if any. Maybe she should invite him to dinner and a movie or a walk around the Quarter. Maybe she should hope he was already gone, so the decision would be out of her hands.

No such luck there. As soon as her eyes adjusted to the dimmer light inside O'Shea's, she saw Nicholas sitting at the bar and talking to Jamey. There was a cigarette burning in the ashtray between them, a half-empty bottle of beer in front of Nicholas and a glass of ice water in front of Jamey, and they were too absorbed in their conversation to pay her much attention—or so she thought. She was halfway down the hall when Jamey interrupted to call, "You got a delivery today, Lainie. Since I didn't have your key, I had them leave it in the hall."

Her furniture. She had forgotten when she'd asked for a

Monday delivery that she would be spending the day away from Serenity. "Sorry about that."

"Give me a minute..." He looked away, giving a nod of greeting to someone she couldn't see, probably a customer. "Give Nicky a minute to finish up here," he went on with a grin, "and he'll help you move it."

"That's not necessary. I can manage. Thanks anyway." She pulled her keys from her pocket as she reached the stairs. Up above on the landing she could see the sofa, stretching from one side of the hall to the other. The two occasional tables were turned upside down on its cushions.

She climbed the stairs, leaned over the end of the sofa to unlock the door and swing it open, then climbed over the arm and inside. She set the tables out of the way in one corner and turned back to the sofa. It was just a bit wider than the doorway, so the only way it was coming inside was on its side. She tried where she was, but couldn't budge it. She climbed over, squeezed into the narrow space behind it and realized immediately that wouldn't work. She was climbing over again, into the hall this time, when she smelled cigarette smoke and knew she was no longer alone.

"I don't need your help," she said ungraciously, looking over the stair railing to where Nicholas stood a third of the way down.

"I didn't come to offer it." A stream of pale, acrid smoke lifted into the air, rising past her, breaking up into wisps, then dissolving into nothing. He followed the drag on the cigarette with a swallow of beer.

"Those are nasty habits, you know."

"So I've been told." After dropping the cigarette into the bottle, he reached between the balusters and set them on the floor near her feet. "Satisfied?"

She purposely ignored the question, not because it was flip and uncaring but because the answer trying to slip out—*It takes a lot more than that to satisfy me*—could too easily provide an opening to a conversation she didn't need to have, not now with any man and never with this man. "If you want to get into your apartment, you'd better climb over now before I turn this thing over."

"I'm not going to my apartment. I came to watch."

Scowling, she turned away. The couch was heavy and took a good deal of maneuvering to get it into the proper position. When it was tilted precariously on its front end, she wiggled into the space between one arm and Nicholas's door, gave it a great shove and pushed it into her apartment. She was setting it upright, a little out of breath and a little damp from the exertion, when Nicholas stepped into the doorway.

"Now that you've proven you don't need it, would you like a little help on the other pieces?"

Since he was gracious enough to acknowledge her accomplishment, she accepted his offer. He brought the chair in by himself, then helped her carry the dresser to the center of the living-room floor. "Thanks," she murmured as she rubbed her hand lightly over the curves of the elaborate mirror. Once it was stripped, sanded and refinished, it would be a beautiful piece. She would leave the rest of the furniture for the next person on the receiving end of Jamey's generosity, but the dresser would go home with her. It was the only thing she planned to take back to Atlanta with her—it, plus a new charity to support and a regret or two.

"You have a bad day at work or are you always crabby in the evening?"

"I'm not..." Her hand grew still on the frame, and she glanced at his reflection in the mirror. He was testing the sofa, settling in, leaning back against the hideous yellow-and-orange cushions. She *was* crabby, in part because of her own reminder that whatever was between them *must* remain strictly business. Then there was the matter of last night. She was annoyed that he'd managed to slip out without her noticing, and she was curious about where he'd

gone and the less-than-friendly mood in which he'd returned. That was all it was—annoyance and professional
curiosity. Nothing personal.

She began removing the drawers and laying them on the
floor. "I'm not crabby. I just had a long day of driving and
waiting, and I didn't sleep well last night."

"I never have trouble sleeping."

"That's because you have no conscience."

"And why would your conscience bother you? You're a
do-gooder who's kind to small children and old women.
What could you possibly do that might cause you sleepless
nights?"

She set the last drawer down, started to sit on the sofa,
then changed her mind and slid into the chair. From his
first comment, she assumed he'd seen her with Mrs. Montoya. Was that what he did during the day? Watch life
taking place outside his apartment windows?

"You're right," she said airily. "I never do anything to
upset my conscience. My actions are innocent, my intentions pure." Except for all the lies she told. Actually, the
reason behind the deception was good and right. She was
trying to keep a man alive. She hated the lies, though, hated
deceiving people whom, under better circumstances, she
could become inordinately fond of.

"Do you plan to work on this tonight?" he asked, giving
the dresser, drawers and tables an all-inclusive gesture.

"If Karen has some stripper over there. Otherwise I'll
have to wait until I can go to the store." Or unless he had
other plans that she could manipulate to include her. She
gave him a sidelong look. "I don't suppose you're planning
to offer your help."

"Why would I do that? You can manage." Before she
could do more than privately acknowledge that he was
right, he went on. "I'm going shopping tonight. Want to
go?"

"To a store that sells stripper?"

"No, to a store that sells clothes. I'm tired of doing laundry every three days. I need some more clothes."

"Okay. Sure." She flashed him a smile. "I have great taste in clothes."

He subjected her to a narrow-eyed look before skeptically agreeing. "Uh-huh. Let's go now so we can get dinner when we're done."

Uh-huh, indeed, she thought as she got to her feet. So her jeans were faded practically white. So maybe everyone in the world didn't think traffic-cone orange was such a great color for a shirt. The jeans were loose enough to comfortably tuck in a .40 caliber semiautomatic—though she'd brought only a little .22 with her—and the shirt was absolutely a hundred and eighty degrees opposite from anything her conservative associates might ever wear. Besides, back home she had a few outfits in her closet that she could guarantee would make an impression on Nicholas Carlucci.

Come to think of it, she had a few things in her closet here that held potential. "Let me change shirts first. I wouldn't want to look like a poor relation or something." She was halfway to the bedroom closet when he called through the open double doorway.

"You don't have to change. We'll just tell everyone you're color-blind."

She took a couple of garments from their hangers, tossed them on the bed, then began unbuttoning her shirt. Suddenly realizing that he still sat in the living room, that he still continued to watch, she forced her features into a frown and somehow injected a note of annoyance in her voice. "Do you mind going away?"

She expected a sarcastic retort. She got a subdued retreat.

When the door closed behind him, she stripped off her shirt and pulled on a sheer top. By itself the tank was indecent, leaving nothing to the imagination. It was also sexy, cool, comfortable and sensual. She pulled a white shirt on next, fastened the buttons, then rolled the sleeves to her

elbows and tucked the tails snugly inside her jeans. For the
final touch, she took a black nylon waist pack from the
closet shelf, slid her gun and some money inside and fastened it around her waist.

A quick look in the mirror confirmed that she had
achieved the look she'd wanted and that everything was
decent. It also confirmed that Nicholas's skepticism had
been well deserved. Bright orange did nothing for her. Soft,
gauzy, barely-there white did.

With a deep breath of anticipation, she walked to the
door, shut off the lights and stepped out into the hall to see
if he agreed.

He was an easy man to distract.

They had talked to Jamey on their way out of O'Shea's,
walked to Decatur to catch a cab and methodically made
their way through the appropriate stores in Canal Place, and
Nicholas didn't remember much about any of it. Even now,
sitting in the lush courtyard of what had long been his favorite French Quarter restaurant, he couldn't recall exactly
what choice he'd made from the menu ten minutes ago.

And it was all Lainie's fault.

She'd layered one shirt over another, the plain outer shirt
left unbuttoned practically to her waist. It was open wide
at the collar, then narrowed in a deep V to the single closed
button, revealing smooth skin up high, a matching V of
gauzy shirt lower. The fabric of the second shirt was of no
substance, thin enough to see naked skin underneath, thin
enough, it seemed, that it would dissolve under his hand.
Combined, the shirts exposed nothing beyond the facts that
she wasn't wearing a bra, that her skin was a creamy gold,
that the golden shade extended unbroken all the way to her
waist. The appeal of the two was in the contradiction. The
thin top revealed. The cotton shirt concealed. The thin one
promised pleasure. The cotton offered protection.

Together they delivered punishment, and all because

he'd implied criticism of the god-awful color she'd been wearing.

He was certainly feeling punished.

She sat across from him, resting her arms on the tabletop, her fingers loosely clasped. She seemed to be waiting for him to speak, but he could think of little to say that wouldn't somehow end in bed. After an evening of watching her like a sex-starved ex-con, he was about ready to hint, ask, offer, suggest, seduce, plead or even pay for relief.

Finally she broke the silence. "If you can afford to shop at Canal Place, why do you live on Serenity?"

"Is that your way of asking if I have money?"

"I know you have money. You just spent more on a pair of pants than all my furniture cost. I'm just curious about why you live in a shabby little place on a dangerous street in a bad part of town when you can afford someplace better."

"Because I don't care."

"About what?"

He shrugged. "The money, the clothes, the apartment, the street, the neighborhood. I don't care about any of it." But somehow the words had sounded truer a week ago. He'd said them then with much more conviction. But there was no reason for the difference. Nothing had changed in the last week.

Except that he'd met Lainie.

Meeting her hadn't changed anything, except that his more frequently occurring fantasies now had a face. The phantom lover who had kept him company for more than five years now had short hair, sweet hazel eyes and a knockout smile. No doubt in tonight's torture she would be wearing some filmy, flimsy, tantalizing bit of nothing, and no doubt he would find it almost as tormenting as the damned clothes she was wearing now.

''When you worked for Falcone, you must have become accustomed to a more luxurious style of living.''

''I did. And when I was in prison, I became accustomed to austerity.''

''But there you had no choice. Now you do.''

''And I choose to live on Serenity. It's my home. Can you honestly say that, when your life got shot to hell, you didn't give any thought at all to returning to Savannah?''

''No, I didn't.'' Her answer was quick and emphatic.

''Not to your father. Just to the place where you grew up. You never considered it?''

''Not for a second.''

''I guess I have better memories of Serenity than you have of Savannah. I never considered going anywhere else. I was born there, I lived there, and if Jimmy has his way, I'll die there.'' His reference to Falcone's threat stole a little of the color from her face. Many people were uncomfortable with thoughts of death, particularly their own. He'd spent a lot of time over the last twenty years contemplating his. It usually brought him a measure of peace, something that had been in short supply since Rena's death.

''Why doesn't the government protect you? You helped them get a conviction, even if he did bribe and intimidate his way out of it. Why aren't they doing something now?''

His gaze narrowed. ''I don't want their help,'' he said, hearing the flat coldness in his own voice. ''All I want them to do is stay the hell away from me.''

''But they owe you—''

''Nobody owes me anything. I didn't do it for them. I did it for myself. I used them to bring down Jimmy in a way that I couldn't do on my own.''

''But—''

''You said you had a long day of driving and waiting today. What did you mean?''

For a long moment she looked as if she wanted to protest, to insist on continuing the conversation. Then she drew a deep breath and shrugged, and damn his eyes, his gaze automatically dropped to her cotton shirt as it shifted, gliding over the thin stuff underneath, teasing but never revealing. When she began speaking, he forced his attention back to her face, but it was difficult to concentrate when he was hot enough to burn and hard enough to break. It was hard—oh, yeah, *real* hard—to pay attention to her talk about playing chair-warmer in the city's waiting rooms when all he wanted to think about her warming was his bed.

Somehow he made it through the rest of the meal, paid the tab and followed her outside. "Want to take a cab or walk?"

"It's a pretty night. I'd rather walk."

It was nine blocks to Serenity, another two and a half to O'Shea's. They traveled the distance in silence, making their way through O'Shea's and upstairs in silence. Lainie was thinking about whatever, and he was thinking about sex. About following her into the apartment and right into her bedroom. About turning on every damn light in the place and removing the cotton shirt and simply looking at her until he couldn't bear to look anymore. About stripping her naked and laying her down and...

"Thanks for dinner."

Her words drew him away from images he didn't want to give up, not yet, not when images were all he had and all he was likely to get. He needed a moment to regroup, to pull himself away from the bed and her naked body, to clear his head and control his desire.

He didn't have much luck at any of it.

She had stopped at the top of the stairs and was facing him. She made no effort to find her keys or unlock her door. She didn't smile uneasily, say a hurried goodbye or look as if she were even remotely considering escape. She simply stood there and looked at him, her expression solemn, her gaze steady, her breathing slow and measured.

He climbed the last few steps and stopped. The bags slipped from his left hand. He let the others fall, too.

For moment after still moment, they simply looked at each other. His throat was dry, his lungs tight, his muscles quivery. In the space of a minute, the temperature in the hall had gone from comfortable to unbearable. Heat suffused his body and seared the air he breathed.

He moved toward her, and she took a step back, leaning against the door behind her as if she needed its support. He reached for the small bag around her waist, snapping the clasp open, dangling it by the long strap until it touched the floor. Next he opened the single button on the shirt and pulled first one side, then the other, from her jeans. There was one more button to loosen, and he worked it free easily, then slid his hand inside the shirt.

The undershirt was soft and silky. She was softer, silkier. He spread his hand flat across her rib cage and felt her breath catch and her muscles tighten. If he slid his hand up and to the right, he would be able to feel her heartbeat, surely faster now, like his own. If he moved it to the back, he could pull her snug against him. If he moved it straight up, he could touch her breast, cover it with his hand, feel her nipple hard against his palm. It was torture not to do exactly that, not to tear off the cotton shirt and the little thin one, not to expose her breasts to his hands and his mouth.

But it would be worse torture to do it. He hardly knew her, but he knew she wasn't a woman to take without care. She wasn't the easy and meaningless type. She wasn't the type a man used for fast, rough, hard, first-time-in-five-years-and-damn-near-ready-to-die sex. She wasn't *his* type.

"All evening long I've been wondering how this shirt would feel under my hands. I've been wondering how *you* would feel." His voice was low, hoarse and none too steady. "That's why you chose it. To make me want... To make me need..."

She laid her hand over his. Her palm was cool, her fingers trembling, as she gently guided his hand up over her ribs and the soft underslope of her breast until his entire palm was curved and cupped and cradled around it.

He squeezed his eyes shut with a muttered curse. He'd never been a breast man or a leg man—just a sucker for pretty hazel eyes. But there was something too damn erotic about touching her this way, about feeling the softness, the swelling, the heat, about holding her so intimately, wanting her so desperately and knowing that, at least to some extent, she wanted him, too.

His eyes still closed, he ducked his head, felt her hair beneath his cheek and automatically brushed a kiss to it. The next kiss landed on her temple, the third on the bridge of her nose, and then her mouth, but only for an instant, only long enough for a taste, and then she was protesting. Every muscle in her body went taut, and she pushed against his chest and twisted her head to free her mouth.

"I'm sorry," she whispered when her voice gained enough strength to be audible. "I'm so sorry. I didn't mean... I can't... I'm so sorry, Nicholas." She slid out from between his body and the door, stumbled on her bag, swept it up and fumbled inside for the keys. "I really am sorry. I wanted... But it really would be—"

He interrupted her babble. "It's okay." He hadn't really expected her to go through with it.

Oh, but some part of him had. The part that was relentlessly hard and throbbing. The part that was hungry for intimacy. The part of him that hadn't been touched in too many years. The part that wanted her too damn much. All those parts had thought, for just an instant when his mouth had touched hers, that this was his lucky day.

But he hadn't had a lucky day since he'd walked onto the LSU campus one hot summer day twenty-three years ago and met Rena.

Bending, he picked up the shopping bags, then turned

toward his door. He shifted them all to one hand while he pulled his keys from the pocket of jeans that were significantly tighter now than they'd been ten minutes ago.

"I'm sorry, Nicholas."

Her voice was low and edged with guilt. His was low and cooler than he meant it to be when he glanced over his shoulder. "It's all right. Forget about it. It's no big deal." When he went into his darkened apartment and closed the door, she was still standing there, looking pale and contrite, clenching her keys tightly in one hand. For a long time he stood beside the door listening, and finally came the sound of metal on metal, creaking hinges, the door closing, the quiet click of the lock turning.

For a time—five minutes, maybe ten—he remained where he was. Then, with a frustrated sigh, he went into the bedroom and flipped on the overhead light. He hung his new shirts, jeans and trousers in the closet, put the shoes on the floor, the socks and underwear on the shelf above. After turning the lights off again, he undressed, swept the empty bags to the floor and stretched out on the bed.

He was accustomed to sexual frustration. He had certainly known his share of it in recent years. But it was different this time. In prison sex had been impossible. Here all he had to do was find a willing woman, and in the city there were hundreds of willing women.

So why was he alone in his bed, aroused like hell and doing nothing about it?

Because he had kissed Lainie Farrell.

And he had liked it. Too much.

Oh, God, he was in trouble.

The door and all the windows were open in Lainie's apartment Tuesday evening, and the fan was positioned to circulate air away from the dresser. She had appropriated a thick stack of newspapers from Jamey's recycling box downstairs to spread over the floor, and now, dressed in her oldest cutoffs and T-shirt, she was preparing to apply the stripper to the piece. She had never refinished anything before, but Karen and Cassie had become experts on the subject since their move to Serenity—since they'd lowered their standard of living, they teased—and they'd given her a few pointers.

She pulled on a pair of rubber gloves, squeezed the thick white solution into a glass bowl, then began brushing it onto the wood. It was a mindless activity that allowed her thoughts to wander, no matter how hard she tried to keep them on the task at hand. Where they wandered, of course, was across the hall.

So much for professional curiosity and nothing personal. Five more minutes of "nothing personal" last night, and she would have been dragging Nicholas to her bed, damn the consequences. It was only the kiss that had brought her to her senses—or maybe robbed her of them. The first kisses he'd given had been tentative, so soft, without substance or promise. The last one had been bold. It had taken, not given. His mouth had covered hers, his tongue had slid into her mouth, and she had panicked. The caresses had been one thing. The kiss had been entirely another. It had been too much, and so she had pushed him away.

She'd felt like a shameless tease, offering, then pulling back when the offer was accepted. She couldn't blame Nicholas for being put out with her. *Forget it. It's no big deal,* in that icy voice had doubled her guilt. For a man in his situation, sex was a *very* big deal.

For her, sex with Nicholas was a very big deal.

Scowling, she poked the brush into the corners, then scooted around to the next side. She had stood there in the hallway a long time last night, wondering what she could have said to explain her actions, wondering for one wistful moment if she couldn't change her mind. Of course she couldn't. She wasn't about to risk the career she'd dedicated nearly fifteen years of her life to for a short-term affair with a man who didn't care whether he lived beyond this week or this month or this year. She wasn't going to jeopardize the case she'd been assigned by getting emotionally involved with the subject—who had, over dinner, made it quite clear what he thought of government interference in his life. Those people he wanted to stay the hell away from him included her.

But it would have been nice. *Nice?* It would have been exciting, toe-curling, intense, powerful and incredible.

Now she would never know.

She finished the third side, then got clumsily to her feet, brush in one hand, bowl in the other, and leaned on the cool marble to paint a heavy coat of stripper onto the carved ornaments that supported the mirror frame and the mirror itself. She was just straightening when she saw Nicholas standing in the doorway, hands in his pockets. He was wearing some of the clothes he'd bought last night—khaki trousers that were neatly pleated, a white undershirt and a white dress shirt half unbuttoned over it. He looked handsome, studiedly casual, hot-blooded.

All evening, he'd told her last night, he had wondered how her shirt would feel, how *she* would feel. She shared the same curiosity now. She wished she could strip off the gloves, walk across the room, unbutton his shirt as he had unbuttoned hers and touch him as he had touched her. He would let her, but she'd damn well better be prepared to wind up naked and underneath him. Hadn't she acknowledged not fifteen minutes ago that she was never going to be prepared for that?

She peeled the gloves off and wiped her damp hands on her shorts. There were still the two tables to strip, but not while he was here. All in good time. Then she smiled faintly. What a difference between their lives. *All in good time* meant he was going to have the most important sexual experience of his life, while she was going to strip a flaking finish from two cheap tables.

"I—I'm sorry." Her face flushed red. She hadn't meant to offer yet another apology. She hadn't meant to do anything at all to remind him of her juvenile behavior last night.

"Yeah. But you're not sorry enough to change your mind, are you?"

The flush heated a few more degrees. "I didn't mean to— It's not that I don't— I really—"

"Hey, if you want to change your answer, just say so. I've got the condoms, and we've both got beds. If you haven't changed it, a simple no is more than enough."

She was unable to answer at all, which was an answer in itself.

"That's an improvement." He gestured toward the couch.

"Thanks." After lying in bed unable to sleep for hours, she had gotten up in the middle of the night, opened the teal sheets she'd bought last night and fastened a makeshift slipcover. They looked like exactly what they were—two king-size sheets tucked over and around a sofa—but anything was an improvement over the putrid yellow and orange of the original upholstery. "Want to sit down?"

He hesitated for a moment, as if he didn't quite trust her or himself, then came inside. He didn't sit, though, but instead circled the room. She stood by the dresser and watched him, seeing what he saw, knowing that anything important—like her gun—was hidden. All he saw was what she'd seen in his own apartment—a space that was occupied but not home. There was nothing on the walls, nothing personal anywhere. All he could say when he finished his inspection was that the place was clean and neat, the bed was made and someone appeared to be staying there. He wouldn't learn anything about her.

There wasn't much he would like about her.

Lately there wasn't much she liked about herself.

Finally he settled on the couch. "Why are you bothering with this stuff?"

As if the fact that he was seated now made it safe for her to sit down, she sank into the chair. "You saw it. It was ugly."

"Yeah, but it's not like you're going to be here long enough to care."

In spite of the heat in the room, a chill washed over her. "Why do you say that?" No one had ever asked her how long she planned to stay on Serenity. Most of them assumed that this was a permanent move, like Karen's and Cassie's, that she was there to stay like Jamey, Reid and the rest.

"You're here because you've had a run of bad luck. Bad luck eventually turns around. Things get better. Eventually you'll get a real job with a real salary, and you'll get out of here. What kind of work did you do in Atlanta?"

She didn't for a moment consider telling him the truth. Hearing that she had been and still was an FBI agent wouldn't go over too well. She didn't offer part of the truth, either—that in her pre-FBI days, she'd been a certified public accountant. The worst CPA in the world could do better than Serenity, unless he'd gone to prison for robbing his clients blind. Instead she reached back even further to her college days at the University of Georgia at Athens. "I was a waitress. Now there's a fun way to earn a living."

"Did you go to college?"

"I went."

"But you didn't finish."

She tried to ignore the twinge of guilt. It wasn't exactly the same as lying. He had made an assumption, and the fact that it was wrong didn't reflect on her. But the fact that she let him believe it did. "I told you that I left home when I was eighteen. My father would have been perfectly willing to pay my expenses for college as long as I came home regularly on weekends, moved back in for summer and breaks and continued to be his perfect little girl. I couldn't do it.''

''You'd been doing it for eighteen years. You couldn't pretend for four more so you could finish your education?''

''No.''

''You'd rather be living on Serenity working for slave wages than suck up to the old man for four lousy years?''

''I'd rather be sleeping under a bridge and selling my body for a dollar a pop than be in the same city with him for four minutes.''

His grin was equal parts amusement and cynicism and all charm. ''You could get more than a dollar. Trust me.''

''So you're familiar with the going rates for prostitutes around here.'' From personal experience? Or old business? Definitely business, she decided. Nicholas was too handsome, too sexy, too full of wicked promise, to ever have to pay for sex.

''Jimmy owns half the prostitutes in the city. He's also got a bunch in Dallas, some in Houston, some in Baton Rouge.''

She knew that. She even knew something about Jimmy's business that Nicholas and no one else on Serenity with the exception of Reid and Cassie Donovan knew: that Meghan Donovan, Jamey's ex-wife and Reid's mother, had for years been one of Jimmy's girls. She'd started working for him in Houston, moved to Dallas to run his operation there and become lovers with him along the way. She was in the witness relocation program now, after betraying Jimmy and putting her son's life in danger, and Jimmy was still doing business as usual. The man led a charmed life.

''Are you suggesting that I should become one of them?''

''You've got potential. You're pretty, and you look innocent. Innocence goes over big with the clientele. Jimmy would put you in one of the escort services so you wouldn't have to work the streets. You'd have a place to live, nice clothes, most days off except when a special customer was in town, and you'd make a hell of a lot better money than you get across the street.''

She couldn't help laughing. "You make it sound like a regular job.''

"It is. But I don't think it's for you. If you can't bring yourself to go to bed with me, you would have some serious problems doing it with just anyone in the world who has the cash. You would have men old enough to be your father, men who want to pretend that they *are* your father, men who are young, old, fat, thin, kinky, boring, selfish, cruel and warped. And you would have no say in the matter.''

Somewhere after the part about going to bed with Nicholas, she lost track of the conversation. After those few moments in the hall last night, it seemed she was destined to obsess over what she couldn't have. Finally realizing that he'd fallen silent and was watching her, his eyes darker than ever, she smiled weakly. "This is a silly conversation. I'm doing just fine here. I make enough money to cover my expenses—''

"Because you don't have any.''

"—and I have a place to live, and I don't ever intend to consider prostitution as a means of support." She also didn't intend to continue discussing sex in any shape or form with him. It was too hard, too tempting. Too cruel.

For a moment he looked as if he wanted to add something, but when he finally spoke, it was about the dresser. "How long do you leave that stuff on?''

She glanced at her watch. "Another five minutes.''

"If I help you clean it up, want to go someplace afterward?''

Her instinct for self-preservation immediately and vehemently answered no, but her cop side stopped the refusal from materializing. She was here to keep an eye on him, remember? If she turned him down, he would probably go anyway, and then where would that leave her? Just how happy would it make Sam and their supervisors if she let Nicholas go out at night alone because she thought it was safer than dealing with the sexual longings that just looking at him aroused in her?

"Yeah, sure," she agreed. Even though she knew it was risky. Even though she didn't want to. Even though she couldn't think of much that she wanted more.

When time was up on the stripper, she gave him one of two putty knives, then went to work scraping the gel and layers of old paint from the dresser. Crouching on the opposite side, he did the same, managing to look perfectly comfortable and to stay perfectly clean.

When they were almost finished, he suggested that she get changed. She was happy to leave the rest of the work to him, since they were working on opposite sides of the mirror and in closer quarters than she found comfortable. She quickly agreed, took clean clothes from the closet and went down the hall to the bathroom. By the time she returned, he was done, and her dresser looked about ten pounds lighter.

"Nice dress."

"Yes, it is." She rubbed a bit of stripper from the marble top with a paper towel. "I can't wait to get it all finished and see how it looks. I think I'll do a dark stain, maybe a—"

"Dress." He interrupted. "Not dresser."

Her face, reflected in the mirror, turned just a little pink. "Oh. Thanks." It was a simple dress, sleeveless and long, a solid teal top with lots of embroidery in a dozen shades of metallic thread, layered over an exotic print skirt. She had paid too much for it but had worn it so much that it no longer looked expensive but rather as something the Lainie he thought she was could afford.

They left the apartment and O'Shea's and walked to the heart of the French Quarter, standing for a time in Jackson

Square, watching the street performers. It was a warm evening, like spring instead of fall. Everyone around was in a festive mood, she was standing in front of St. Louis Cathedral with the fragrance of roses in the air, and she was with a handsome man. Could life get much better?

Yeah, it could. For starters, Nicholas could be just a man—not an ex-con, not her assignment. She could be just a woman, and this pack around her waist could hold nothing more important than a vial of perfume, a key to a hotel room and the requisite sex-in-the-nineties condoms. Jimmy Falcone could disappear from the face of the earth. All the world and all the problems outside Serenity and the French Quarter could cease to exist.

Bending close to be heard above the surrounding laughter, Nicholas asked, "You like oysters?" At her nod, he took her hand, pulled her through the crowd and started toward a side street. Once they were away from the tourists, he didn't release her, at least not for a block or more. She regretted that he did then.

The bar he took her to was compact, squeezed between a T-shirt shop and an antique store. There were fewer than a half-dozen tables inside, all but one of them occupied. They took the one.

"Why did you come to New Orleans?"

He had ordered a dozen oysters and tea before asking the question. Lainie wished he hadn't asked it all. "Because I was looking for someplace different."

"Someplace better." So he remembered that they'd had this conversation Saturday. "But why New Orleans? Why not Charleston or Charlotte or Mobile? Why not stay closer to home?"

She tried to think of the best answer she could give, the one that would ring true with him, that would make him quit wondering and asking. She couldn't tell him that she'd never had any desire in her life to visit New Orleans. She came from gracious, old and Southern. She preferred the modern, cosmopolitan New South of Atlanta. At least, until recently she had.

She could tell him that she'd come with a man who had given her such sweet promises before leaving her stranded and broke in a strange city with no way to get back home and no home to get back to. She could say that she'd come because of a man, because of a relationship gone bad that had driven her away from everything she knew and into this strange new place. But some perverse part of her didn't want him to think that any recent man had been that important to her. She didn't want to pretend heartache and sorrow.

She accompanied her answer with a shrug. "I'd been in Atlanta a long time."

"Five years isn't so long."

"I beg your pardon. Tell me about the last five years of your life. How long did they last?"

He grinned. "A lifetime."

She moved her arms from the table as the waiter brought the oysters on a bed of ice. She picked up her fork and one damp, gritty shell, prying the mollusk free and letting it dangle from the fork. "I wasn't particularly satisfied with my life in Atlanta," she went on and realized that that much, at least, was true. "One day I decided to make a change—a big change. I'd never done anything foolish or reckless in my life, so I decided it was time. I gave notice on my apartment, quit my job and came here. I chose New Orleans because it was as far as I could go at the time. The bus ticket took practically all the money I had, but I figured that with all the tourists, I could get a decent job, find a place to live and start all over again."

Finally she ate the oyster, savoring its cool, fresh flavor with just a hint of lemony tartness. Nicholas let her eat two more before prompting her to go on. "But?"

She smiled ruefully. "Finding a job took time and money—two things I didn't have much of to spare. And I didn't count on the cost of living. Even a cheap motel adds up to a lot. The only apartments I could afford were either in areas where I didn't want to live or so far out that getting to work was a problem. Then I heard about Kathy's House. I showed up one day, looking for help, and Karen offered me a job.''

"Just like that. A stranger."

Lainie nodded. They had been prepared to use a little influence. The agent in charge of the Falcone case was Remy Sinclair, and his wife, Susannah, was a nurse at the center. They could have trusted her to get Lainie an in with Karen, but Remy hadn't wanted to involve Susannah unless there was no other way. Lainie had tried it on her own first, and it had worked. Karen had been happy to give her a job and, a few weeks later, a place to live.

"Any regrets?"

Plenty. She shook her head.

"Even though it hasn't been easy here?"

"It hasn't been so hard. I found a job and a place to live that I can afford. I've met some nice people, and I like my work." She smiled as she speared another oyster. "Hey, I'm not living under a bridge and selling my body to anyone who's got the money. It hasn't been hard at all.''

Chapter 4

From the oyster bar they went to a club that advertised the best blues band in the Quarter. It was an intimate place, dark and smoky, with a shapely blonde serving drinks to customers interested in the music, not in talking. It was the sort of place where Nicholas could spend an entire evening—exactly the place where he *had* spent Sunday evening. He'd even sat at the same table, in the corner facing the doors, his back to the brick wall, his gaze mostly on the street. He'd never made it to Bourbon Street and the bar where his friend Monique had worked. The music had drawn him in here, and he had stayed the rest of the evening.

Beside him Lainie was sitting forward in her chair, arms on the table, eyes closed. She was pretty and innocent, he'd told her earlier, and it was true. With her ultrashort hair, delicate bone structure and easy smile, she did, indeed, project innocence. Right now, though, right this minute, everything about her put him in mind of sex, not innocence. The way she absorbed the soulful music. The way she swayed from time to time in rhythm with the tune. The way her mouth slowly curved into a sensuous smile. The way her eyes needed a moment to bring him into focus when she opened them and smiled that sensuous smile at him.

When he spoke, his voice was husky and thick. "Want to dance?"

Her smile faltered. Her gaze didn't. Dancing, for all its innocence, could be dangerous. Like her. Dancing to music like this meant getting intimately close, moving in a lazy, indolent manner better suited to a bedroom on a hot New Orleans night than a public place like this. It meant touching, rubbing, holding, tormenting. It meant tempting themselves and fate.

He didn't think she had the nerve. He hoped she didn't. He prayed she did.

All serious now, she rose from the table, walked a few feet away, then waited. He gathered his courage, then joined her.

The dance floor was small, bordered on three sides by an arc of tables, on the fourth side by the platform where the band performed. Nicholas reached for her, and she came willingly into his arms. He clasped his hands behind her back. She slid one arm around his neck and rested the other hand on his upper arm. They fell into the same easy rhythm as if they'd done it a thousand times before. Making love to her would be the same way, he suspected. All new but as familiar, as natural, as breathing.

She nestled her cheek against his throat, and her fingers on his arm slid around to the underside. His muscles tightened automatically, there and everywhere else. He had asked for this, he reminded himself as desire began building deep in his belly, as his arousal began swelling against her belly. He had known what would happen, had known he couldn't touch her without wanting her. It was pure torment...and purer pleasure. He had never felt so intensely, had never wanted so desperately, even though he knew it was futile. After last night's rejection, she wasn't going to suddenly forget her misgivings, whatever they might be, and acquiesce tonight. Still, he wanted this. He needed it. Tonight, alone in his bed, he would pay the price, but right now he just might die without it.

The song went on forever, a mournful tune that wrapped around them in a smoky haze. His mouth brushing her ear, he murmured, "The whole time I was in prison, I had these dreams of a woman with no name, no face, nothing of substance, but last night it was you...and you didn't pull away. We were in your bed, and I was inside you and—"

She stumbled against him, pressing hard against him and he sucked in a taut breath. He was accustomed to the discomfort of purely physical arousal, more than accustomed to the dissatisfaction of his only means of relief. This was something more. This was beyond easing with a few erotic thoughts and a little dexterous handwork. This was painful, unbearable, and it was going to remain unsatisfied until she took pity on him.

And if she never did? Some other woman would, and Lainie could be his erotic thoughts.

The music stopped, and slowly their dance ended. She didn't release him, didn't pull away, didn't lift her gaze from the vicinity of his chest. She just stood there, body to warm body, barely breathing, not moving. He freed one hand and raised her chin, but she still refused to look at him. Was she afraid of what she might see, of what he might expect? Or afraid of what he might see?

"Let's go home." He turned her toward the door, then followed her, one hand still on her waist, between the tables and through the open French doors. They'd covered half the distance back to Serenity in silence before she stopped on a street corner and faced him.

"I can't..." She shrugged helplessly.

His smile was a little cynical and a lot wistful. "Don't

turn me down until I ask. It's hard on my ego. I don't expect you to..." He mimicked her shrug. "It was just a dance, Lainie, nothing more."

After a moment, she nodded and began walking again. With a frustrated shake of his head, he followed her. *Just a dance. Nothing more.* Right.

When they reached the block that O'Shea's was on, it was his turn to stop on the corner. He muttered a curse that brought Lainie up short. She looked back at him, puzzled, then followed his gaze to the car parked in the middle of the block ahead. It was a limousine, black, beyond elegant into ostentatious. Only one man routinely traveled New Orleans' tougher neighborhoods in such a car. Only one man had the power, the influence and the reputation to make such an undertaking safe.

"Do me a favor. Go to Kathy's House and wait there."

"Whose car is that?"

"Falcone's. Go on. I'll let you know when he's gone." He gave her a little push toward the street, but she didn't go willingly.

"Falcone's not interested in me," she protested. "He's not going to pay any attention to me."

"Jimmy's interested in anyone within a mile of me. He'll be particularly interested in a woman I've had dinner with. Just go to Kathy's House, Lainie, and let me handle this alone."

Reluctantly she stepped off the curb, crossed the street and, with a backward look at him, quickly covered the distance to the women's center. He waited until he saw her climb the steps to the veranda, then he began moving again.

The limo's engine was running, the driver waiting behind the wheel. Nicholas would like to take that as an indication that Jimmy didn't intend to stay long, but he knew from experience that it wasn't. The old man wanted to always be prepared for a quick getaway, should the situation demand it. Such planning had saved his worthless hide from arrest or worse on a number of occasions.

Drawing a deep breath, Nicholas walked through the first set of doors at O'Shea's. He saw Falcone right away but ignored him and headed for the bar, where Reid was filling in for Jamey. He was wiping the counter with a damp cloth and keeping a close eye on their first-time customers, as were all the regulars. "You notice you have company?" he asked, his voice low, his tone blank.

"Yeah. Have they been here long?"

"Maybe ten minutes."

"Give me a beer, would you?" He'd ordered only one drink at the club and he hadn't finished it because he'd been too preoccupied with Lainie. He wasn't ashamed to admit that he needed a little courage before he walked across the room and faced Jimmy Falcone for the first time in a long time.

Reid pulled a cold one from the cooler and popped off the lid before sliding it across the bar. He didn't offer a glass. Nicholas had done enough drinking in O'Shea's for the bartender to know he didn't use glasses.

Picking up the bottle by its neck, he turned—and came to an abrupt stop as Lainie walked in the door. She smiled at Eldin and spoke to old Thomas and Virgil, then came to the bar, climbed onto a stool in the middle and greeted Reid warmly.

So much for favors. She hadn't given him more than five lousy minutes, though at least she'd had the sense not to speak to him. Gritting his teeth, Nicholas ignored her and made his way across the room to a table against the wall. Jimmy sat on one side, Vince Cortese on the other. Another of Jimmy's goons stood against the wall a few feet away, his black suit coat unbuttoned, just a glimpse of a pistol in a shoulder holster visible in the dim light.

Pulling a chair from a nearby table, Nicholas turned it around, then straddled it. "Hey, Jimmy. Vince."

His old boss hadn't changed much. His hair might have gotten a little grayer, and there were a few more lines around his eyes, but he didn't look five years older or long since betrayed. He was several inches shorter than Nicholas and probably twenty pounds heavier, but not much of it was fat. He was solid, tough, the kind of guy you'd think twice about taking on in a fight even if you were taller, younger and lighter on your feet. He was dressed in a suit that was custom tailored in outrageously expensive fabric, fine leather shoes, a linen shirt and a silk tie. There were another two dozen similar suits in his closet; two dozen linen shirts, all in white; two dozen silk ties, all conservative, and a dozen pairs of identical shoes.

The gold nugget ring on his right hand caught what little light was available and flashed as Jimmy clasped his hands. "Nicholas. I expected a visit from you when you got back."

"A visit? Why? What would I say?"

"You could start with 'I'm sorry.' You could explain what I ever did to you to deserve such treatment. You could explain why you tried to destroy my life."

I'm sorry. It was hard to offer an apology when the only thing he was sorry for was the fact that he hadn't succeeded. He was sorry Jimmy had managed to buy and bribe his way out of the convictions. He was sorry the bastard was walking around free, still prospering. He was damned sorry that he hadn't taken the easier way out twenty years ago and put a bullet between his eyes. But he wasn't the least bit sorry that he had betrayed his boss.

"I treated you like a son, Nicholas. I took you in, gave you a home, paid you a substantial salary and made you a part of my family, and you turned on me. Why?"

"I earned that salary. I kept you and everyone who worked for you out of jail more times than I can remember."

"And the whole time you were working to try to put me

in prison for the rest of my life. Why? What did I do to deserve that?''

"You kill people, Jimmy. You profit from others' misery. You destroy lives."

"You never minded sharing those profits."

Nicholas couldn't argue the point with him. Maybe on some nobler level he had objected to being paid with dirty money, but it had been a necessary part of his quest for revenge. That was how his business—Jimmy's business—was conducted.

"You should have come to see me. You should have shown me some respect. You're going to have to pay for that, Nicholas." With a signal to the men, Falcone got to his feet. For a moment he stood looking down at Nicholas. There was genuine affection in the old man's eyes and, underneath it, sorrow. Nicholas was reminded of what he'd told Lainie a few days ago. *He could…tell you he loves you and mean it with all his heart, then put a bullet in your brain.* That look left him more sure of it than ever. "You're going to have to pay for a lot of things, Nicholas."

They left then, Vince in front, the other guy bringing up the rear. Nicholas turned to watch them go, but as soon as they'd disappeared into the car, he turned his attention to Lainie. She was still sitting at the bar, watching him openly, her expression grim and concerned. He rose from the chair and scraped its legs on the concrete floor as he slid it into place, then started toward her.

For a moment she sat motionless, then apparently she decided that retreat was the best course of action. She slid to the floor, murmured something to Reid, then started for the stairs.

Nicholas followed her. "I told you to go across the street."

"I went."

"I told you to wait there."

She stopped halfway up the stairs and faced him. "I

didn't want to wait there, Nicholas. I wanted to see what was going on here. I didn't speak to you. I didn't look at you. I didn't give the slightest hint that I knew you. Falcone never even noticed me."

"He noticed." The bastard noticed everything. Considering that several of his business ventures exploited attractive women, he had certainly noticed Lainie.

"What did he want?"

He climbed the stairs, pushed past her and went to his door. She followed as far as the landing. "It was private business."

"I heard him say that you would have to pay. He was threatening you, wasn't he?"

"I didn't hear a threat."

"Oh, come on, Nicholas—"

"He wanted to know why I hadn't been to see him since I got out, why I hadn't paid my respects to him. He's big on respect, you know. He doesn't get it from the people who count, but he damn well expects it from the rest of us. He thought I might like to offer an apology for everything I did, and he wanted to know why I'd done it. And, yes, he said I would have to pay for my sins."

"Sounds like a threat to me."

For a moment he simply looked at her—so pretty, so innocent, so damned desirable. Jimmy had all but stated that Nicholas's days were numbered. A dying man deserved one wish, didn't he? He already knew what his wish would be: Lainie. One night, from sundown to sunup, in her bed, seducing, using, giving, taking, pleasing, tormenting, fulfilling. One night in Lainie's bed, and he could die, maybe not happy, but satisfied. Just one night. Surely she and Jimmy would allow him that.

He turned the key in the lock and swung the door open, then looked at her again. "It didn't sound like a threat to me," he disagreed. "It sounded like a promise."

* * *

When Karen sent Lainie out of the neighborhood on errands Wednesday afternoon, she took advantage of the opportunity to arrange a meeting with Sam. In jeans and a chambray shirt, he looked like most of the other men wandering the aisles of the building supply superstore. He was pushing a cart that held a variety of tools and gadgets, which surprised her. She hadn't figured that he'd know a hammer from a screwdriver. He didn't seem the sort to go in big for manual labor.

"This is neat, isn't it?" he greeted her as she studied samples of wood stain. "A toy store for adults."

"Yeah, it's great. What do you think of this?"

He glanced at the stain she'd singled out and shrugged. "Kind of ugly. I hear your neighbor had company last night."

It wasn't ugly. It just didn't have the depth and life her beautiful dresser required. The mahogany next to it, though, was a rich, dark hue with deep red undertones. It would be perfect. She picked up a quart, then located an applicator sponge in the next section. "Yeah," she replied grimly. "The man himself."

"I don't suppose you got to sit in."

"No." After scanning Karen's list, she set out to locate the supplies, all the while talking quietly to Sam. She repeated Falcone's one comment that she'd personally overheard and Nicholas's version of the rest of the conversation.

"Are you sticking close to him?" Sam asked when she was finished.

"Yeah."

They walked the length of one aisle in silence before he found the nerve to broach the next subject. "You know, Lainie, you were picked for this job for two reasons."

"Because I'm a good agent and…?"

"Well, for three reasons. You're from out of town, so there's minimal risk that either Carlucci or Falcone could ever recognize you, and…" He shrugged uncomfortably.

"You're a pretty woman. A pretty woman stands a much better chance of getting close to Carlucci than a man does. But there's a risk of getting *too* close. Don't jeopardize your career or your case by…well…" His face flushed. "Oh, hell. Don't fall for the guy, okay? Don't get involved."

Clenching her jaw, Lainie stared straight ahead. *Don't get involved.* Jeez, he made it sound so easy: Move in next door to the guy, draw him out, spend time with him, deal with the fact that he's been celibate for more than five years and also with the fact that he's sexually attracted to you, but don't get involved. Don't let him kiss you. Don't let him touch you. Don't let him seduce you with looks and with dances and with husky, erotic talk about making love with you. Be a professional. Don't get personal.

She was doing her damnedest, but she wasn't sure she was succeeding. When he'd kissed her outside her door, it had taken her only a moment to come to her senses and stop him. Last night she'd needed half the walk home to say no. The next time he touched her, the next time they danced, the next time he looked at her in that dark, intense, sensual way of his, who could guess when—or *if*—she would remember to say no?

Forcing her thoughts in a different direction, she added the last item on Karen's list to the cart, then started toward the checkouts. "Tell me something, Sam. If Carlucci were a woman and I were a man, would we be having this conversation?"

"It has nothing to do with sex—"

"It has everything to do with sex."

"It has nothing to do with gender," he amended. "We're asking you to spend a lot of time in very close contact with a man whom even our own Shawna finds damn near irresistible."

Shawna Warren was one of the agents who had worked with Remy Sinclair on the Falcone case. She had given

Lainie a detailed briefing on the case and its principals. She was around forty, pretty but very professional, very ambitious, very aggressive. No one who knew her would be surprised if her ambitions included being the next head of the bureau. It did surprise Lainie, though, after spending a few intense days with her, that Shawna even noticed gender. She seemed the most job-oriented, advancement-obsessed and relationship-deficient person Lainie had ever met.

And yet she had noticed Nicholas.

Of course, he was a hard man to ignore.

"I'm just saying don't forget why you're there," Sam went on. "Don't let pleasure interfere with business."

With no more acknowledgment than a curt nod, Lainie began unloading her cart, separating her purchases from Karen's. Sam's warning annoyed her—not because she was an adult fully capable of making rational and right choices without prompting from her superiors, but because she was in danger of doing exactly what she was being warned against. Because she felt guilty. She should request to be removed from the case, but what would that do to her career? Reputation aside, would they even let her pull out now? She was already in place on Serenity and in Nicholas's life. How difficult would it be to remove, then replace, her?

She paid for her purchases, pushed the cart aside and scooped up the bags. "I'll be in touch."

Sam nodded as he removed his wallet. "Take care."

His farewell made her smile grimly. She was trying. She was seriously trying.

After finishing the rest of her errands, she returned to Serenity. As she pulled into Karen's driveway, Nicholas came out of the house and closed the door behind him. He circled to the back and was approaching as she got out with bags in hand. "What are you doing over here?" she asked, ashamed that she was hoping he'd come looking for her, grateful even if he hadn't that he'd found her.

"Jamey said Karen wanted to talk to me."

"About what?" Setting the bags on the ground, she unlocked the trunk, then picked up as many bags as she could carry. Automatically he took the heaviest ones from her.

"You're nosy, aren't you?"

"Well, I can't think of anything Karen would want from you besides your legal expertise or your money. I don't know how you feel about money and charities, but you've already made it clear that you're not willing to offer legal advice."

He gave her a steady, smug look. "Shows what you know. There are a lot of women out there who want something other than my money or my legal advice. They just want my body."

"I'm sure they do." She was one of them. But she wanted more than just sex. She wanted... Too much to even think about, especially when she couldn't have anything.

She led the way through the back door and the kitchen and into a small storeroom down the hall. There she began unpacking the food donations she'd picked up from a local women's club.

"What's with all the food?"

"Most of it's for the school. A lot of the kids don't get to eat as regularly as they should, so the center offers breakfast and lunch. Some of it's given to the residents, when they have unexpected expenses, when they get sick and can't work or there's too much month left at the end of their money."

"How do they pay for it?"

"With work, usually. They can help out here at the center, volunteer at the school, pick up trash, plant flowers, paint their houses—anything that benefits the community."

"Not a bad system."

She emptied the last paper bag, then folded it and added

it to the stack on one shelf. "No, it's not. Give people something to care about, and they will. I've seen photographs of the befores, and every day I see the afters. The center is making a big difference. Of course, with a legal advisor and maybe a nice little chunk of change, they could accomplish even more."

He didn't respond to that, but followed her outside again. "How long till you get off?"

She glanced at her watch. "Technically I'm off now. I usually quit sometime between four-thirty and five, but I missed lunch today, so I can take off a little early. What do you have in mind?"

"Just a walk."

She opened the trunk again for the last six bags, then slammed it shut with her elbow. "Okay. I guess I can spare a little time away from my dresser." They carried the last bags in, three each, then Nicholas waited in the kitchen while she returned the keys to Karen. That done, she took a few minutes to leave her own shopping bag at the bar with Jamey, then rejoined Nicholas on the sidewalk.

She expected him to turn toward Decatur, but instead he headed deeper into Serenity. They passed the Donovans' house next door to the bar, still dilapidated and in great need but greatly improved over the pictures Cassie had shown her. The original owner of the house had just walked away one day, leaving it to fall into disrepair and the city's hands. Reid had bought the place for practically nothing, and they'd begun their effort to turn it from a neglected eyesore into a home. For a young couple who worked full-time and had little time or money to spare, they were making admirable progress.

That was what she would do, if she were the down-on-her-luck Lainie that everyone believed her to be. She would save every extra bit of her salary and one day buy one of the three dozen or so abandoned houses in the neighborhood. With hard work and some of the donated building supplies that Karen was always panhandling for, she would fix it into a pretty little place all her own. She'd never lived in a house, not since the day she'd left home twenty-one years ago. Dorms, apartments, a condo while she was married, then back to apartments. It would be nice to have a house again, with a yard for a garden like her mother used to tend.

"I used to live in that house." Nicholas stopped as he gestured to a gray house across the street. It was three stories with a broad porch and a single door in the center, and it went without saying that it was shabby. At one time it had been a single-family home, but about the time Serenity's general decline had begun, it, like most of the other big houses, had been chopped up into apartments. As far as Lainie knew, only Karen's and the Donovans' houses had escaped that fate. "We had the apartment in the left front corner. It was one room, with a tiny refrigerator, a hot plate, a sofa that made into a bed for my mother and a bunk-size mattress on the floor for me. We shared a bathroom with two other families. My mother did dishes in the bathroom sink."

The window he pointed out was boarded over, making it impossible to tell if anyone lived there now. She hoped not. She hoped even the poorest person on Serenity could afford better. "Did you ever try to find your mother?"

"Try how? She had no friends and no family but me and the father who disowned her. She didn't have a driver's license or a car. She worked the sort of job where people come and go, where they quit with no warning and are forgotten about the next day. Do you know how easy it is for someone like her to disappear?" Shoving his hands into his pockets, he kicked a crushed beer can and sent it skittering across the sidewalk. "I used to think she would have a change of heart and come back for me. A couple years of living with Father Francis relieved me of that notion. At some point I decided that she was probably dead."

"Why did you think that?"

"Because, up until the day she disappeared, she was the mother least likely to pull such a stunt. She was a good mother. She gave up a lot for me." He shrugged. "Plus the fact that she didn't take anything with her. Everything she owned except the clothes she was wearing was still in the apartment."

Maybe she had left everything deliberately—had wanted an entirely new start with nothing, not even clothing, to remind her of the past. Or maybe she'd gotten tired of the burdens of her life and had freed herself, like Lainie's mother, through death. Maybe she hadn't planned to disappear at all. Maybe she'd had a perfectly innocent reason for sending Nicholas to the church after school that day, and someone had grabbed her off the street, leaving her body where it would never be discovered, at least not while it was still identifiable.

It would be tough not to know. Her mother's suicide had been tremendously hard, but if Elaine had simply disappeared one day, never to be heard from again... That would have been impossible.

"The Wades—Reid's in-laws—lived in the same house. They moved away while I was in school. They were among the lucky ones."

"So Cassie didn't grow up down here, but Jolie did."

If the long, steady look he gave her was any indication, when he'd told her about his initial sexual experience, he hadn't expected the name to mean anything to her. If he'd thought she could connect the name to any particular person, he probably wouldn't have mentioned it at all. "What do you know about Jolie?"

She leaned back against the abandoned storefront behind her, feeling the setting sun's warmth in the soft brick. "She's a pretty little green-eyed blonde and the best reporter you've ever known. She's married to the U.S. Attorney, and..." She didn't mean to let her voice get husky.

It slid into the lower register of its own will. "She was your first."

When he continued to look at her, she shrugged. "This is Serenity. It's impossible to live down here without hearing certain names. Jimmy Falcone is one. Vinnie Marino is another. Nicholas Carlucci, of course. And Jolie Wade. You two are Serenity's homegrown claim to fame. You're the success stories."

"Jolie's been a big success, but me—I haven't succeeded at anything."

"You got out. You got an education. You had a career that you were damn good at. They say you were a brilliant attorney." High praise, considering that it came from the opposition—Smith Kendricks, Remy Sinclair and Shawna Warren, all lawyers themselves.

"How brilliant do you have to be to get a guilty man off?" He gave a scornful shake of his head. "All I succeeded at was making a mockery of justice. It's hardly anything to be proud of."

She couldn't argue the point with him because he was right. He'd used his education, experience and understanding of the law to subvert the system. He'd made it possible for the bad guys to go free, unpunished for their crimes. His ten-year career as a mob lawyer wasn't a source of pride.

They began walking again, Nicholas pointing out old familiar places. There was the barber shop where his mother had taken him for haircuts, the restaurant where they had splurged on special dinners out, the corner grocery where he had worked as a teenager, saving every penny he could for college. How different their lives had been, Lainie mused, listening to his reminiscences and calling up a few of her own. She had begun making regular trips to her mother's beauty salon when she was six, and expensive dinners out had been a twice-weekly event. She had never given a moment's thought to working when she was a teenager, but even if she had, her father would have forbidden it. As for college, it was true that she'd required financial aid and as many long hours at her waitressing job as she could manage, but that had been her choice. Her father would have paid every penny if she had continued to play the dutiful daughter.

They passed the park and walked to the end of the street. Once the road had continued on through a few barren blocks of trees and ditches, but long ago those blocks had been broken up and left in great chunks, a pile here, another there. A guardrail fastened with reflectors stretched from one side of the street to the other, and a chain-link fence, hanging in vandalized strips, made a halfhearted effort to block off the marshy area beyond.

As they crossed to the sidewalk on the opposite side, Nicholas gestured toward the house on the end. "I always liked this place."

Lainie stopped on the curb, hands in her pockets, and studied the house. She could understand why. The house was big and square, with the main level a good six feet above the ground and reached by twin staircases that met in the middle. The broad porch was sheltered from sun and rain by a deep overhang, and there were plenty of windows, six across the front and an equal number on each side, for ventilation. Of course it needed paint, new windows, major repairs and a dump truck to haul away the debris and garbage from years of neglect. Once fixed up, though, it would be, like Karen's house, like the Donovans' house would soon be, a source of pride and beauty.

"Why don't you buy it?"

The look he gave her was just short of derisive. "And what would I do with it? It's not fit for anything but tearing down."

"You could fix it up. Live in it." When his look turned scornful, she shrugged. "That's what I would do. I would paint it, replace the windows—"

"Replace the roof, rescreen the windows, rebuild the chimney, repair all the damage from vandalism and neglect, rewire it, replumb it, convert it from multiple apartments back to a single-family home, remodel it, modernize it."

She continued as if he hadn't interrupted in that cynical tone of voice. "But first I would clean out the yard and all those great planters, and I would fill them with flowers so it would be beautiful while I worked at making the house beautiful."

"And what would you do all alone in a place like that?"

It was a big house with a huge lot, much too big for just one person. But it would be perfect with all the rooms and all the space for a large, loud, boisterous family—one thing she wasn't likely to have at this late stage of the game. One thing she still, from time to time, found herself wanting. Especially lately. "I would buy the lot next door, too," she said, deliberately turning from thoughts of family, "and start my own business—a nursery with a greenhouse and acres of flowers, plants and trees. I would donate flowers to everyone on Serenity who wanted them, and I would hire only people who lived here, and I would make it Serenity's first wildly successful commercial venture." If she were going to stay here forever. If she had the freedom to do something risky and exciting. If she were the Lainie Farrell he thought she was.

With a shrug that made clear his opinion of her idea, he began walking again and, after giving the house one lingering look, she followed him. She couldn't blame him for being skeptical. After all, she wasn't going to stay here forever, she wasn't going to throw away the career she'd worked long and hard for to risk everything in the craziest of ventures, and she wasn't the Lainie he thought she was.

Even though, right this moment, she wanted to be. She wanted it more than anyone could imagine.

Nicholas let himself into the apartment and closed the door behind him. The sounds of life from downstairs—the television, conversation, Sean O'Shea's delighted laughter—immediately faded into stillness. Nothing but the lazy whir of the fan blades broke the silence. Only a few days ago, he had told Lainie that the apartment suited him exactly the way it was, and he had meant it. Was it possible that he'd changed his mind in so short a time? Because the place certainly didn't suit him this evening. It felt cold, impersonal, unwelcoming. Like a prison.

He gazed around the living room, though there was nothing to see but a little dust in the corners, then went into the bedroom, tugged off his shirt, kicked off his shoes and stretched out on the bed. He turned onto his side so he could see the photograph on the night table, but he didn't pick it up. The last rays of light coming through the window touched it, making it the bright spot in the room, the way Rena had always been the bright spot in his life. She had accepted him in a way few people had, had loved him in a way no one ever had, and she had paid for it with her life.

He had thought he would never get beyond that knowledge and the guilt that accompanied it. Lately, though, he'd spent entire periods of time where he didn't feel the guilt, where he didn't even think of her. Of course, that made him feel guilty in an entirely new way, even though he knew Rena would be the first to approve. She would have been disappointed at the way he'd lived his life without her, would have fiercely disliked the choices he'd made— the mistakes he'd made.

He reached toward the picture, but didn't touch it. *Love, Rena.* For more than twenty years that love had kept him going. It had driven him to become a better lawyer than a punk from Serenity had any right to expect. It had compelled him to gain Jimmy Falcone's attention, his respect, his trust. It had steered him down the wrong path, through the wrong choices, into a nightmare of hatred and a need for revenge that had almost destroyed him. It had sent him to prison and left him with nowhere to go but home. Her love and the value he'd placed on it had turned him into a man who didn't deserve her love.

He was a man who didn't deserve much of anything. But Jamey and his family still offered their friendship, and Lainie...

He rolled onto his back, feeling a familiar sense of sharp-edged frustration slice through him. He wasn't sure exactly what Lainie was offering, but he knew too well what she *wasn't* offering, what he wanted, what he was starting to need with an intensity that was damn near painful: her body. He'd had plenty of opportunities to find release else-where, but for reasons he didn't care to understand, he found it impossible to look any farther than across the hall. Yes, he wanted sex—hell, after more than five years with-out, he *craved* it—but before he settled for some stranger, before he gave in and accepted nothing but purely physical satisfaction, he wanted a chance with *her.* Every minute he spent with her, every time he looked at her, every conver-sation he shared with her, just made him want her that much more. No one else. Just her.

And that sounded like serious trouble.

So did the voice at the door. "Hey, Nicholas." There was a soft rap on the door. "Come and have dinner with us."

"Us" no doubt included the O'Sheas and the Donovans. They'd all been gathered around the bar when he and Lainie had come in from their walk. He had left her down there and come up here to brood, not in the mood to see how easily she fit in with the small group that constituted the closest thing to friends he had in this world. He hadn't wanted to see Jamey with his wife and Reid with his, hadn't wanted to see the intimacy they shared and know that, when the evening was over, he and Lainie would each be as alone as two people could be. He hadn't wanted to know that she could change that if she wanted but that she didn't want.

He wondered why she didn't want an affair with him, if her objections were something he could overcome. Was it simply because she hadn't known him long or she didn't feel she knew him well? Was it something in her past—a man who'd treated her badly, someone she still loved? Or was it *his* past? Maybe she didn't mind living next door to a disreputable, dishonest ex-con ex-mob lawyer. Maybe she didn't mind spending time with him, sharing meals, dances or a few inches of all too personal space a couple of nights ago in the hall, but she drew the line at actually doing the deed. Maybe the idea of getting down and dirty with him was just a little more than she could stomach. After all, she was a respectable woman who was simply having a run of bad luck. She wasn't the sort of woman to settle for a man like him, not when she could easily find a hundred men a hundred times better.

Or maybe she just needed coaxing. Seducing. Tenderness. Reassurance. Maybe she liked to believe when she had sex with a man that it meant something more than the obvious. Maybe she needed the emotional connection as much as he needed the physical.

Unfortunately he'd never been very good at emotional connections. His connection with Rena had gotten her killed.

Across the empty room, there was another knock, then the door slowly swung open. "Nicholas?" She came through the living room, stopping in the wide doorway six feet from the bed, leaning one shoulder against the jamb. She had changed from work clothes into a hot-weather dress, a fitted little thing that was sleeveless and short and left exposed too much creamy golden skin. The dress was perfectly suitable for going out on a date, shopping with friends or on a walk through the Quarter. It was just as perfectly *un*suitable for standing in his bedroom door, where all he could think about was taking it off of her slowly, so damn slowly that he just might die in the process.

"Karen's bringing dinner over, and she's invited us to join them. Interested?"

Interested? Oh, darlin', he was interested, all right. But not in Karen. Not in her dinner. Not in anything outside this room right now. "I don't think so."

She came closer, stopping at the foot of the battered iron bed. The bed in her apartment was iron, too, a little more ornate and painted bright white by the previous tenant. He was haunted by nighttime fantasies of her in it, naked, hot and needy. Now he would be haunted by dreams of her here, too. "Come on, Nicky," she coaxed, her grin charming. Her use of his childhood nickname should have sounded silly, should have provided a symbolic dash of cold water to his libido. Instead it sounded incredibly erotic.

Sitting up, he swung his feet to the floor. The movement made his body tingle and tighten and left him surprisingly aware of the slightest sensations. "Why don't you come over here and persuade me?"

The grin slowly faded, and her eyes took on a hazy look. She wanted to take him up on his challenge, wanted to walk around the bed and right up between his thighs and do whatever it took. He believed that in his soul. But she didn't move except to wrap her fingers tightly around the thick iron of the footboard while she stared at him.

Finally he looked away, feeling grim and sore, wishing he hadn't said a word, wishing he'd pretended that the mere sight of her didn't leave him feeling achy and aroused, wishing he'd ignored the heat and the hunger.

One long moment drew out, followed by another. Sometimes it amazed him how time that involved pleasure could pass in the blink of an eye. Those few minutes outside her apartment Monday night when he'd touched her, when he'd kissed her, had lasted mere seconds. These few minutes were going to last a lifetime.

At last he stood, walked in a wide circle around her and went to the window to stare out. "Is it because of who I am?" His tone was harsh, angry. In the past twenty years he hadn't given a damn about who and what he was, hadn't given a damn what that meant to anyone else, whether it caused them to scorn him, distrust him, despise him, hate him.

Tonight he cared.

"No. It's because of who *I* am."

He turned to face her. "I don't care who you are. I don't care what you did before you came here. I just want you."

"You shouldn't."

"It's too late for that, darlin'."

She stood motionless for a long time, looking utterly miserable, her knuckles white where she gripped the rail so tightly. If he uncurled her fingers and lifted her hands, he would smell the iron in a wide band across her palms. He would see bits of rust and flaked paint rubbed off onto her skin. But if he lifted her hands, he wouldn't be thinking of smelling or seeing. Only touching. Caressing. Tormenting. Pleasuring.

After a moment, he moved toward her. He knew it was a mistake, knew he should send her away, lock the door behind her and crawl into bed with the covers over his head until this need was gone. But he walked to the end of the bed, stopped beside her and touched a bit of skin where the wide strap across her shoulder ended. "Who are you, Lainie?"

She tried to smile. "No one you'd want to know."

"You're wrong. I do want to know you. In every meaning of the word." He realized as he said the words that they were true. He liked being with her, even if he didn't touch her, even if he knew he would be going home alone when the evening was over with nothing to get him through the night. Hadn't he sought her out today, deliberately delaying his meeting with Karen until it was time for Lainie to get off work, until she could spend time with him? Didn't he find himself listening for her on the stairs or in the hall? Didn't he stand at the window when she was working outside and watch her, want her?

Stubbornly she shook her head. "You can say that now because you don't know who I am. You don't know what I am. If you did know…"

With his hands on her shoulders, he pulled her away from the death grip on the bed and turned her to face him. "What would I do if I knew? Judge you? Condemn you?" He shook her gently. "For God's sake, Lainie, look at me. I'm a convicted felon. I've been to prison. I spent my entire career working for the mob. I worked with people who killed other people for a living. My boss ran the drug trade, the prostitution, the protection, the money laundering, the gambling, and I made it all possible. Who the hell am I to criticize what anyone else has done?"

"You don't understand," she whispered.

"No, I don't, and if you won't explain it, I can't understand. But I understand this—it doesn't matter. Nothing you ever did could possibly matter."

Instead of reassuring her, his words saddened her. Instead of trying to fix whatever he'd said wrong, he forced a smile. "Let's go downstairs and eat. If Karen's half as pushy as Jamey says, she'll bring the food up here if we don't."

Once more she tried to smile. It wasn't much of a success. "Karen's not pushy. She just likes to get her way."

So did he. If that meant slowly seducing Lainie, if it meant forgetting that he'd been without sex for a lifetime, if it meant taking his sweet time and winning her over one word, one touch, one promise, one kiss at a time, then that was what he would do. Even if it killed him. Of course, it wouldn't. Succeeding would kill him. Lying naked with her, kissing her, touching her, filling her, satisfying her, finding his own satisfaction inside her... It would be the sweetest death any man could ask for. Then Jimmy could have his revenge. Nicholas wouldn't care, because he would have had Lainie.

Or maybe he would care entirely too much, because he would have had Lainie.

Backing away from that possibility, he turned his shirt right side out and pulled it on, stepped into his shoes and followed her at a safe distance down the stairs. In the broad hallway below, three tables had been pushed together and food had been laid out. There was a platter of muffalettas, made on round Italian loaves and cut in quarters, heavy with meats, cheeses and olive salad, and bowls of salad and vegetables for Jamey's vegetarian daughter-in-law. Jamey and Karen sat on opposite sides at one end, with Sean in his high chair between them. Reid and Cassie were also on opposite sides in the middle, leaving the last two chairs for Nicholas and Lainie. Also on opposite sides.

He would rather sit beside her and run the risk of bumping her every time he moved than across from her, where every single time he looked up from his plate, she would be the first—the only—thing he'd see.

He sat down in the empty chair next to Cassie. Though her oldest sister had been his girlfriend for three sweet years, Cassie was young enough to be his daughter. There were eleven Wades between her and Jolie, every one of them a better kid than the average Serenity Street product. Though Jolie's overprotective parents and unending supply of siblings had been a pain back then, he had envied her. He had often wondered what it felt like to have a family. Back then, everyone on Serenity had had a family, even Jamey—though his father had been a drunk and his mother had been a drunk and chronically depressed. Only Nicholas had been alone, and he had hated it. Finally, after years of practice, he'd gotten used to it, but now he was starting to hate it again. He was starting to crave companionship, starting to hate the long, empty hours alone in his world.

Damn Lainie for it.

She was subdued across from him, trying to unobtrusively scrape the olive salad from her sandwich, probably wishing she'd gone from his apartment to her own or, more likely, that she'd never set foot in his. He would apologize, but the only regret he felt was that she hadn't accepted his challenge and crawled right into bed with him. At least, then she wouldn't be worrying about offending their hostess by not eating part of the meal. Then she wouldn't have had to worry about anything except surviving the passion for hours and hours and...

Everyone was looking at him, and he realized that someone must have spoken, though he couldn't remember hearing a voice—at least, not one suitable for the dining table. No doubt, somewhere in his rich fantasy life was an entire audio section—soft whimpers, breathless pleas, helpless, shuddering little moans, all in Lainie's honeyed Georgia drawl. Clenching his jaw, he looked questioningly around the table, his gaze settling on Karen, who was leaning forward to see him.

"I asked if you'd given my suggestion any consideration," she patiently repeated.

"What— Oh." She'd made the same suggestion this afternoon that Lainie had made the day she moved in—that he volunteer his legal services at the women's center—and he had offered the same response. He was a disbarred lawyer who had been convicted of multiple felonies. Karen had reminded him that, even disbarred, he could provide legal advice for free and then had gone one step further: she had suggested that he make an effort to get reinstated. She had refused to take no for an answer, had insisted that he think about it, but he hadn't. His desire to practice law was dead. He had nothing to offer anyone, especially the sort of women in trouble who frequented the center.

"Look, if you need a volunteer to clean up or paint or something like that, fine. But I'm not a lawyer anymore. I can't help anyone with their problems. I can't give advice—" He broke off as Lainie looked up and met his gaze. Her expression was steady, blank, uninvolved, and still she somehow managed to convey disapproval. Well, damn it, he didn't care what she thought.

Yeah, right.

"I can't," he said quietly, to Lainie, not Karen. She held his gaze a moment longer, then looked down again at the food on her plate. Through the rest of the meal, she didn't look at him or speak to him.

When dinner was finished, Jamey took Sean to the bar and Nicholas and Reid returned two of the tables to their original places out front while the women cleaned up. Nicholas came around the corner in time to see Lainie disappear up the stairs. Instead of following her, he retreated, taking a seat on a stool at the bar.

"Aren't women wonderful?"

Nicholas scowled at his friend. "I've never understood them."

"Son, you don't have to understand them to appreciate them."

He supposed that was true. He certainly didn't have Jamey's experience to know. He'd had only two real relationships, and he had completely understood both women. Jolie had been just like him—ambitious, hungry, driven to get out and make a better life for herself—and Rena had been everything he'd thought he wanted to be. Average, normal, happy with the simple things. In Baton Rouge, she had wanted a job that she didn't hate, a little of his time during the day and to sleep beside him at night. Her plans for the future had included a small wedding back home in the family church, a house and eventually kids with whom she could stay home while he worked and paid the bills. If they could have managed those small dreams, she would have been blissfully happy.

Instead she had stayed at a job she'd hated, because *he* had needed the money. She had wanted to quit, and he had persuaded her to stay another few months, just until the semester was over, just until summer came and he could get a job to take up the slack. But the semester had never ended and summer had never come, not for Rena. One rainy March night the job had killed her. Jimmy Falcone had killed her.

Nicholas had killed her.

Hating the morose mood creeping over him, he forced his thoughts back to the real subject: Lainie. He didn't understand her at all. What was in her past that she thought so horrible that he, the biggest loser in Serenity history, would be put off by it? And why did she care whether he played lawyer for free for Karen's clients? She wasn't one of the women in need of legal advice. If she were, she must know he would help her.

Maybe she thought he was selfish. Maybe she'd convinced herself that, in spite of all his failings and flaws, he had at least one decent quality. Maybe she'd thought he was a more generous man than he really was. Maybe, for her, he could be...if the idea didn't repulse him so damn much.

"What's between you two?"

Nicholas waited as Reid and Cassie said their goodbyes, then headed out the door, holding hands as if they couldn't bear not touching. Newlyweds, Jamey and Karen often joked with a chagrined shake of their heads, but they were no better, and they were much older and past the one-year mark in their own marriage. "Remember when we were that young?"

Jamey grinned. "We were never that young." Almost immediately he sobered. "I know you helped Reid out a number of times when he was in trouble. Ever since you came back, I've been meaning to thank you for it.''

''Jimmy got the kid into trouble. Paying me to get him out seemed only fair.'' He had hated like hell to see his old friend's only son get tied up with Falcone—had even tried to talk him onto the straight and narrow a time or two—but the boy had been bitter, angry and unwilling to listen. He'd needed to make his own mistakes, to set his own priorities. If respect, family, friends and living past the age of twenty were important, there were choices to be made. Nicholas had been half surprised to hear that Reid had made the right ones.

''So...what's between you and Lainie?''

It was a simple enough question that Nicholas couldn't begin to answer. He was no more sure what was drawing them together—besides sex, of course—than he was of what was keeping them apart. With a bewildered shake of his head, he gave the only answer he could offer. ''Damned if I know.''

But he intended to find out.

Chapter 5

Lainie stayed in bed Saturday morning hours after she ordinarily would have been up and about, lying on her side, staring out the window at the rain that darkened the sky and washed clean the glass and screen. Like most Southerners, she usually tolerated rain as the price to pay for living in the South. Some rains, like the gentle spring showers that her mother had always anticipated for the health and well-being of her garden, depressed her. Others, like the endless heavy rains that accompanied distant hurricanes, wearied her. Some, on hot summer days, she actually enjoyed, putting on shorts and old sneakers and going for a walk, splashing through puddles, getting herself good and soaked before heading home.

Though there was nothing gentle about this morning's rain and it was months past spring, it was depressing.

With a sigh, she slid out of bed, shoved her feet into a pair of canvas sneakers, grabbed an armful of clothes from the closet and left the apartment. Nicholas's door was closed, his apartment quiet—always quiet. The bathroom door at the end of the hall was open. The air was warm, damp, just short of steamy, and smelled of soap and shaving cream. Wherever he was now, he'd recently been in the shower, which was an image she didn't need this morning.

Scowling at herself, she brushed her teeth and washed her face before getting dressed. After finger-combing her hair, she deemed herself as ready to face the day as she was ever going to be, hung her nightshirt on the back of the door and headed downstairs for breakfast. Halfway down the stairs, she became aware of the music—low, mournful, so perfectly fitting to the gray skies and the downpour of rain.

She stopped in the kitchen and found a pot of coffee, freshly brewed and fragrant. After pouring herself a cup, she started back to her apartment, but somehow her feet turned left out of the kitchen instead of right. Somehow they moved totally against her will down the short hall, around the scarred wooden counter and into the bar.

The television on the wall was tuned to a twenty-four-hour blues channel—no commercials, no distractions, just uninterrupted music. The lights were off, the ceiling fans running, the four sets of French doors open to admit the sound and the sweet, clean scent of the rain. Straddling a chair at a table in front of one door was Nicholas, a cup of coffee, a plate of beignets and an ashtray in front of him. Smoke rose from the ashtray in a thin wispy trail, pulled one way by the nearest fan, pushed another by the gentle breeze through the door.

For a long time she remained where she was, far enough away to escape his attention, near enough to the hall to slip upstairs. That was what she should do—run, not walk, down the hall and up the stairs, where she could lock herself in her apartment and not come out again. There she might be safe. But she wouldn't count on it. There she could escape Nicholas, but not herself. Not her thoughts of him. Not her desire for him.

It wasn't fair. Back in Atlanta, through her job, neighbors and helpful friends, she'd met plenty of suitable men and hadn't been the slightest bit interested in any one of them. No, she had to go and fall for Nicholas, the most unsuitable of them all. It just wasn't fair.

But life wasn't fair, her mother had always told her. It certainly hadn't been fair to Elaine Ravenel. She hadn't wanted so much—a good marriage, a happy family, a comfortable home and a lovely garden. The marriage had never been good, the only happiness the family had ever found had been when Frank was away, and the beautiful old house had been filled with fear, tension and despair. In the end, even the garden had let Elaine down. Like her, it had withered and died.

Lainie wished this attraction to Nicholas would wither and die, but woman's intuition warned her that it wasn't going to happen. Things were going to get much worse before they got better.

Over by the doors Nicholas picked up the cigarette and took a deep drag. She smelled the smoke on the breeze, a faint, pleasant aroma. It drew her away from the bar, across the room and around the empty tables to his table. She chose the chair against the wall, facing him with the thick brick wall at her back. She set her coffee on the table and sat down, drawing her feet onto the seat, watching him watch the scene outside.

His hair was damp, slicked back from his face, and the legs of his jeans were turned deep indigo by rain. A dripping jacket hung over the back of a nearby chair, and waterlogged tennis shoes had been kicked underneath it. He'd gone to the Café du Monde for breakfast, bringing the hot beignets back to cool into greasy lumps on a bed of powdered sugar. If he had knocked at her door and asked her to go with him, she would have. She would have enjoyed such a start to a dreary Saturday morning.

He pushed the plate toward her in silent offering, and she chose one of the beignets. She ate it, scattering sugar all across her shirt, and licked her fingers clean before finally speaking. "Appropriate music for the weather."

"I like rain," he said in a tone that indicated the opposite.

"I had hoped for sunshine on my day off."

He dismissed her with a wave of his hand. "The sun will come out soon enough. What did you have planned that you can't do in the rain?"

"Nothing." She hadn't really made any plans. She had thought she might spend the day away from Serenity, playing tourist and seeing all the sights. She needed to buy some groceries, do a load or two of laundry and maybe mail a few postcards to friends back in Atlanta. Truth be told, she needed to do anything that would keep her mind off her job. Off Nicholas.

So why was she sitting here across from him?

"How's your dresser?"

"It's coming along." After dinner Wednesday evening, she had stayed up late into the night, sanding the wood until it was as smooth as glass, taking out her frustrations on the flat surfaces of the dresser. She'd saved all the intricate curlicues for the next night when she was calmer, when there wasn't such a risk of sanding the curves right off. It had been hard work and good therapy—for as long as she'd done it. But it hadn't stopped the frustration from returning once she'd quit. It hadn't ensured restful, dreamless nights. It hadn't done a damn thing for her desire.

"If you asked nicely, you could probably persuade me to help with it."

Though there was nothing the least bit provocative in his voice or his manner, she couldn't help but remember Wednesday evening, when he'd sat on his bed wearing

jeans and nothing else and had made a similar suggestion.
Why don't you come over here and persuade me? Did he
have any idea how powerfully he'd tempted her? Did he
even suspect how desperately she'd wanted to do just
that—persuade him. Entice him. Seduce him. She still
wanted… But nothing had changed. She was an FBI agent.
He was her job. Anything personal between them would be
grounds for losing that job.

Her voice was too husky for the teasing tone she was
striving for when she replied. ''There's just no limit to the
things you might do if a person asked you nicely, is there?
Except, of course, what you're trained to do—offer legal
advice.''

He ignored the last part. ''Not a person, Lainie. *You.*''

His gaze was dark and unwavering. It made her body
hot and achy, caused her hand to tremble when she reached
for her coffee and made her throat tighten so the lukewarm
brew was difficult to swallow. She needed to step outside
and let the rain wash away this fever, but if she did, no
doubt she would sizzle. Besides, it wouldn't ease this need.
Nothing would but the one thing she couldn't have from
the one man she shouldn't want.

Through sheer will, she broke free of his gaze and turned
to stare out the door. Water had pooled in the street, rushing
and eddying with no place to go. The yard at Kathy's
House was under several inches of water, which poured in
miniature waterfalls all along the curb into the street.
''Does O'Shea's ever flood?''

''It has before. Every place on Serenity has flooded except the cottage.''

''The cottage?''

''At the end of the street. It's a Creole cottage.''

Mention of the house provided a vivid reminder of how
different they were. They had stood side by side Wednesday evening and looked at the same house, but where she
had seen a house that could be a home, he had seen a place

deserving only of destruction. Less than an hour later in his bedroom, they had looked at each other, and he had seen an affair worth pursuing, while she had seen the ruination of the career that was the one constant, the one thing of importance, in her life. Her family was gone, her marriage fallen apart, her relationships with men on what seemed like permanent hold, but her job was always there. It filled all the empty spaces—well, most of them. It satisfied her.

At least, it always had. Until she had come here.

Across the street, a slender figure wearing a trench coat and huddled under a sunny yellow umbrella hurried toward Decatur. On the veranda at Kathy's House, Karen's dog Jethro lay stretched out in front of the door, his chin resting on his paws, his tail occasionally swishing through the air. Otherwise, the street was quiet and still. Everyone who could remain dry inside was doing so.

She wanted very much to go out.

"Want to take a walk?"

Her gaze jerked back to Nicholas. Had he read her restlessness? Did he share it? She should tell him no—should come up with some excuse, someplace she needed to go. She should work on the dresser or the two tables she'd bought. She should do anything besides go out all alone in the rain with him.

No, she should do anything besides stay in all alone with him.

"Let me get my slicker." It took her only a moment to retrieve the slicker, bright pink with a pink and yellow plaid lining, from the closet upstairs. It took him only the same moment to close and lock three sets of doors and put on his shoes. He was waiting, jacket in hand, by the open doors when she returned.

Before they'd gone half a block, every place on her body that wasn't covered by the slicker was soaked. She combed her hair back and let it drip down her neck rather than pull the hood forward. It restricted visibility and distorted the sounds around her. Besides, this morning she wanted to be wet. It felt good. Fresh. Clean.

"You ever miss Atlanta?"

She blinked back raindrops to look at him. He was as wet as she was—wetter, actually, since he wore jeans while she was in shorts—but while she felt like a drowned rat, he looked incredibly handsome. Sexy. Dangerous. She couldn't forget that this was one case where appearances weren't the least bit deceiving. He *was* dangerous—to her career, her future, her heart.

"No," she replied, not happy to realize it was the truth. In the weeks she'd been in New Orleans, particularly the last one, she hadn't missed a single thing about Atlanta. Not her routine eight-to-five days in the office. Not her quiet, air-conditioned, high-security apartment. Not her neighbors or her friends, her unvarying schedule week in and week out, her money, her car, her higher standard of living, nothing. She didn't miss Atlanta at all, and she wasn't looking forward to her return.

But, of course, she would go back. When she finished this job, there would be nothing left for her in New Orleans. Nicholas would hate her or he would be dead.

She smiled thinly. She'd never before found herself wishing that someone she cared about would live to hate her, but she hoped Nicholas did.

"So you plan to stay here. You're happy here."

"You sound skeptical. In all your years on Serenity, were you never happy?"

"I was happy with my mother."

"But not since then?"

He shrugged. "At times, I suppose."

Times with Jamey, Lainie suspected, and, of course, with Jolie Wade. Did the U.S. Attorney's wife know what a feat she had accomplished in making Nicholas Carlucci happy? Would she even care, or was he a long-ago-and-best-forgotten part of her life? Nicky, the punk, the bad boy, every parent's nightmare and every teenage girl's fantasy. *She* had harbored a few such fantasies when she was a kid, but they had never been more than wishful dreaming. In thirty-nine years her only fantasy come true had been the one where she escaped her father and the lovely old house on the square.

Nicholas could be the second.

They reached the end of the street and turned toward Divinity. Its five blocks held more houses, more abandoned storefronts and three churches, all boarded up and forgotten. The first, according to the crooked fading sign, was the A.M.E. Zion church, where most of Serenity's black residents had worshiped. It was a simple building, its wooden planks once painted white. The paint was mostly gone now, the wood faded to a silvery gray, and only jagged shards of the colored glass windows remained. The second church was brick and had housed the Baptist congregation. Its windows were shattered, too, and the inside had been gutted by fire. Only the charred remains of pews and a tall cross remained. Both buildings looked even more forlorn in the rain.

The last was St. Jude's.

Nicholas stopped on the sidewalk in front of the gate and stared at the building. Beside him, with water dripping from her nose and chin, Lainie gave the church grounds the same intense study. The walled compound was stucco over soft red brick, with only two entrances—this gate for foot traffic and a wider gate at the opposite end for cars. The church itself was straight ahead, a tall building with high arched windows depicting biblical scenes in stained glass. Wire grates protected the glass from hurled rocks or bottles, keeping it mostly intact, and the massive, ornately carved double doors were too sturdy for vandals to do much harm. Obscenities and gang slogans had been sprayed on the walls, and the yard was barren, but for the most part, St.

Jude's had survived its abandonment in better shape than its neighbors.

Nicholas pushed the gate open, disrupting the steady flow of water down the sloping sidewalk to the street. When he walked inside, she followed, looking around at the cobblestone walkways, the rectory in the distant corner and the empty fountain with a statue in its middle. In the dirt halfway between the gate and the rectory was a memorial—a small white cross, plastic flowers bleached of color by the sun and a bow that had lost its shape and dragged limply in the mud.

"Kids used to come in here and play. Their mothers thought they were safe on church grounds, even if the church had long since abandoned them. One day about eight years ago, there was a shooting. Some punk had looked at some other punk the wrong way, and the second one blew the first one away. Unfortunately a five-year-old boy got in the way. He died right there."

Lainie looked away from the sad little flowers to Nicholas. His face was expressionless, but his eyes weren't. The look in his eyes was dark and angry over the pointless loss. Deliberately she changed the subject. "So this is where you grew up."

"Part of the time. That was my room." He pointed to a corner window on the second floor of the small house. "I had a cot and a chest for my clothes. There were no curtains on the windows, no rugs on the floors, no pictures on the walls. There was no television, no radio, no books to read but the Bible. Father Francis was short on affection and long on penance, forgiveness and suffering for your sins. It was good preparation for prison." He said the last with a faint smile that didn't extend beyond the corners of his mouth.

It must have been a sad place for a little boy to live. As if losing his mother hadn't been enough for a six-year-old to bear, he'd had to bear it here, in a place as unwelcoming as any she'd ever seen with a man undeserving of the title of father. The state should have taken him into custody, should have placed him with foster parents or found an adoptive home for him. How big a difference would that have made in his life? If loving parents had taken him away from Serenity, if they'd given him a happy, healthy upbringing, if he'd had all the advantages and benefits that every child in the world deserved, what kind of man would he be today?

Possibly not half the man he was now. Adversity often brought out the best in a person. If he'd been able to achieve his goals without hard work, effort and determination, he might not have worked as hard, might have set easier goals. He might not be the man she spent too much of her time obsessing over.

Stepping past him, she walked along the uneven stone path to the fountain. It was a half-round, curving out from the back wall, tiled in blues, pinks and greens that had long ago lost their brilliance. There were cracks where age and neglect had taken their toll and smashed places where vandals had done their own damage. Dirt, trash and weeds filled the bottom and rose around the feet of the headless, handless statue there. The hands lay in pieces in the mud. The head was probably sitting in some kid's apartment nearby, a grotesque trophy celebrating a juvenile act of destruction.

"That's St. Jude. He's the patron saint of hopeless causes. Appropriate, don't you think?"

Lainie gave him a chiding look as he joined her. "Does everyone in the world think of Serenity and its people that way?"

"Everyone except Karen and Cassie."

"And me. I haven't met any hopeless causes yet."

"You've met Vinnie Marino. He's about as hopeless as they get." His voice lowered a note or two. "You've met me."

The rain fell harder, stinging her face, dripping inside her jacket, sending a chill through her, but she didn't seek shelter. She simply stared at him for one moment, then another, before slowly raising one hand to his face. His jaw was smooth, cool, the muscles working. She slid her hand up until one fingertip touched the corner of his eye, then let it slide down his jaw again, breaking the contact bit by bit, first with the heel of her palm, then the midsection, then her fingers. "You're not hopeless, Nicholas," she said quietly.

She started to turn away, but he caught her hand and pulled her back, using his grip to pull her snug against his body. His intent was clear in his eyes, darker than ever, but he didn't act on it right away. "Most people would disagree with you. Most people think I'm way beyond hope and way beyond help."

"Most people are wrong."

"No. If they were wrong, I wouldn't be doing this..." He used one arm around her waist to hold her close and slid his free hand up into her hair, tilting her head back, exposing her throat to his mouth. When his first kiss landed at the base of her throat, heat raced through her. She knew she shouldn't let him continue, shouldn't let him leave a second kiss a little higher, a third one a little higher still. She knew that if she let him *really* kiss her—mouth to mouth, tongues, heated, demanding, wicked, raw lust—*she* would be the one beyond help. *She* would be the hopeless cause.

But she couldn't stop him. If her life depended on breaking free of him at this very moment, she couldn't do it. She wanted him, needed him, craved him too much.

He toyed with her, reaching her jaw, brushing his mouth across her ear, touching her cheek, then finally taking her mouth. It was a simple kiss, perfectly chaste, perfectly respectable. If he stopped right there, maybe she could survive. Maybe she could walk away with her future intact.

But, of course, he didn't stop there, for which she was practically tearful in her gratitude. He drew her closer, held her tighter, as if he could join with her right there, as if the setting and their clothing were minor barriers easily overcome, and he slid his tongue into her mouth, thrusting, seeking, claiming.

She was lost.

All she could do was cling to him. When he moved her against the wall, she was grateful for the support. When he opened the snaps that secured her jacket with one savage pull and slid his arms inside, she welcomed his touch. When he moved his hips suggestively, erotically, against hers, she whimpered, wordlessly pleading, helplessly needing—

And then he stopped. He pulled back, returned for one little kiss, then unwound her fingers from his jacket, turned and walked a few yards away.

"Nicholas..." Her protest had no substance, no sound. She didn't try to find her voice, didn't try to call him back. However strong her disappointment, whatever his reason for stopping, it was best for both of them. Her job left no room in her life for this particular man, and even though he'd insisted that he wanted her in spite of who and what she was, she knew how quickly that would change when he learned that *who she was* was an FBI agent, that *what she was* was a liar, a deceiver and a cheat.

Still, for a time she leaned against the wall, seeking the strength to let the moment pass and the courage to not call him over and plead for more. Just one more kiss, one more touch from his hands, one more moment pressed intimately close, arousal to long-unsatisfied arousal.

When she thought she could trust herself to not do anything rash, she moved away from the wall, pulled her slicker tight and went to stand near him—not close enough to touch, just in his general vicinity. "How long has the church been empty?" Her voice sounded strained, thick, out of place.

"Fifteen years." His was strained, too, and he didn't look at her. Instead he scowled hard at the church. "People just quit coming. The church blamed crime rates, the crises everyone down here was facing, the economic depression and everything else in the world, and some of that probably did play a part. Crime was bad. People were afraid to get out on the streets. They were losing their jobs, their homes, their families and their faith. They needed the church more then than they ever had, but they were turning away."

"Because of the priest?"

His smile was cynical. "Father Francis treated his best parishioners the same as his worst sinners. *He* was pious and holy, and everyone else was going to hell."

"For a man of God, he was hard and unforgiving." The comment came from behind them, startling Lainie. She hadn't heard Luke Russell's approach, although Nicholas clearly had. The man looked less like a preacher than any she had ever met. He was dressed in faded jeans and, under an open jacket, a brightly colored tropical shirt that looked out of place in this somber scene. His hair was a little too shaggy, the look in his eyes a little too worldly, his overall appearance a little too unholy. Still, Karen was convinced that he was exactly what Serenity needed.

"You planning to put this place to good use?" Nicholas's tone was overtly detached. If the minister heard the skeptical undertones, he gave no sign of it.

"It seems the best choice. The other churches are in sorry shape."

"So you're really going to open a church down here." Lainie gazed past him to the church. Maybe it would be good for the building. Maybe regular services, prayers and singing could alleviate the dark sense of desolation that hovered inside the compound. Maybe children playing once more on the grounds would shatter the stillness that surrounded them. Maybe having an outlet for their spiritual needs would help bring peace to Serenity.

Or, she thought as gunshots rang out in the near distance, maybe not.

Luke looked toward the open gate and the little bit of street it showed. "Sometimes it seems almost like a normal neighborhood. You can forget that it's not safe to be on the streets."

Especially for Nicholas, Lainie silently agreed. He was convinced—and the FBI and the U.S. Attorney's office agreed—that Falcone would make his death a personal issue, but the old man could surprise them all. He could pay someone like Vinnie Marino a few thousand bucks to turn Nicholas into just one more victim of senseless violence, an innocent in the wrong place at the wrong time.

"When do you plan to open the doors?"

Nicholas's question made the minister grin. "Not for a while. We don't even have permission to come in here yet. When it's a go, I'm sure Karen will let you know."

"As she hands out the hammers, shovels and ladders," Lainie replied dryly.

That made him laugh, a full, deep, rich sound. Too many people on Serenity never laughed. "She knows how to get things done." As he started to walk away, he gestured toward the smaller building behind Nicholas. "I understand you and Jamey lived here for a while. The rectory's open if you want to take a look around."

She would like to go in and climb the stairs to the corner room with no curtains, no rugs, no comforts or affection. She would like to see the place that had helped turn little Nicky Carlucci into Nicholas Carlucci, attorney for the rich and corrupt. But if she went, she would go alone. She knew before he refused Luke's offer that he had no desire to set foot inside his former home. To him, this place was nothing that a church should be—not a sanctuary, a place of worship or a haven from the problems of the world. It was just a place of bad memories.

Once the minister disappeared behind the church, Nicholas gestured toward the street. "Ready?"

With one last glance at the rectory, she nodded and followed him out the gate.

Walking in the rain had lost its appeal by the time Nicholas and Lainie turned onto O'Shea's block again. He wanted nothing more than a hot bath and dry clothes—except maybe a warm bed, a willing body and no clothes. If her reaction back there at the church was anything to judge by, it wouldn't be long before Lainie would be willing. The way she had responded to his kisses... It had been *almost* as good as sex. Of course, the sex, once they finally got to that point, was going to be incredible. He didn't have the slightest doubt.

"Looks like Jamey opened early."

He looked ahead and saw that the doors to O'Shea's were open and light spilled out, a soft yellow glow in the dreary day. From the day Jamey had taken over the bar twenty years ago, the doors had opened at ten a.m. and stayed open until two a.m. six days a week, and he'd been there every hour. Since he'd married Karen, the bar was open only from noon until midnight, and closed on Sundays, holidays and every time there was a function going on at Kathy's House. This morning it wasn't yet eleven. Why the early opening?

The instant he stepped through the door behind Lainie, he saw why. Jamey was sharing a table and conversation with guests: Smith and Jolie Kendricks. He would like to think that Jolie was simply visiting old friends. She'd known Jamey all her life, and she'd first met his wife back when Karen was married to her first husband, a New Orleans cop Nicholas had often faced in court. But it was a miserable day, and Jolie hated Serenity too much to drop in for a casual visit. On a day like today, she would surely rather be home—a few significant miles away in a much better part of town—with Smith and the kids.

So this visit was probably business. Kendricks's business. Nicholas's business.

He pulled his jacket off and hung it on a doorknob so the water dripped outside. Lainie, looking more than a little uneasy, did the same. Her hair was soaked and dripping, and her soft cotton shirt was damp in interesting places. Though he'd deliberately ended the kiss too soon—to prove to himself that he could, to avoid the appearance that he was pushing her, to give her time to adjust to that much before he asked for more—if they'd come home to an empty place and he'd seen her looking exactly the way she did right now, he would have been seriously tempted to pick up where he'd broken off.

It was Kendricks who finally broke the silence. "Pleasant day for a stroll."

"We had the streets to ourselves." He wished they had the bar to themselves, at least for the seventy-five minutes remaining before O'Shea's official opening. The things they could do in seventy-five minutes…

"Why don't you guys get dried off and changed?" Jolie's smile was none too bright. "Then we can talk."

Lainie started to move, but Nicholas didn't. "I doubt Lainie's interested in anything we might have to say."

"Then she and I can talk while you talk to Smith."

He wasn't sure he cared for that idea, but he *was* sure that he had little say in the matter. Jolie was stubborn and used to getting her way—a large part of what had made her such a good reporter. As the top federal prosecutor in eastern Louisiana, Kendricks was also used to getting his way. He would say what he'd come to say, alone or in front of Lainie. Nicholas preferred to be warned of his impending death alone, without the woman he was trying to seduce close enough to hear every word.

"Give us ten minutes." He gave Lainie a nudge toward the back of the bar, then followed her, their shoes squeaking on the floor.

Down the hall and up the stairs, she remained quiet. As she unlocked her apartment door, though, she gave him a difficult-to-read look. "She's very pretty."

"Jolie? Yeah, I guess so."

"You guess so," she scoffed. She pushed the apartment door open, and he caught the scent of cinnamon and cloves. His own apartment smelled of dust and emptiness. "You were intimate with this woman, and you don't really notice how pretty she is?"

He moved close enough to smell her own particular scents and to feel the soft puff of her breath on his chin. "I was intimate with a teenage girl and, yes, she was pretty. But that was another lifetime." He moved another step closer just to torment himself. "I noticed that you're pretty."

For just one moment he thought she was going to press against him, to cling to him the way she had at the church, in the way that he'd never imagined he would like but did. Unfortunately she didn't. Instead she backed away. "Get changed. I'll see you downstairs." With that she closed the door in his face.

Nicholas stood motionless for a moment, then, swearing softly, went down the hall to the bathroom. He stripped and dried off, then wrapped the towel around his waist for the trip back to his apartment. Lainie's door remained closed.

Dressed in warm, dry clothes, he went downstairs, stopping behind the bar for a beer before joining the others at their table. Jamey excused himself, got his jacket and returned to his house across the street. Nicholas watched him go before facing the Kendrickses. "Well?"

It was Smith who answered. "I understand Falcone came to see you last week."

Nicholas didn't respond. The government spent a great

deal of money and effort to monitor Jimmy's movements. Kendricks no doubt knew the exact date, hour and minute of Jimmy's visit, who had accompanied him and how long they had stayed, where they had been before they'd come here and where they had gone when they'd left. He obviously had a pretty good idea of what was said while they were here.

"Did he want to make his threat in person?"

"He wanted to talk. Just like you."

"I want to talk about his promise to kill you. Was that what he wanted to talk about?"

"He wanted to talk about respect. About forgiveness. About paying for my sins."

Smith and Jolie exchanged somber looks, then he said, "The offer for protection still stands."

Nicholas finished his beer, then tilted the bottle from one side to the other. He had never asked exactly what their offer entailed. It could be as simple as placing him under twenty-four-hour surveillance or as complicated as taking him into protective custody. Either one would play hell with his plans for a personal life. Seducing Lainie wasn't the easiest task he'd ever attempted. With a constant audience, it would be impossible.

With his luck, their plans could be as drastic as placing him in the witness relocation program. They could give him a new identity and a new life far from Serenity and New Orleans, but a new life was one thing he'd never wanted. No matter how miserable things had gotten, he had always been satisfied being Nicholas Carlucci, Serenity Street punk. He would never be happy as anyone else, would never be happy anywhere else.

"My refusal still stands."

Jolie leaned forward, resting her arms on the table. "Don't be an idiot, Nick. You know Jimmy better than anyone else. You *know* he'll keep his promise."

"So maybe the feds should try to stop him before he does."

"Maybe *you* should cooperate in stopping him. It's *your* life, damn it."

"And I have to live it my way. I don't want the government's protection. I don't want anything from them. I'll deal with Falcone on my own."

"He'll kill you," Smith said flatly.

"He'll try."

"He's just playing with you," Jolie needlessly pointed out to him. "He's making you wait, giving you a false sense of security. When you start to think that maybe he's forgotten you, when you think that maybe it's okay to do something with your life, when you've got something worth having, *then* he'll act. Then he'll kill you."

As she spoke, Lainie came around the corner and started toward them. Her hair was still damp, but she'd changed into a dress the color of turquoise whose fibers were surely all elastic, because that was the only way it could cling and shift and give with her natural, easy, too damn sensual movements. Her timing, with regards to the conversation, couldn't have been more perfect. *Something worth having.* She certainly was.

Not that he had her...yet. Not that he was certain he wanted her for anything beyond sex and short-term companionship. Not that he thought there was any possibility of keeping her. Not him. Not a woman like her.

She sat down in the chair Jamey had vacated and extended her hand first to Jolie, then to Smith. "I'm Lainie Farrell. I work over at Kathy's House."

Nicholas gave Jolie a chance to complete the introductions before he spoke. "Lainie lives upstairs. She's another of Jamey's charity cases." First had come Reid, then Cassie, then Nicholas and Lainie. Once she had moved on to a better life and he was gone—not necessarily dead, just gone—Jamey would find someone else who needed a cheap roof over his head. His old friend had quite a social conscience—but then, he had always looked out for others, even when they were kids. "If you have enough time to mind other people's business, Jolie, why don't you do some fund-raising for the women's center so they can pay their employees a living wage?"

"Pardon me for thinking that forty-three is too young to die."

"Hey, I'm not dead yet." At his flippant reply, shadows darkened Lainie's eyes, and he silently cursed Jolie and Smith for coming here, for forcing the issue when she was around. "Look, you want to talk about something else? Fine. Otherwise, this visit is over."

He was surprised when Smith rose from his chair, circled the table and helped Jolie to her feet. He had expected more of an argument, but he was relieved not to get it.

"If you change your mind…"

"I won't."

Kendricks looked from him to Lainie, then back again. "Situations change. If yours does, let us know. In the meantime, be careful. I agree with Jolie. Forty-three is much too young to die. Lainie."

Nicholas didn't turn to watch them leave, but instead spun the empty beer bottle in slow circles on the table. After a half-dozen rotations, Lainie caught hold of it and tugged it from his hand. "They're worried about you."

"I can't live my life waiting to see what Jimmy might do."

"Waiting for the inevitable, you mean."

"The only inevitability around here, sweetheart, is you and me in bed." He watched a flush darken her cheeks and felt a corresponding heat spread through him. They were both mature, capable adults, with a lifetime of experience between them, and yet she could still blush. He could still respond like an infatuated kid.

"You're awfully sure of yourself." Now she was the one

making the bottle twirl, letting it slow to a stop before giving it another spin. When it stopped, pointing directly at him, he intercepted her hand as she reached for it and drew her out of the chair and around the table.

"You owe me a kiss."

She pulled against him but not hard enough to free herself. "I don't owe you anything."

"You spun the bottle. The rules say you have to kiss whoever it points to."

"That's a silly game. I was too grown-up to play it even when I was a kid."

He drew her across his lap, not straddling it, the way he would like—her dress was too short and too snug—but sitting sideways, hands folded in her lap, prim and proper, considering that his arousal was growing and straining against her. "You should never be too grown-up to play kissing games." He drew his fingers down her bare arm, making her shiver and shift against him. "Just one kiss, and I'll let you go." But that was a lie. One kiss of the right kind, and he would carry her upstairs to one bed or the other and never let her go.

For a time she simply looked at him, her hazel eyes steady, and then she touched him. She combed her fingers through his hair, sliding all the way down to his nape, then brushing just the tips of her fingers around to his jaw. Bracing herself with her other hand on his chest, she bent closer, moistened her lips, then stiffened. In an instant, the playfulness, the seductiveness were gone, and tension had taken its place. "I'm sorry. I can't," she whispered, jumping to her feet, hurrying toward the back of the bar.

He stood up, too, but she was already disappearing around the corner. "Lainie, wait—"

A moment later, her apartment door slammed. A moment after that, the Kendrickses drove past on the flooded street.

He went upstairs and tried the door. It was locked. "Lainie, open the door."

There was silence inside.

"Come on, it's no big deal." Just maybe the biggest deal in his life. He'd gotten himself into a hell of a mess—damn near desperate to end too many years of celibacy and determined to end it with only Lainie, who couldn't decide whether she wanted him. At the church her answer had been a definite yes. In spite of the rain and the peculiar location, he had no doubt that he could have taken her there. If he hadn't preferred the comfort of a bed over the frantic hurry-up-and-explode they were building to, if he hadn't wanted all the time in the world for looking, touching, kissing, pleasuring, if he hadn't wanted the privacy for something special, something meaningful, something memorable, he could have already ended this long, painful phase. But he had wanted more, and now she didn't. She *couldn't*.

Frustrated, he banged the door hard enough to rattle it on its hinges. "Damn it, Lainie!"

Absolute silence.

For a long time he stood there, hearing nothing but his own uneven breathing, feeling nothing but his own restless edge. Finally he went downstairs to the kitchen, where he fixed a sandwich he didn't particularly want, and then to the bar, where he pulled up a stool behind the bar, popped the top on a can of soda and ate lunch to the lonesome accompaniment of rain beating down.

At five minutes till twelve, Jamey made a repeat dash across the street. He left his jacket near the door, combed the water from his hair, then settled on a stool on the opposite side of the bar. Without waiting to be asked, Nicholas fixed a glass of ice water and slid it across.

After the silence had dragged out, Nicholas finally broke it. "You want me to get out of here?"

Jamey looked surprised. "Why would I want that?"

"At least it would stop the feds from coming around here."

''Smith? Nah. He and Jolie come down here pretty often, either to the center or to see Cassie and Reid. Remy Sinclair and Michael Bennett come by a lot, too. Michael's wife helps out from time to time, and Susannah, Remy's wife, is one of Karen's full-time nurses.''

Now that was news. He'd probably seen Susannah Sinclair—Duncan when he'd known her—a dozen times or more when he'd watched at the window for Lainie, but he'd never recognized her. Of course, he'd never *really* known her. Like so many others, she had been just one more of Jimmy's pawns. After one attempt on Sinclair's life had failed, leaving him wounded and in need of nursing, Jimmy had persuaded Susannah to take the job by kidnapping her younger brother, then offering to trade the kid's future for information regarding Sinclair's habits and movements. The information was meant to facilitate a second, hopefully successful attempt to get rid of the FBI agent who had long been a thorn in Falcone's side.

Unfortunately for Jimmy, he had chosen the wrong go-between. Nicholas had had no desire to play a role in anyone's death, particularly the FBI agent who was his best chance at seeing Jimmy punished. He had deliberately distorted Susannah's information, had left out certain details and completely fabricated others. Unfortunately for Sinclair and Susannah, Jimmy had gone around Nicholas and had almost succeeded in killing them both anyway.

''Have you even considered Smith's suggestion?''

Nicholas scowled at Jamey. ''I don't need protection. The FBI has somebody watching Jimmy twenty-four hours a day. If he decides to come after me, they'll know.''

''They could have someone watching you without your agreement, couldn't they?''

''They could, but they haven't.'' He grinned. ''A stranger in this neighborhood draws more than a little attention. He would be real easy to avoid.'' It wasn't as if he were new to the surveillance game. Most of the time he'd worked for Falcone, he'd been under the FBI's microscope. It had provided him with something of a challenge there toward the end, when he'd begun passing evidence and documentation of Jimmy's crimes to Jolie. Giving both Jimmy's watchdogs and the feds the slip had added a little danger and excitement to the process.

Changing the subject, he gestured toward the street. "You get many customers on a day like this?"

"Not too many. There are a few who need a drink more on a day like this, but most of them stay home. That's where I'd be if I had a choice."

"So go on home. I'll watch the place."

Jamey gave his offer about a moment's serious thought, then grinned. "Are you serious?"

"I've got nothing better to do."

"Oh, Nicky, you're a sad man." He slid to the floor. "There's a price list posted, some of the regulars have an account, and you know your booze. If you have any problems, give me a call."

It was that easy—no protests, no worries. Just a simple offer, and he had a job for the day.

Not much of a job, he acknowledged later in the afternoon. Lainie remained silent and locked away upstairs, the rain continued to fall, no customers came in, and the hours crawled past. He caught a football game on TV, even though he didn't care much for the sport, and watched part of a movie before wandering over to settle at a table near the door. Periodically the rain let up enough to allow the excess water to flow down the street and empty into the ditches there; then it seemed to come harder and faster than ever, rising to the top of the curb, once covering nearly half the sidewalk in front of O'Shea's. Major portions of the city were flooded, creating an emergency of minor proportions, but down here on Serenity all was quiet. People didn't expect help from the city's pumping stations or from God or nature. They just quietly coped.

He'd been sitting at the table for well over two hours, playing solitaire with a well-worn deck of cards Jamey kept behind the bar, when the car first drove past. Jimmy had a whole garage full of expensive automobiles, but he had never sat inside any of them. The limo was his only form of transportation. Even when he got arrested, he always found out about the warrant and turned himself in before the cops could show up to haul him off to jail in the back of a patrol car.

The car was barely moving but still created a wake. Nicholas watched the little ripples of water washing high up onto the sidewalk as the car passed out of sight. The driver would go to the end of the block, turn around and come back at the same slow pace. Just giving Nicholas the message that Jimmy hadn't forgotten him? He knew that. Jimmy never forgot a slight, real or imagined—and Nicholas's had been very real.

In less than five minutes, the limo returned, stopping in the middle of the street directly in front of Nicholas. The press of a button sent the back window silently down, giving him a glimpse of the darkened interior of the car before Jimmy leaned forward. He didn't speak. He simply stared at Nicholas for a long, still moment, the look on his face one of pure sorrow. Then, in the space of an instant, his expression went blank, he leaned back, the heavily tinted window went up again, and the driver pulled away.

Goodbye. That had been the message. Now the games would begin. *He's just playing with you,* Jolie had told him. Jimmy loved cat-and-mouse games. Playing with his victim—keeping him off balance, giving him days, maybe even months, of peace, then tormenting him, never letting him guess when or how it would happen—would bring him almost as much satisfaction as actually killing him. It would be business well done.

Well, Jimmy was going to have settle for just the killing this time. The game wasn't going to work. Nicholas didn't care when he did it or how or where. He didn't give a damn about any of the details, didn't even give a damn about the final result. Dying six months from now wasn't going to be any more punishing than dying tonight. He was ready. He'd been ready ever since he'd knelt on a wet Baton Rouge street and watched the only woman he'd ever really loved die before his eyes. He was ready.

So why did his hand tremble as he played the two of hearts on a black three?

Why were the muscles all through his body knotted and taut?

And why did he feel tremendous regret at the thought of Lainie?

He heard her footsteps in the back hall an instant before she entered the bar. He didn't turn to look at her but continued with his game, moving a black seven to a red eight before playing the red six on the bottom of the deck. As she came to a stop somewhere close behind, he picked up the deck, counted out three cards and turned them faceup on the table.

"What was he doing here?"

She must have been sitting on the ugly sofa in her apartment, staring out the window in exactly the way he passed too much of his time. Usually, though, he was looking for her. What had she been looking for?

He played another card before answering. "Just making his presence known."

"Did he say anything?"

"Nope. He didn't need to."

After a long, still moment, she came around and sat down on his left. She was still wearing the turquoise dress, but she'd added a jacket, ivory, long, ending only an inch or two higher than the dress. The sleeves were long, too, meant to be folded back and cuffed, but she wore them down, covering all but the tips of her fingers. In spite of the jacket, she looked cold. Well, he had a remedy for that, but damned if he was going to offer. Not yet, anyway.

"Why are you so dead set against accepting the government's help?"

The five of diamonds he'd been looking for turned up in playing position, and he moved it into place, which allowed him to move one column and turn over the last ace. He added it to the three above before glancing at her. "I think I've said all I want on the subject."

"Say it to *me*. Tell *me* why you're willing to sit back and let that man kill you."

"I've told you before. I don't give a damn." He gave her long, bare legs a long, leisurely look, then grinned. "Of course, if you want to give me a reason to live, I'd be happy to consider it."

Her scowl was proportional to his grin. "How about the fact that people care about you? Jamey and Jolie and Smith—"

"What about you?" He wasn't grinning now, and the cards lay forgotten in his hand. "Do you care about me, Lainie?"

For a long time she stared at him, her eyes wide with dismay. Her lips parted, then compressed, then she drew a deep breath and gave the answer he wanted to hear. No, the answer he *didn't* want to hear. "Yes, Nicholas. I care, too."

Chapter 6

"Did you know that you're standing on the east bank of the Mississippi facing east?"

Lainie looked over her shoulder at the man who had spoken with more than a little wariness. She had expected Sam to show up, as usual, for this Wednesday afternoon meeting. She was disconcerted to see Smith Kendricks instead.

"It's because of the way the river loops around the city. You can stand here and watch the sun rise over the west bank."

She turned her gaze back to the river and the twin bridges rising high above it. "Where is Sam?"

"I told him I would fill him in." As the U.S. Attorney, that was his prerogative. He could get as involved in an investigation as he and the FBI wanted. There was no question that the Falcone case had long been personal for him and, with his good friend Remy Sinclair the case agent, no question that he was going to be very involved. "What happened Saturday afternoon?"

Her muscles tightened and her face started to warm before she realized that he was referring to Falcone's visit, not to her tremendous lapse in conduct. He hadn't seen her sitting on Nicholas's lap after he and his wife left O'Shea's, hadn't seen her bend to kiss him. If he had, she would have heard from him long before now. She would have been stood at attention in her boss's office and given a blistering reminder of exactly what constituted professional misconduct. She probably would have been yanked off this case and sent back to Atlanta in disgrace, and Nicholas would have official protection, whether he wanted it or not.

Even though Smith hadn't seen her, she had fortunately seen him when he, Jolie and the O'Sheas had come out of Kathy's House. The brief glimpse had been all she needed to remember who she was, why she was there and how much she had to lose. It had been enough to send her fleeing for the safety of her room, where she had brooded and worried until she'd seen the car on the street.

She'd been brooding and worrying even more since she'd seen the car on the street.

"According to Nicholas, Jimmy was just making his presence known. He drove by, turned around, stopped in front of O'Shea's, rolled the window down and let Nicholas see him, then left."

"There was no conversation?"

She shook her head.

"Any sign of Jimmy since then?"

Another shake.

"What does Nick do with his time?"

"Not much. As far as I know, he doesn't go anywhere. I see him sometimes during the day just standing at the window. Yesterday he helped me plant some flowers at Kathy's House." She'd been on her knees in front of the long raised bed that stretched from one end of the iron fence to the other, with breaks for the center gate and the driveway where it entered and had once exited, when he'd joined her. Flat after flat of pansies in shades of violet, deep purplish-blue and white had stretched across the yard, donated by a local nursery, and he had remarked that, if she stayed around, in another year or two she could be planting her own pansies, grown in her own nursery.

There wasn't much chance of that. Staying was out of the question—her job and her life were in Atlanta—and raising flowers had been her mother's dream, not hers. It was a nice dream, though—fixing up the cottage, filling its huge yard with every sort of flower, tree and shrub that flourished in New Orleans' tropical climate, living and working with people she had come to like and respect, contributing to a community that she believed she could enrich. Oh, yes, it was a sweet dream.

She didn't deal in dreams, though, but hard realities. If she failed to protect Nicholas, neither Serenity nor New Orleans would be bearable. If she succeeded in her job, he would make staying impossible. He would send her back to Atlanta and would never want to see her again.

"What about nights?"

She blinked, then focused on Smith. "Nights? He usually spends them with me." At his faint smile, she felt a flush heat her cheeks. "I mean the evenings, of course. The last couple of nights, around nine o'clock, he's taken over the bar so Jamey could spend some time with his family." Before nine, he'd been in her apartment both evenings. They'd eaten dinner on the slip-covered sofa, then spent the rest of the evening working on her dresser and tables. She was great with the finish sanding between coats, while his talent lay in meticulous, bubble-free applications of polyurethane. In a different world, she could have her gardens and he could build quite a business refinishing fine old furniture. He could help her plant and she could help him sand, and together they could accomplish anything.

But this was the only world they had, and in this world, she was an FBI agent, and he was an ex-con disbarred lawyer with whom she was prohibited any association at all except in the performance of her duties. That kiss in the rain Saturday had been enough to tarnish her so-far spotless record. Another one or two like it, and she would be out of a job. Who would hire her then when the FBI had fired her for professional misconduct?

"Have you talked to him about accepting protection?"

She gave him a dry look. "The subject isn't open for discussion. He says he doesn't give a damn. Period."

"He hasn't given a damn about much of anything for a long time except seeing Jimmy punished."

"Why did that mean so much to him? He risked his life. He went to prison. Why?"

"The only reason he ever gave was that Falcone killed someone. We went through all the deaths attributed to Jimmy, and we couldn't make a connection."

She watched a piece of trash float by in the muddy brown water. "Maybe it wasn't directly attributable to him. Maybe she overdosed on drugs bought from his people. Maybe she was one of his girls. Maybe she gambled away more than she could afford to lose." There were plenty of ways people like Jimmy Falcone killed, many of them too round-about or distantly connected for the law to hold him accountable. But Nicholas could.

"Why do you say she?"

Her choice of pronouns had been subconscious, but she would have made the same choice if she'd given it any thought. "He sacrificed fifteen years, his career and maybe even his life to this vendetta. Such an extreme need for vengeance must have been fed by tremendous grief or sorrow or guilt. What greater sorrow for a man than to lose the woman he loved?"

It was the obvious conclusion. Of course Nicholas had loved some woman. He was a grown man. It was only natural. And of course his love had been powerful, strong enough to drive him for ten years or more, intense enough to make him believe that life without her wasn't worth living. That was why he refused the government's protection. That was why he didn't give a damn about where he lived, how he lived or even if he lived. Obvious…but she didn't like it just the same.

She hated being jealous of an unknown dead woman, hated the sense of defeat she felt. How could she compete with a ghost? How could anything she had to offer compare with the memory of his one great love?

She *wasn't* competing, she reminded herself sternly. All she had to offer Nicholas was protection, nothing more, nothing less. His past love life was none of her business, and his future love life, if he had one, was sure as hell none of her business.

"Talk to him when you get a chance. Try to change his mind about accepting our help. I trust you to keep an eye on him, but knowing Jimmy, I'd feel more comfortable if Nick were in a more secure place."

"I'll try, but he may not listen." Or he might repeat his suggestion of Saturday afternoon—*give me a reason to live*—and she might make an effort. If she succumbed, if she was that weak, that foolish, her only hope was that they would both live to regret it. "I'd better get back. I've been gone too long."

"Are these meetings difficult for you to arrange?"

"No. Karen sends me on errands pretty often. I'll just tell her I got lost." It wouldn't be entirely a lie. Thanks to Nicholas, she was feeling more than a little lost right now. Offering a grim smile in place of a goodbye, she headed for the parking lot where she'd left Karen's car. The interior was fragrant with the smell of day-old bread and rolls, another donation to the center.

She drove through downtown and the Quarter, making all the right turns without thinking. She was becoming accustomed to the city, familiar with its streets and traffic. She was starting to feel at home there—which had very little to do with the city and everything to do with Serenity, with Kathy's House, with her job. With Nicholas.

As she slowed for the turn onto Serenity, another car rolled to a stop there. It was common knowledge in the neighborhood that the car was stolen, but it was so battered that the owner had probably failed to report it. It looked and sounded one step away from the junkyard, but it provided adequate transportation for the punks who had stolen it.

Trevor Morgan was behind the wheel. He didn't even look in Lainie's direction, but Vinnie Marino in the passenger seat did. He made a big show of it, leaning forward and glaring at her all the way past. At the last second, just before he passed out of her field of vision, he grinned and made a grand kissing gesture, followed by an obscene one. The second gesture didn't bother her. The kiss sent shivers of revulsion down her spine.

Classes were letting out at the school as she parked in the lot behind Kathy's House. Cassie and Jaye Stephens, who taught the upper grades, were lining their thirty or so students in the grass, preparing to walk them home. In the beginning, the escort had been necessary, the only way some parents would agree to let their children attend. Lately the streets seemed safer, but the practice continued and probably always would.

Lainie was backing out of the car with an armload of bakery bags when Nicholas joined her. "You've been gone quite a while for a simple errand," he remarked as he took her bags and freed her to reach inside for the remaining half dozen.

She tried to ignore the little pangs of guilt inside. "Was Karen concerned?"

"No. She just didn't think it should take so long."

"I got lost." The lie flushed her face, but she was far enough behind him that he wouldn't notice. "My sense of direction is okay, but I guess I don't pay enough attention.

Like the day I walked past the furniture store without noticing it.''

"You were upset that day.'' He slowed until she had no choice but to fall in step beside him. "Were you upset today?''

"No. Just lost.''

"Next time ask me to go along. I never get lost.''

"I bet you don't,'' she murmured as she maneuvered the door open, held it for him, then followed him inside.

Most of the bread went straight into the freezer in the utility room. The remaining loaves and the waxed paper bags holding two dozen cinnamon rolls went onto the counter in the kitchen. After returning Karen's keys to her and repeating the lie about losing her way, Lainie went outside with Nicholas on her heels. "Is there any particular reason you were looking for me?'' she asked as she started toward the storage shed in the back corner.

"I got bored in the apartment.''

"And I'm supposed to do something about that?''

The look he gave her was teasing and tempting, and she expected a response to match. He controlled the urge, though, and said, "Actually I was looking for the key to your apartment. I thought I'd put the last coat of polyurethane on the tables so you wouldn't have an excuse not to go to dinner with me tonight.''

Barely breathing, she looked at him a long time. The key to her apartment. It was a simple enough request. After all, he'd spent plenty of time there. He'd done most of the hard work on the tables. It wasn't as if he were likely to steal anything—wasn't as if she had much of anything worth stealing. The Lainie he knew would probably hand over the key without the slightest hesitation.

But he didn't know the real Lainie, the one with the badge, credentials and pistol hidden in the bottom of her backpack in the darkest corner of the closet. And while she knew she could trust him not to take anything, she *wasn't* sure she could trust him not to do a little snooping. He was a curious man, and she had a lot to be curious about.

She picked up a pair of gardening gloves, shook them, then tugged each one on. "Funny. I don't remember being invited to dinner tonight."

He shoved his hands into his jean pockets as he leaned against the jamb. "Will you go to dinner with me tonight?"

"Yes, I will. See how easy that was? You didn't even have to bribe me by finishing the tables."

"So I'll do it anyway. Like I said, I'm bored."

"So do something important."

"I assume you have a suggestion."

She smiled coolly. "You could help Karen track down the owner of the apartment building the Williamses live in. The tenants are having some real problems, and the management company doesn't want to do anything besides collect the rent."

"Easy job."

"Maybe for an experienced lawyer. I bet you could find out the information and still be ready to go to dinner around six."

For a moment he simply looked at her, then, with a grin, shook his head. "All right. You win this time—but only this time."

"Oh, don't count on it," she said softly. "You'll get bored again or you'll want something from me again. Who knows what you might agree to next time?"

When she started to leave the shed with gardening tools in hand, he blocked most of the doorway so she had to pass indecently close. For just a moment, he stopped her, his hand warm on her arm, his breath warmer on her temple. His mouth brushed her forehead, her cheek and finally her mouth as he softly, hoarsely answered. "And who knows what you might give me in return?"

He kissed her then—tender, sweet and incredibly possessive, as if he had every right, as if she belonged to him and only him. When he broke off, too soon—or was it too late?—he cupped his palm to her cheek for a brief caress, gave her a gentle smile, then walked away without a look back.

Lainie stepped back into the shadows inside the shed, the back of one gloved hand pressed to her mouth—to capture the feel of the kiss, to stifle the half laugh, half cry bubbling up inside her, to send a calming message to her unsettled stomach. He was going to be the ruin of her with those kisses, those touches and all those sweet temptations.

She just prayed that, as a result, she wasn't the death of him.

Lainie had been right. Uncovering the name of the errant landlord hadn't taken more than a single phone call, though, frankly, Nicholas had cheated. His call had been to a private investigator whose business he'd supported during his years with Falcone. In no time at all, thanks to computers and a friend at City Hall, the PI had called back with a name, address and telephone number. Karen had been grateful, even though it had been a nothing job. Now they could go on to their next step, she had said with great satisfaction. He hadn't asked what that was, afraid he would hear the word lawsuit, along with a few other unwelcome words, like advice and help. He wasn't in the help-giving business anymore.

Not that he ever had been—at least, not legitimate help to people who truly needed it. To his knowledge, he had never defended an innocent man. Early in his career, there had been those who had claimed innocence, though he'd never believed them. Once he'd started working for Jimmy, none of his clients had bothered with the lie of innocence, except in court.

All those years in school, all that hard work and money, all that effort to become one of the best lawyers in the damn state, and all he had done was manipulate the system to set guilty people free so they could go out and rob, steal and kill again. It was a depressing thought.

Rolling onto his side, he deliberately avoided Rena's picture and checked the clock. For the five years he was in prison, time had never really mattered. He'd gotten up when he was told to, had eaten not when the clock or his stomach had said it was time but when the guards said it was, and he'd gone to bed when they decreed. For the first few weeks out, he hadn't cared about time, but lately he was starting. He wanted to know when it was time for Lainie to go to work, when it was time for her to come home. This evening he certainly wanted to know when it was time to meet her for dinner, and so he had finally set the clock to the proper hour.

She was expecting him in ten minutes. He had heard her come up the stairs forty minutes ago, had heard her get into the shower soon after. That had been both pleasure and pain—lying in bed still naked from his own shower, listening to the water run on the opposite side of the wall and knowing that she was naked, too.

Rising from the bed, he got dressed, ran his fingers through his hair, locked up the apartment and crossed the few feet to her door. "It's open," she called, and he hung the jacket he carried over the stair rail, then turned the knob, letting the door swing in on its own weight.

She was standing in front of the dresser in the living room, fastening earrings in place, sliding a half-dozen silver and gold bangles onto her right wrist, fixing a substantial looking gold cuff around her left wrist. She was wearing jeans that fitted more snugly than her favorite pair and one of the two white shirts that still gave him restless nights and heated dreams. Unfortunately it was the wrong one— or, if they really did want to go anywhere but straight to bed, the right one.

Finished with the jewelry, she smiled at him. "You look nice."

He gave his clothes—khaki trousers with his own white cotton shirt—a glance, then shrugged off her compliment. In the years he'd worked for Jimmy, he'd worn suits of silk or linen every day. His former boss had believed in dressing the part you were playing, and Nicholas's role had been that of successful attorney. He'd never faced a prosecutor whose clothes were better chosen, had never faced a single juror who ever might have guessed that he'd come from the poorest part of the city. He had looked the part, and he had become what he'd pretended to be.

He had no pretenses left. He was an ex-con with more money than he ought to have and nothing else. This was as nice as it got.

"Before we go, could you help me move the dresser? I tried to scoot it, but the legs wouldn't scoot and kept bowing."

"Grab that end." He took hold of the marble top, lifted and followed her into the bedroom. The waist pack she carried instead of a purse was on his end, sliding with each step they took. Just as they set it down, it reached the edge. He reached for it, but she pulled it away a little too hastily, he thought, and quickly secured it around her waist. "What do you carry in there?"

"The usual. Makeup, tissues, breath mints, money, keys." She grinned. "You know. Women's stuff." She adjusted the dresser an inch or two this way, another inch that way, then bent to make sure the legs were straight.

While she was busy, his attention drifted to the only other piece of furniture in the room—the only piece he had any interest at all in: the bed. It was a double, like his, in better shape than his and unmade. There was nothing frilly or fussy about it. The sheets were white, as was the loosely woven blanket, and the comforter was yellow and white stripes. It was inexpensive, quilted in a puffy diamond pattern that was slightly off-kilter with nylon thread that tended to give up its stitches easily. It was the sort of comforter that, after a year's use and a year's washings, got relegated to picnics in the yard and pallets on the floor.

"That looks great, doesn't it?"

He moved to study the dresser. The marble was in fair shape, and she'd done a good job on the wood. It bore little resemblance to the twenty-five-dollar eyesore the furniture store had delivered a week and a half ago. The mirror could use a little resilvering or, better, complete replacement. The image it reflected—him, her, the bed—was slightly distorted, wavy, softening around the edges before disappearing. "You do good work."

"We," she said, correcting him. "You did a lot of it yourself. Ready?"

He led the way out, picking up his jacket, waiting for her to lock the door, then slide the key into her pocket. When he had approached her this afternoon about working on the tables, he had expected her to hand the key over without hesitation. Instead she had simply looked at him for a long time before none too subtly steering him away from the idea. Had she been thinking of all the things in her apartment he could snoop through, all the secrets she had hidden? Did she think he would stoop to that?

He wasn't offended. The final coats of finish for the tables wouldn't have taken long, and she must have brought a few personal things with her—mementos, souvenirs, the sort of things sentimental women didn't leave behind when they moved on. Maybe when he was done, he *would* have looked for them and through them. There were things he wanted to know about her, and he'd learned from Jimmy to take advantage of whatever opportunity presented itself. When else would he be alone in her apartment, free to intrude on her privacy? When else would he be given the chance to find out something, anything, about her life before New Orleans?

They left the bar and headed for the restaurant, a quiet little place in the heart of the Quarter. There were fewer than a dozen tables, several of which were afforded privacy in the dining room's odd little nooks and crannies. Their table was in the courtyard, once open to the hot Louisiana sun, now glassed in and surrounded by brick walls and lush plants. The only music was the water falling in the central fountain, the only intrusion the waiter who took their order, then served their drinks.

"I never knew this place was here."

"You've only been here a few weeks. You can live a lifetime in New Orleans and never know everything."

"How did you discover it? Someone special bring you here?"

He shook his head. Jimmy had introduced him to the place. The old man had planned many a crime here, and Nicholas had prepared many a defense.

"There must have been someone special at some point," she persisted, her smile sweet and inviting all sorts of confidences. "Surely you've been in love a time or two."

"Or two," he agreed. "As much as I was capable, I loved Jolie."

With a shake of her head, she brushed that off. "Doesn't count. You were a kid having sex for the very first time. Of course you loved her."

"Did you love your first?"

Her expression sobered. "I never had a chance to have a first at home. My father insisted on putting the fear of God into every boy I went out with. They would have died before sullying his precious little girl. After a while, they quit asking me out."

"So you waited until you left home."

"I moved to Athens because I had friends going to school there who would let me crash on their floor. My first night in town they took me to a party, and…" Her shrug was uneasy, her smile a little sad, more than a little ashamed. "I never even knew his name."

It seemed perfectly reasonable to him. With her mother

dead and her brother gone, living four long years with only the father she despised who loved her too much, she must have been desperate for some semblance of normalcy in her life. Teenage girls away from home in a college town for the first time got a little wild, and they certainly had sex with teenage or slightly older boys. She'd just wanted to be like other girls—at least, until she'd done it.

The smile tightened and lost its shame but gained no pleasure. "So now you know two things about me that I've never told anyone else. Let's get back to the original subject—you being in love."

How she'd lost her virginity and how her mother had lived and died. To most people they would be nothing but stories, one unremarkable, the other sad. They meant more than that to Lainie, though. Shame and sorrow, significant times in her life and, therefore, very personal. It said something of her feelings for him that she'd shared them with him. It made him a little uncomfortable. It touched him.

And it aroused him like hell.

"Jolie does count," he disagreed. "We were together a long time. It wasn't just sex."

"Okay, but that was when you were a kid. As an adult, as a man, have you ever been in love?"

He shifted his gaze to the brick wall a dozen feet ahead. It was old, original to the building, the brick soft and red. Some sort of vine had been planted along the base, and it spread up and out in a fan, sinking its roots into the mortar, attaching its tendrils to the face of the bricks. Maybe someday the vine would become too invasive, its roots chinking the mortar the bricks needed to stand, and it would destroy the wall. Or maybe the vine strengthened it, the roots become a part of its support. Did Rena—knowing her, loving her, losing her—strengthen him, or was she going to someday destroy him? He suspected the answer was both. It had been her memory that had gotten him through the last twenty years, and it was the things he'd done in her memory that were going to get him killed.

Unless he decided to fight Falcone one last time. But this time it wouldn't be for Rena. It would be for himself. And Lainie.

"Yes," he replied at last, meeting her gaze again. "I've been in love. Have you?"

She flashed that uneasy smile again. "I was married, remember?"

"And you woke up the next morning and realized what a tremendous mistake you'd made. You didn't love him, did you?"

"I did." His steady gaze made her shift and admit, "I thought I did. I tried." She didn't pause more than a second. "What about the woman you loved? Where is she now?"

He didn't have to answer. In all these years he'd never told anyone anything about Rena. All Jolie knew was that there'd been a woman. Jamey didn't know that much. Nicholas hadn't wanted to share her with anyone while she was alive, and once she was dead, she had remained his private sorrow. She had been too special, too important, to entrust her memory to anyone around him. There had been a practical reason for his silence, as well: if anyone who worked for Falcone had made the connection between him and Rena, at best, he never would have been allowed within a mile of Jimmy. At worst, it would have meant his death.

He was good at not answering. He'd been doing it for years. So it was with some measure of surprise that he heard himself saying, "She's dead. She died because of me." He waited a moment for that to sink in, then quietly added, "Now you know something that I've never told anyone else."

He waited for her to respond. Her expression was as still, as serious, as it'd been before he'd answered. She hadn't shown any shock at hearing that Rena was dead or any revulsion on hearing that he was responsible. She had probably already guessed the first and suspected that he blamed himself for it. She probably didn't believe him, probably thought that he was accepting guilt where there was none. Now she would want proof, explanations, details, answers.

For a long time she didn't say anything. Then she laid her hand lightly over his. "Life is tough, isn't it?"

He had expected more questions, more demands. Instead she'd offered understanding. Again he was surprised.

Life is tough. It sure as hell was.

But a woman like Lainie could make it a little easier.

After their meal, they moved on to the blues club where they had shared their first dance. They sat out the first few numbers, then she rose from the table, silently extended her hand and, when he took it, led him onto the dance floor.

It was sweet, erotic, tormenting. The night was cool, the music was hot, and this thing between them—this need, this hunger—was damn near unbearable. Nicholas tried to enjoy the dance for exactly what it was—intimacy of the public variety, their bodies pressed together, her breasts against his chest, his arousal against her belly, every movement stirring a raw ache inside. He tried not to think of what it could but wouldn't lead to: him and Lainie, alone and naked, exploring, learning, moving together, wicked, wild sex, passion, desire, satisfaction. She wasn't ready for all that yet.

He was beyond ready.

Halfway through the second song, she tilted her head back and, with an effort, focused her hazy gaze on his. "Did you dance with her like this?"

He shook his head. Only in bed, the very first night they'd met and a thousand times after that. He'd never had such riches in his life, not physically and never emotionally. Rena had loved him from the beginning, and it had never wavered right up until the end.

He wondered if Lainie could ever love him.

As he gazed down at her, somewhere off toward the doors a light flashed. Tourists, trying to capture the Quarter's night life on film, as if memories wouldn't be enough. He was living proof that memories could last a man a lifetime, but he was ready for some new ones. He was tired of only remembering what it was like to be happy, loved and in love. He wanted to know again. He wanted to feel it, wanted to live it again, and he wanted to do it with Lainie.

Bending his head, he nuzzled her ear and sent a shiver through her that he felt in his own body. His mouth directly above her ear, he murmured, "Darlin', unless you're willing to go to the nearest bed with me right now, I can't take any more of this. It's your choice."

For a moment, she continued to move with the music. Then, with a reluctance he could feel, she stopped and took a step back. It put only a few inches' space between them, but it was enough. It made her answer disappointingly clear.

He gestured toward the doors, then followed her through them. As the night's humid chill replaced the smoky warmth of the bar, she pulled her jacket tight and held it with her arms across her chest. He was grateful for his own jacket and for the lower temperatures that provided his body with a little badly needed cooling.

Lainie didn't speak until they reached Jackson Square. There she walked to the wrought iron fence, wrapped her fingers around a bar and stared at the statue of Andrew Jackson. When she finally broke her silence, her voice was unsteady. "I'm not playing games with you, Nicholas."

He didn't think she was, but he didn't say so. A little guilt on her behalf could work in his favor.

When he didn't respond, she turned around and leaned against the edge of the masonry wall that supported the fence. "I want to make love with you, but I can't."

"Because of who you are. What you are."

She nodded unhappily.

"Exactly what does that mean, Lainie? Were you the head of the Dixie Mafia? Were you a crook, a drug addict, a prostitute? Are you a nun? Do you have a husband and ten kids back in Atlanta wondering where the hell Mama has gone?"

She shook her head.

"Those are the worst things I can think of, and they don't matter, so the secret you're hiding doesn't matter, either. It can't affect the way I feel about you. Whatever it is, it can't make me not want you." A new possibility occurred to him, and he moved to stand only a few feet in front of her. "Were you with some bastard who mistreated you? Are you afraid it'll happen again? Are you afraid I'll hurt you?"

"No," she whispered, and he believed her. He had never seen fear in her eyes, not even when they'd gotten as close as two people could get without completing the act. There had been only desire, need and, at times like these, regret.

Frustration propelled him away, then he came back to lean beside her. "Can you tell me one thing? Do I stand a chance? Because I don't want to reduce what's between us to just sex, but it's been a hell of a long time for me, darlin'. I'll wait if there's a chance, but if there's not..." He stared hard at the benches in front of them and the trash collected underneath before gathering the courage to look in her face and finish. "I've got to find someone else."

She stared at him, her eyes wide, her expression one of hurt and dismay. Abruptly she jumped to her feet and took off. He let her go and for a moment sat there damning himself. Who was he kidding? He didn't want anyone else but Lainie. No matter how many times she said no, he would wait, because eventually she would have to say yes. Eventually she would learn to trust him, to love him, and with that the last barrier, whatever the hell it was, would have to come down.

As he got to his feet, he felt every one of his years in his bones and double the number in his soul. He turned the corner she'd rounded and started toward Decatur, expecting to see her somewhere just up ahead, waiting for him, but the sidewalk between Chartres and the next street was practically empty. He picked up his pace until he was running, sliding to a stop at the light, searching the street to his left for her. The ivory jacket she was wearing should stand out, even in the night, but he saw no sign of her.

His heart rate increasing, his panic level rising, he spun to look behind him and saw her leaning against the fence, her head bowed, her arms tight across her stomach. He bowed his own head for a moment and said a silent prayer of thanks, then took a few steps toward her. "Let's go home, Lainie."

When she looked up, he saw the sign of threatening tears that she hadn't quite controlled. He quickly looked away. If she cried, he would have to comfort her, and there was only so much torture a man could endure in one evening.

While he waited for her to join him, he stepped to the curb and flagged down a cab, opening the back door for her, sliding in beside her. He gave the cabbie O'Shea's address, and the shriveled little man twisted in the seat to face him. "I don't go to Serenity."

Of course not. No one with good sense or other choices went to Serenity. He was there because he lacked good sense, and Lainie thought she had no other choices. "The corner of Serenity and Decatur will do."

With a nod, the driver faced forward again, waited for a slight break in traffic, then swung the cab in a wide arc. It wasn't wide enough, of course. He had to back up, pull forward and back up again, all the while ignoring the impatient honks from the traffic he'd stopped in four lanes. Less than five minutes later, he deposited them at the end of Serenity and was on his way back for a more lucrative fare.

As they approached O'Shea's, Nicholas finally broke the silence. "I never got around to telling you that I've taken a job. I'm now officially the evening bartender at O'Shea's. Tonight was my last free night for a while." He had hoped to spend it doing something special, and he had. Any time with Lainie was special. But he surely had hoped for a more satisfying ending to it.

"That's nice," she murmured. "Jamey can use the time with his family, and you need—"

He quietly interrupted. "I need *you,* Lainie."

"Time with other people." She stopped just before the bar and faced him. "Thank you for the dinner. Enjoy the job, and..." She looked away, then back, smiling the unsteady sort of smile that begged to be kissed away. "Good luck finding someone else." With that she made another quick escape, into the bar and no doubt straight upstairs to the safety of her apartment. He could follow her, could bang on the locked door, apologize, beg and plead, but it wouldn't do any good. He had screwed up really good this time. It would take some effort to make up for it.

Tonight he just didn't have the energy.

It was past time for a decision.

Lainie had tried to busy herself with normal tasks when she'd come in. She had removed her makeup and brushed her teeth, put the tennis shoes she'd kicked off in the living room in the bedroom closet, gathered up the newspapers that had served as drip cloths underneath the dresser and put away her clothes in the freshly lined dresser drawers. Her gun, slipped from its holster to prevent rusting, her badge and her credentials were in the top right-hand drawer, under a pile of socks, superficially hidden but easily accessible in an emergency.

All that had taken less than twenty minutes, though, and she'd been left with nothing to do but think, and nothing to think about but Nicholas. Her job. Her future, or lack of one.

She had already crossed the line with regards to her job. She suspected she had started across it the afternoon she'd moved in here when Nicholas had invited her to join him for a drink. But so far she hadn't done anything she couldn't turn back from. She had come close—too close tonight, last Saturday, the Monday before—but she could still save her job and herself.

But she was no longer sure that saving her job and saving herself were the same thing. Saving her job meant keeping her distance from Nicholas, emotionally as well as physically. Saving herself just might mean getting as close to him as humanly possible.

It was a risk, no denying that. Making love with him would almost surely mean losing her job. And for what? A short-term affair? A long-term one with no promises for the future? Or maybe so much more. Maybe making love would lead to just that—creating love where there had been none, building the desire, need, caring and concern into something that would last a lifetime. Maybe this next step could lead to the future she had long dreamed of and long ago given up on.

And maybe it could lead to heartache.

But not pursuing it would definitely lead there. She couldn't stand back and watch him turn to another woman. It would destroy her.

She didn't have many options. She could end this relationship right now and break her heart but keep her job. She could have an affair with him for as long as the assignment lasted, keep it her most intimate secret and try to hold on to the job when it was done. She could become lovers with him and tell him the truth; he might love her anyway, and she could trade the job for happily-ever-after with him. Or they could become lovers, he might hate her for the truth, and she would lose both him and her career.

Four possibilities, and only one happily-ever-after. Not very good odds.

With a morose sigh, she walked to the window and stared out at Serenity. Maybe she wasn't being fair to him. He'd said he didn't care if she'd been a crook, a drug addict or a prostitute. He'd insisted that whatever she was hiding didn't matter to him. He'd argued that nothing she'd done in the past could affect the way he felt about her now. Maybe the fact that she was an FBI agent *wouldn't* matter to him. Maybe the lies she'd told and the deceptions she'd practiced wouldn't change the way he looked at her, thought of her, wanted her.

Maybe. But she was pretty sure that, in his eyes, being an FBI agent was a much graver sin than being a crook, drug addict or prostitute. She'd heard the derision in his voice, had seen it in his eyes. She didn't think the knowledge that she was one of the damned was going to change his opinion of them. It would just change his opinion of her.

But he was an intelligent man and a brilliant lawyer. He was capable of seeing both sides of every case, of using rationale and logic, of seeing that, like him in his vendetta against Falcone, she'd done something less than honorable but for the most honorable of reasons. Yes, she had deceived him, but she'd done it to protect his life. He would have to forgive her.

She hoped. She prayed. She was risking her future on it.

Down on the street Jamey came into the light, crossing to the other side, going through the gate at Kathy's House. A glance at her watch showed that it was ten minutes before midnight. Either he'd closed early or Nicholas, who had never come upstairs, was doing it for him.

She watched as Jamey disappeared into the big house. The downstairs was dark, but dim lights burned on the second floor, where their living quarters were. Sean was probably tucked in his crib, snoring softly, but Karen was awake in their bedroom. She always liked to know that Jamey was home, she'd told Lainie, and that another day on Serenity had ended safely. They would talk, maybe make love, maybe go right to sleep, but whatever they did, it would be together. Lainie envied them their togetherness. It seemed so perfect.

But no one would have pegged them for the perfect couple when they'd first met. Karen had been the widow of a hero cop, a social worker, a do-gooder as they called her down here, and Jamey had been the slightly disreputable owner of a shabby bar in a lousy part of town. She had wanted to save Serenity from itself, and he had wanted to save it from her. She had been determined to make a difference, and he had been determined to make her leave. But somewhere among all their disagreements and differences, they had fallen deeply in love. Nothing could tear them apart.

Nicholas had loved like that before. Not even death had weakened his love for the woman. Maybe he could love that way again. Maybe he could love Lainie like that.

It was time to find out.

Turning away from the window, she walked to the door and swung it open. A dim light was on in the hallway. Brighter lights burned downstairs, where music played to the accompaniment of running water. She paced halfway down the hall, turned back, decided against going downstairs, paced again, then finally slid down to sit on the floor at the top of the stairs. She scooted into the corner, with the wall supporting her back, drew her knees to her chest and waited.

The water stopped, but the music continued. Maybe he was having one last drink and reading the newspaper Jamey always left on the bar. Maybe he was playing a lonely game of solitaire. Maybe he'd left the music on and gone out to find the someone else he'd warned her about. Maybe he'd already found her. Not all of O'Shea's customers were men.

There were a number of attractive women in the neighborhood, any one of whom could have stopped in for a drink, friendly conversation and a friendlier invitation. Maybe—

The music went off and the light filtering up the stairs dimmed as the lights in the bar were shut off. The bottom half of the stairwell went dark as the light in the hall down there was shut off. She heard only one set of steps on the stairs. He was alone, she realized with a rush of tremendous relief.

He rose out of the shadows, dark, distant, scowling. His steps slowed when he saw her, and at the landing he stopped, looking down at her, studying her face. She let him look as long as he wanted, let him see all he could see. Whatever it was, it was enough. After a couple of very long, very still moments, he offered his hand. When she took it, he pulled her to her feet, then wrapped his fingers tightly around hers.

She was already very close to him. She moved a little nearer and raised her free hand to his face. She brushed her fingertips across his cheek, along his jaw, then leaned forward and touched her mouth to his. For a moment, he remained still, unresponsive; then, with a groan, he took her mouth in a hungry, hot, demanding kiss that stole the breath from her lungs and replaced it with searing need that made her heart race and her muscles quiver.

He ended the kiss too soon, pushing her back, holding her face in his hands. "Do you want this?"

She nodded.

"I don't want any regrets, Lainie."

She smiled shakily. "I'll only regret it if we don't." It was true. Whatever happened—losing this assignment, losing her job, facing the future alone—her biggest, most serious regret would be if she didn't take this chance. If she didn't trust Nicholas. If she didn't give him all she had to give, if she didn't accept from him all that he could give. If heartache followed, at least she would know that she'd tried, that she'd loved him the best she could. Maybe it wouldn't be enough, but it was something.

"Do you have—" He broke off, shrugged, and she smiled a little. He hadn't been so reticent the last time the subject had come up. If she wanted to change her answer, he'd told her in her apartment that night, just say so. *I've got the condoms, and we've both got beds.*

She shook her head. "Why don't you get them? I'll wait."

With a shake of his own head, he reached inside her apartment to twist the lock on the door, then closed it and drew her by the hand into his own apartment. He locked that door, turned on the overhead light and pulled her into the bedroom, where he left her at the foot of the bed while he went to the closet.

The windows were open, bringing the night's cooler air into the room, along with the scent of the not-too-distant river and the delicate fragrance of nearby flowers. The bed was neatly made, with a faded quilt smoothed from side to side and tucked over two pillows at the top. The night table beside it held a clock and a photograph. She hadn't thought of Nicholas, with his bare walls and single duffel to hold an entire life, as a photograph sort of person, which meant this one was special. It was *her.* The woman he'd loved and still loved, even though she'd been dead five years or more.

Deliberately she shifted her gaze away from the photo. She would look at it later, if she had the chance, but not now. She couldn't deal with the other woman right now.

He tossed a small box on the bed, then came to stand behind her, his hands rubbing the chill from her arms, his body sharing its heat with her. Sliding his arms around her, for a moment, he simply held her, and she knew that, no matter how wrong this seemed, it wasn't. It was quite likely the most *right* thing she'd ever done in her life.

She turned in his arms, and Nicholas bit back a groan.

His muscles were taut, his arousal relentless. It had been so long, well over eighteen hundred nights and, beyond being his last time, that one hadn't been anything special. The woman had been an acquaintance whom he'd occasionally seen for just that purpose, while she had used him for occasional matters of financial or legal significance. At the time, it had been a satisfactory arrangement. He couldn't imagine settling for so little now. He couldn't imagine settling for less than everything. For less than Lainie.

Holding her close with one arm, he worked free the buttons on her shirt, then pulled it from her jeans, unfastening the last two buttons, sliding the garment off her shoulders. She was naked underneath. Her breasts were full and would be heavy in his hands. Her nipples would react quickly to his caresses, would respond with great pleasure to his kisses. All in good time. After he looked at her. After he kissed her.

"You're a beautiful woman."

He simply stated the obvious, but it pleased her, bringing a shy smile that made her look innocent and untouched, even though she was half-naked in his arms, even though her lower body was in intimate contact with his, even though in a few more torturous minutes they were going to get even more intimate.

He moved to sit on the bed, pulling her along to stand directly in front of him. The position was perfect for kisses, and he pressed the first one to her stomach, just above the waistband of her jeans. The next landed on her rib cage, the third on the satiny skin of her breast. A tiny moan escaped her, and he looked up to see her head back, her eyes closed, her lips parted—an expression of pure pleasure and growing need. "You like that?" His voice was thick as he touched her breast. He stroked it, rubbed it, first ignoring, then concentrating on, the hard crest of her nipple, his fingers tickling, teasing, pinching and soothing.

With a helpless cry, she reached for him, and he took her into his arms, kissing her hard, pulling her onto the bed with him. With his tongue in her mouth, he struggled with her clothes, with his own clothes. Blindly he found the box he'd left on the bed, freed one of its packets and, without breaking the kiss, without breathing, without thinking, purely by instinct alone, he managed to get it in place, then rolled so that she was underneath him.

Her body accepted his in one long stroke, taking all of him in a snug fit that couldn't have been better. For a moment he squeezed his eyes shut, breathing heavily, his heart thudding in his ears, every muscle and nerve quivering, begging for release. When her own muscles tightened deep where she sheltered him, he groaned. "Ah, damn, don't... Not yet... I want..."

She stroked his arms, his sides, his chest, his back, starting a trembling that rocketed through him, building a hunger that he couldn't control. He tried to hold back, tried to concentrate on anything that would slow the intensity, but when she began moving underneath him, he couldn't stop from responding, thrusting into her, in and out, hard, deep, fast, for only a moment, then two, and then release, pounding, rushing, incredible. It wasn't over, though, not hardly. Just a little something that he'd had to get out of the way before the real business of their lovemaking got started.

He needed only a moment to catch his breath. As soon as he did, he kissed her, sliding his tongue inside her mouth, claiming her, possessing her in exactly the way he'd been dreaming about ever since she'd moved in across the hall. He kissed her and seduced her, aroused her, coaxed and guided and pushed her. Her body was slick and hot, her muscles quivered, her breathing came harder, and her voice turned raw and hoarse as she pleaded, whimpered, demanded everything.

When she came, it was sweet and sharp, her body clenching hard around his. It was exactly the little push he needed to trade torment for pleasure, to let his muscles relax, to let satisfaction wash over him in hot, draining waves.

It had been well over eighteen hundred nights since he'd experienced such relief and, he acknowledged as he bent to give her one last, sweet kiss, it had been well worth the wait.

Chapter 7

Nicholas turned off the living-room light, then returned to
the bed. He didn't stretch out beside Lainie, though, where
he'd lain the last half hour. Instead he freed one pillow
from the quilt, propped it behind his back at the foot of the
bed and watched her. Enough light came through the windows to clearly show the round line of her breast, the nar-
rowness of her waist, the curve of her hip. It was enough
light to arouse him, enough to please him.

She slept on her side, hands folded under her head, un-
mindful that she was naked. He had known the minute he'd
come up the stairs and seen her there that she had changed
her mind, that she was willing to give them the chance he'd
asked for. He'd wondered why, not that it mattered. He
was no idiot. He would never turn down or even delay
something he wanted so desperately while he looked for
answers why. Why didn't matter. That she was here did.

Her body was soft now, completely drained of tension.
It gave him a tremendous sense of power to know that, in
the space of a heartbeat, he could change that. He could

touch her, and her muscles would go taut. He could kiss her, and her breasts would swell, her nipples harden. He could touch her more intimately, could part her thighs and kiss her, stroke her, fill her, and her entire body would stiffen and—

"I would ask what you're thinking, but I believe I can make a pretty accurate guess."

His arousal didn't embarrass him. Lately it had become his most common state around her. Now that he'd made love to her, now that he'd acquainted himself with the tight, snug heat inside her and with the incredible, heartbreaking satisfaction to be found there, it would probably become a permanent condition. "I thought you were asleep."

"And miss this? That would be sad." She scooted back at an angle, facing him more, and smiled. "You're incredible."

"I was thinking the same about you."

Her smile turned shy again, then wavered and disappeared as her expression sobered. "I'm sorry about this evening."

He thought back to the disappointment he'd felt when she'd pulled away from him in the club, the frustration when he'd questioned her and gotten no answers, the fear when he'd thought she'd gone on home alone, to the discouragement when he'd seen the tears in her sweet hazel eyes and the quiet desperation when he'd interrupted her on the sidewalk outside. *I need you, Lainie.* He still did. God help him, he might always.

"What made you change your mind?"

She shrugged, and her breasts swayed enticingly. "I've never wanted anyone the way I want you."

It was a sweet answer but not entirely the truth. Obviously she had come to terms with the background that she was convinced he couldn't accept. Would she ever confide in him? It didn't matter. Though he wanted to know everything about her, he didn't need to. As long as she was dealing with it, as long as it was no longer an obstacle keeping them apart, it could remain her secret.

"And, of course, there was your threat to find another woman."

"It wasn't a threat, sweetheart. Just a statement of intent." He hesitated. "I wouldn't have done it. If I'd wanted just sex, I could have had it a hundred times since I got out of prison. I wanted more. I wanted this. I wanted *you*."

For a long moment, she simply looked at him, her gaze never wavering. Then she rose to her knees, claimed a condom from the box spilled on the floor and put it to good use, then moved astride his hips, taking him deep and tight inside her. "You've got me," she murmured in his ear. "For as long as you want."

She made love to him, her fingers wrapped tightly around the slender iron posts on the footboard, riding him until neither could bear it anymore, until they both exploded, and when their breathing calmed and their skin cooled, she did it again, coaxing him to a last, lazy, satisfyingly exhausted climax. This time they both slept, arms wrapped around each other. Sometime in the night he woke long enough to set the alarm so she could get to work and to tug the quilt from underneath them so he could cover her.

Daylight came too soon, though. He tried to ignore the alarm, tried to bury his head deeper into the pillow, but the beeping went on. At last, too tired to be believed, he sat up, realized they'd slept at the foot of the bed and slid out from beneath the covers to shut off the clock. For just a moment, he hesitated there, his hand resting on the frame holding Rena's picture.

Before last night, he'd never made love to a woman without suffering a little guilt and a lot of regret, without wishing in his soul that it was Rena. This morning he felt a stab of guilt because last night he'd felt none. He had brought Lainie to his bed, had made love to her, held her, slept skin-to-skin beside her, and not once had he wished she was Rena. Not once had he given even a moment's thought to Rena.

He had always believed she was a once-in-a-lifetime gift. Few men deserved one woman like her, and none deserved a second. But Lainie was such a woman—such a gift. He sure as hell didn't deserve her, but he had her—for as long as he wanted, she'd said. Maybe for forever. He wouldn't feel guilty for such good fortune. Rena would understand.

Giving the photo a gentle touch, he returned to the foot of the bed. Lainie had turned onto her side and snuggled deeper under the quilt. He slid under, tucked the multicolored cover under her chin, then lay on his side, his head resting on one hand, and watched her. After a moment, her eyes narrowed, then relaxed. Then her nose twitched. Frowning, she finally opened one eye, then both eyes, and sleepily smiled. "I thought someone was watching me." She patted his cheek with one warm palm. He caught it and guided it to his mouth for a slow, lazy, wet kiss that made her shiver. "Good morning."

It *was* a good morning, the best in twenty years.

"Is it time to get ready for work?"

"You have twenty minutes before you're late."

"Think I could call in sick?"

"And do what?"

Letting her eyes drift shut again, she smiled. "Make love all day."

There was a thought to make a man hard. He hadn't indulged in the luxury of an entire day with nothing to do but satisfy a lifetime of longing in more than twenty years. He wasn't sure he could survive...but what a way to go. "With Jamey downstairs this afternoon? You're not that quiet." Even half asleep and lying naked beside him, she blushed just a little. He couldn't resist teasing her. "Don't be embarrassed. I like all those little sounds you make. They're exactly what I imagined in my fantasies."

The smile came back, seducing him. He was wondering

just how much they could accomplish in twenty minutes when she finally sat up, taking the quilt with her, yawned and began looking for her clothes.

With a sigh, he picked up his own jeans. "I'll make some coffee while you get dressed." He left her sitting on the side of the bed, her hair standing on end, sleepily trying to deal with clothes and looking too desirable for his own good.

Downstairs he started the coffee in the kitchen, then headed toward the bar to turn on some music. He was half-way there when he noticed an item out of place on the bar. It was an envelope, large, dark yellow, balanced against the telephone, and it brought him to an abrupt halt. He had closed up for Jamey last night—had swept the floor, washed the glasses, locked all four sets of doors and wiped down the bar. Just before going upstairs, he had moved the phone, emptied his ashtray and turned off the lights. He had set the telephone on the counter underneath the bar.

And now it was on the bar again.

So Jamey had come over early this morning and left something, he told himself, but the uneasy shiver creeping down his spine wasn't convinced. Slowly he forced himself to walk the last half-dozen feet to the bar, to reach out and pick up the envelope. It was addressed to him, and it wasn't from Jamey. Not once in his entire life had Jamey ever called him Nicholas. *Not once.*

The flap wasn't sealed but folded over and secured with a clasp. As he straightened the thin metal pieces, he walked around the tables to the doors, checking each set in turn. The last set on the left was unlocked. He twisted the knob, and the door swung open easily. But he had locked it, damn it. He *knew* he had.

He closed and locked the door, then returned to the bar before emptying the contents of the envelope. It didn't hold much—a handful of photographs and a slip of paper with a typewritten message. He didn't need more than the first line to recognize it as a prayer, one Father Francis had required him to learn by heart, to the patron saint of hopeless causes. It had been altered here, though, with some words crossed out and others penciled in ...*the name of the traitor hasn't been forgotten...*

He set the paper aside and picked up the photographs. They measured five by seven inches and were poorly lit, but the subjects were easy to recognize: him and Lainie. One was a shot of them entering last night's restaurant, another in Jackson Square at the moment when he had brought that hurt look into her eyes by saying that he would find another woman. The third one had been taken in the club when they were dancing. He remembered the flash and thinking that some foolish tourist was trying to capture nightlife in the Quarter. He'd been wrong.

"Nicholas?" Lainie's voice came from the stairs, accompanied by the solid thud of tennis shoes on bare wood. Quickly he shoved everything back into the envelope and slid it behind a stack of trays underneath the bar before turning to watch her approach.

She was dressed in faded jeans and a white T-shirt, tucked in snugly with the short sleeves rolled up a few times. No one could tell by looking at her that she'd gotten only a few hours' sleep last night. She looked well rested. Energized. Beautiful. Oh, hell, yeah, she was beautiful. God help him, if anything happened to her...

Nothing would. Jimmy wanted *him*. He had no interest in Lainie.

"I've got to take the coffee with me. I'm running late."

"It'll be ready in a minute." Grateful that she was in a hurry, that she didn't have time for a cup of coffee with him, time to notice that he was acting oddly, he reached out to stroke her hair, then slid his hand down to cup the back of her neck. Gently he pulled her to him, just holding her tight for a moment, then giving her a slow, leisurely kiss that stirred hunger and fire and incredible need.

When he finally released her, for a moment she remained utterly motionless. Then, with a shiver, she gave a little laugh. "Who needs coffee? You just got my blood pumping."

He stroked her mouth with his thumb while issuing a command. "Come home for lunch."

The lightness disappeared, and she looked as serious, as intense, as he felt. "All right." No questions about why, no excuses, just simple agreement.

He gave her another, quicker kiss, then stepped around her and went to the kitchen. When he returned a moment later with coffee, his in a mug, hers in a foam cup, she was still standing in exactly the same place. He wrapped her hands around the cup, then turned her toward the doors. "You're running late, remember?"

"Right. Late. Lunch." With a quavery smile for a good-bye, she crossed the room and let herself out. He stood where he could watch her cross the street, climb the steps to Kathy's House, then go in. He waited until the door closed behind her before he turned back to the bar and retrieved the envelope, carrying it and his coffee to a table, emptying it there.

...the name of the traitor hasn't been forgotten... Sometimes Jimmy operated with exquisite subtlety. Sometimes his message couldn't be clearer if it were printed in capital letters across the front page of the *Times-Picayune*. This little prayer was his reminder that he hadn't forgotten Nicholas or his promise to kill him. A few years ago Nicholas had welcomed the idea of his death. As recently as a few weeks ago he had been ready for it. This morning he wasn't. Give me a reason to live, he had challenged Lainie, and she'd done it. This morning, for the first time in more years than he could remember, he wanted to live to die of old age.

This morning he was afraid.

Maybe he should call Smith Kendricks or Remy Sinclair.

Maybe he should rethink their offer of protection. But that would mean giving up the freedom to have a life. Submitting to having every move scrutinized by the feds. Subjecting the people in his life to their intrusion. It would be a quick and easy way to bring his relationship with Lainie to a premature end. Satisfying lust with an audience always nearby wouldn't be easy. Anything more—like falling in love—would be damn near impossible.

And it wouldn't guarantee his safety. Jimmy was accomplished at getting his way. When Remy Sinclair's investigation nearly six years ago had gotten too close for comfort, Jimmy had gone out and bought himself an FBI agent—Sinclair's partner, no less, who had been more than happy to keep Falcone informed on the bureau's case in exchange for having his gambling debts wiped clean. Travis Wilson had gone so far as to shoot Sinclair on a wharf during a bust and was now serving a life sentence in a maximum security prison, too afraid to implicate Jimmy in anything.

If Nicholas had protection, Jimmy would find a way around it, or he would simply lay low until the government's budget for protecting ex-con informants ran out. Considering Nicholas's reputation with the bureau, that wouldn't take long. With the exception of Kendricks and Sinclair, most cops held him in as low esteem as Jimmy or lower. Jimmy was dirty, but at least he displayed some loyalty to the people who worked for him, while Nicholas was dirty and had shown none.

The best thing he could do was keep Falcone's latest message to himself. He would stay close to home and be more alert to what was going on around him when he did go out. He would maintain a profile so low that Jimmy would be forced either to forget that he existed or to be a lot more public—and therefore much more at risk—in extracting his vengeance.

Jimmy didn't like risk. He'd spent most of his adult life learning to minimize it, hiring people to do his dirty work for him, cultivating their loyalty and buying their silence, then hiring other people—like Nicholas—to try to keep them out of jail. He got his own hands dirty only in the most important instances, only when the betrayal was so personal that to allow someone else to avenge it for him would be an affront to his honor.

Nicholas was such a case. Jimmy wanted to take care of him himself. He wanted to look Nicholas in the eye when he killed him. He would probably do it at his own estate. The place was heavily guarded, and people were coming and going at all hours. There were no neighbors close by to observe the goings-on, and there was plenty of land to effectively dispose of a body or plenty of privacy for loading it into a vehicle for disposal.

So all he had to do was stay away from Jimmy's estate, and he just might stay alive.

Of course, if men with guns invited him to accompany them to visit his old boss, he would find it hard to turn them down, especially if anyone else was around when they offered the invitation.

Leaving the table, he retrieved his cigarettes, lighter and ashtray where he'd left them last night, then came back and sat down. With the first draw from the cigarette bitter in his lungs, he picked up the photograph taken in the club. His arms were around Lainie, he was gazing down at her, and she was looking up at him. She had asked about Rena and dancing. He had wondered about Lainie and love. The shot had been taken from the doorway, showing one side of his face, one side of hers. Even in the bad light, even with the limited view, it was easy to see that they were looking at each other like two people who should be naked and alone.

She was looking at him in a way Rena never had.

Across the room the door opened, and he reached automatically for the pictures, dropping the one he held on top.

When he recognized Jamey, he drew back. He could trust his friend with the warning.

Jamey detoured by the bar to fill a glass with water. In all their lives Nicholas had never seen him drink anything stronger than soda, not even as a teenager. Maybe it was because his old man had been a drunk, maybe because he'd seen so many lives on Serenity destroyed by liquor.

He pulled out the chair opposite Nicholas. For a moment he simply looked at the items scattered across the table. When he spoke, his voice was quiet. "Father Francis would frown on rewriting the prayer to St. Jude."

"Father Francis frowned on everything."

"That he did." There was another silence before Jamey asked, "What is this?"

"A message from Jimmy."

"How did he deliver it?"

"One of his people let himself in sometime during the night. He picked the lock on the door over there."

Jamey glanced at the eight glass doors that stretched across the front of the bar, then turned back. "Maybe you should close and lock the shutters at night."

Each set of doors had its own wooden shutters. Though they had been installed back when the building was new to protect the glass doors from hurricane-force winds, they had been more useful in recent years for protection from vandals who roamed the streets. Lately Serenity had gotten safe enough that the shutters remained propped open. If he started closing them now, would Lainie wonder why?

"You didn't hear anything from your visitor?"

"I was preoccupied."

Jamey picked up the top photo, the one Nicholas had been studying, and saw in a glance all he needed to see. "Uh-huh. You know, if he got in here unnoticed, he could have easily gone upstairs."

"You think that hasn't occurred to me?" That had been another part of Jimmy's message. *Look how close we can come without being seen, without getting caught. We can come right into your building, right up to your apartment—hell, right into your bedroom—and no one would know.*

"Does Lainie know?"

Nicholas shook his head.

"Don't you think she should?"

"Jimmy won't hurt her."

"Are you sure?"

"As sure as I am about anything." But what if he was wrong?

He wasn't. He *knew* Jimmy. Yes, innocent people sometimes got caught in his crossfire—like Rena—but this was a special case. Jimmy had had five years to plan Nicholas's death, and those plans didn't include enduring the heat of an investigation into an innocent woman's death.

"Look, whatever's between you two is none of my business. But if there's even a remote chance that her life is in danger, she has a right to know. If she chooses to stay, fine. If she chooses to end the relationship... It's her decision, Nicky. You can't make it for her."

If he were totally, one hundred percent positive, he could disagree. He could keep this threat to himself and keep Lainie from worrying unnecessarily. But he wasn't one hundred percent positive. There was always the remote chance that Jimmy would tire of the game and simply order one of his men to take Nicholas out. There was always the chance that Lainie could die right alongside him. A minimal chance, too small to calculate, but a chance all the same.

Jamey was right. He had to give her the chance to leave him...even though her leaving just might kill him and deny Jimmy his satisfaction.

He shook out another cigarette, lit it from the one that had burned to the filter, then stubbed the first one out. He inhaled deeply and blew the smoke out in a long, thin stream that drifted up, turning blue when the sunlight hit it. Then, disliking the taste in his mouth—though he knew it had nothing to do with the cigarette and everything to do with fear—he laid the cigarette in the ashtray and didn't reach for it again. "I'll talk to her," he said grimly.

Lainie bent over the sink, splashed cool water over her face, then reached blindly for the towel hanging on a nearby hook. For a long time after she straightened, she kept the towel over her face, then finally let it slide away and stared wide-eyed at herself in the mirror. It was five minutes until twelve and Nicholas was expecting her any minute. At three o'clock it was Smith Kendricks who would be expecting her. She had called from Karen's office this morning to arrange a meeting with him, and he had suggested the Moon Walk. Overlooking the Mississippi River just a short distance from Jackson Square, it would be easy for her to reach and yet she wasn't likely to run into anyone she knew there.

She was going to tell Smith everything. It was the best rule of unprofessional conduct: confess before you're found out. Don't wait until the case goes sour and they're looking to lay blame. Whatever happened in the future, whether she tried to save her job or tendered her resignation, she didn't want her relationship with Nicholas hidden like a dark, shameful secret waiting to be discovered.

Besides, telling was the right thing to do. There was a problem with Smith's case—*she* was the problem—and he had a right to know. If, God forbid, they failed and Falcone got to Nicholas anyway, it wasn't fair to Smith or Remy Sinclair or to the bureau itself to find out too late that their agent had been romantically involved with their subject. They were responsible for this case, responsible for Nicholas's *life,* and they had a right to know everything, even the personal little details about lovers.

So this afternoon she would confess her sins. But right now it was time to indulge them again.

She ran a comb through her hair, spritzed on cologne, then left the bathroom and went down the hall to Nicholas's apartment. She started to knock but froze when she saw that the door was ajar. With a sudden case of nerves and a wish for the gun locked up across the hall, she hesitantly pushed the door open, then relief swept over her.

Nicholas was standing at the window, watching her. The quilt from his bed was spread on the floor, and lunch was waiting—a bowl of fruit, a round loaf of bread and chilled bottles of flavored water. Beside the water was a small cardboard box, a little the worse for wear after last night's careless handling.

With a smile, she closed and locked the door, kicked off her shoes, and began pulling her T-shirt free of her jeans as she walked toward the quilt. With a faint smile of his own, he met her there, his own shirt hitting the floor the same time hers did. His kiss was demanding and possessive, his caresses less than gentle, as the fever began burning. Her arousal grew sharp, raw, with a desperate edge, as if all the relief of last night had never happened, as if this need could never be satisfied.

They struggled with their clothes and each other, sinking together to the floor, tugging, resisting, caressing, tormenting. She gave him a moment to deal with his protection before she pulled him achingly closer. He gave her a moment to adjust to his presence within her before he began moving, thrusting deeper, harder, faster. It ended too soon, but not before she shattered, not before he did, too.

Minutes. Mere minutes, and they lay exhausted, their bodies slick, their breathing ragged. She lay on her back, staring at the ceiling, forcing slow, deep breaths into her lungs. He lay on his stomach beside her, his forehead resting on her shoulder, his thick black hair damp where it circled his face and rested on his neck. She stroked it, tangled her fingers in it, then used a handful to gently lift his head. "Hi."

He slowly smiled, such a simple act to send such pleasure through her. It warmed her all the way through, made her feel happy and hopeful and *right*. It convinced her that she'd made the right decision, that any future worth living was worth living with this man. She could lose her job, her income, her comfortable life. She could lose everything, but as long as she still had Nicholas, she would be all right.

He kissed her, a sweet, gentle taste, then returned her greeting. "I missed you."

"I've only been gone four and a half hours."

"Four and a half hours that you could have been with me."

"One of us has to work for a living."

"Hey, I've got a job, too. I'll be starting this evening at six."

"And I'll miss you while you're working and be waiting when you come upstairs."

He moved over her again, worked his way inside her again, even though her body was tight, even though his was starting to soften. The first few strokes put an end to that. She could feel him swell to fill her. Once he was hard, once she could take no more, he became still, supporting himself on his elbows, looking down at her with an intensity that made her quiver. "For how long, Lainie? How long will you wait for me?"

The question was too serious. She answered it with a bit of a laugh anyway. "Hey, neither of us is planning on going anywhere, right? At least, I'm not."

He stared at her a moment longer, then abruptly lowered his head to kiss her while his body quickly, uncontrollably finished inside her. For a long time he was still, then he pulled away. He left the room, scooping up his jeans as he went, and came back half dressed to sit beside her. He was carrying an envelope. "Last night, sometime during the night, one of Jimmy's people came into O'Shea's and left this on the bar. I found it when I went down to make coffee this morning."

She stared at him, a lack of understanding making her feel dull. When he offered the envelope, she slowly sat up, looked around for her clothes and settled on his shirt. She pulled it over her head and down past her hips before taking the envelope. It was a plain manila envelope, the kind sold by hundreds of outlets in the area, and was addressed simply with his first name in block printing that was devoid of any identifying characteristics. As for fingerprints, they would find Nicholas's and now her own, maybe Jamey's, but probably not anyone else's.

Before she opened it, she looked at Nicholas. "What do you mean, one of them came into the bar? You mean before closing?"

He shook his head.

"You mean he broke in?"

A grim nod.

"While we were up here…?"

He nodded again, and she swallowed hard. She had felt an overall sense of well-being and safety last night, while danger had crept closer than it ever had before. She'd heard nothing, felt nothing, sensed nothing, out of place. A fine protector she'd been. His life and maybe her own had been in danger, and she'd been too lost in their lovemaking or sleeping too soundly in his arms to hear a thing.

But even if she hadn't been with him, even if she'd been alone in her own apartment, she comforted herself, she still wouldn't have heard anything. She still would have been sound asleep.

Opening the flap, she looked inside the envelope before sticking her hand in. Trying to ignore the foreboding sending chills down her spine, she pulled out the thin sheaf of papers, read the prayer and its revisions, looked at the photographs and silently whispered a prayer of her own. "Can I give this to Smith Kendricks?"

"I'm not accepting their protection. For the first time in fifteen years, my life is my own. I can't turn it over to them."

"I understand that." And, though she wasn't sure she could explain it to anyone else, she did. "Still, the government needs to know about this. They need to know that Jimmy's made another threat so they can step up their surveillance of him and his people."

The silence that followed lasted so long that she was sure he intended to refuse. "Please," she added softly.

Finally he shrugged. "Do what you want with it. There's something else we need to discuss, Lainie. I don't think we should see each other anymore."

Once more she stared at him, positive she couldn't have heard him correctly, convinced by the sudden emptiness inside her that she had. She wanted to shriek her refusal, to insist that he was wrong, to fling herself into his arms and convince him that, damn it, he needed her. Instead she swallowed hard, forced herself to remain calm and quietly asked, "Why?"

"I honestly don't believe Jimmy would hurt you, but as long as there's even the slightest risk, I think it would be best if you kept your distance."

She unfolded her legs and got to her feet, quickly pulled on her jeans, then stripped his shirt off and replaced it with her own. Once everything was zipped and tucked, she walked to the nearest window, faced him and leaned against the sill. "So you won't let the FBI tell you how to live your life, but you will let Jimmy Falcone." She folded her arms across her chest. "Or maybe Jimmy's not the issue here at all. Ten minutes ago you couldn't get close enough to me. Once you'd gotten what you wanted, suddenly you think I should keep my distance." She made the suggestion to provoke him. She didn't believe for an instant that he'd wanted only sex from her—did she? Was there just the tiniest bit of doubt deep in her heart? Was there some insecure little part of her that needed to hear him deny it?

He didn't look the least bit provoked as he stood and advanced on her. In fact, he looked mildly amused as he caught her wrists and pulled her with him, snug between his thighs as he leaned against the wall. "If sex was all I wanted, darlin', you and I both know I would have gone somewhere else in the beginning, because getting it from you wasn't the easiest thing I'd ever done. But," he added in a husky voice heavy with promise, "it was the best."

"Then how can you push me away?"

He touched her face so gently. A month ago she never would have believed that a man with his reputation could be so gentle. "If anything happened to you, it would destroy me. I've been through this once before, Lainie. I can't live through it again."

She laid her hand over his. "Nothing's going to happen to me. You said yourself that this is personal with Jimmy. I don't mean anything to him. He's not going to mess with me."

"Unless you get in his way."

"Is that what happened with her?"

He became very still, not even breathing for a time. Then finally he sighed deeply and said, "Yeah. She got in his way."

"Do you want to talk about it?"

Again he became still before offering a simple, quiet, "No."

She wasn't disappointed. She hadn't been holding her breath anticipating that he might confide in her. She wasn't anxious to hear about the woman he'd loved so much that he'd risked his freedom and his life to avenge her death. She didn't want to wonder if there was a chance that he might ever care half as much about her. She told herself all those things, but she lied.

He held her a moment longer, then pressed a kiss to her forehead and pulled her back to the quilt. "Let's eat before you have to get back to work."

The bread was freshly baked, still warm in the center, and the fruit was sweet and juicy. She wondered where he'd gotten it, where he had wandered off to on foot and alone, knowing that Falcone's people had been watching him. Had he considered the danger and thought he could be careful enough to balance it, or had he been unconcerned? Did he still not give a damn whether Falcone killed him? Was he still so accepting of his own death? Hadn't everything that had happened between them given him even a small reason to change his mind? Hadn't their lovemaking meant anything to him?

She couldn't ask, not yet. All she could do was pass everything on to Smith Kendricks, try to keep a closer eye on Nicholas and pray.

When she finished eating, he sent her off to work with a slow, lazy kiss that stole her breath and turned her muscles weak. The next few hours both dragged and rushed. Her professional side was anxious for the meeting with Smith so she could turn over the envelope and its contents. Her personal side dreaded it. She arrived at the Moon Walk ten minutes early, the envelope in a plastic grocery bag to protect it from further fingerprints, and paced uneasily back and forth between the steps leading to the Quarter side of the levee and the longer stairs leading down on the river side. She had just turned at the top of the stairs when she saw Smith approaching.

He came to stand beside her, gazing out over the river. "It's a pretty day, isn't it?"

"Yes, it is." She'd been outside the better part of the day, but she hadn't noticed the weather. This morning she'd been preoccupied with coming clean about last night. This afternoon she'd been disturbed by the contents of the envelope and the method of its delivery. Always she was disturbed by Nicholas.

"You said you needed to talk."

She glanced around, saw an empty bench flanked by other empty benches and gestured toward it. She sat on the edge, dangling the bag by its handles between her knees. Smith chose to lean against the big, boxy planter at its end.

All the way over here, she'd sought the right words to say what she had to say, but they had eluded her. Now, with his dark gaze steady on her, she grabbed the first words that came to mind. "I was told that I was picked for this job for two reasons—because I'm from Atlanta, so no one here would recognize me, and because..." She faltered, the same way Sam had when he'd made the comment to her. "Because I'm a woman, and a woman would stand a better chance of getting close to Nicholas than a man would. Of course, I'm not supposed to get *too* close, because that would be unprofessional."

His gaze never wavered, not through her jerky little speech or the silence that followed it, until finally he looked away to the river and went straight to the heart of her comment. "How close are we talking?" He sounded embarrassed by the question.

No more than she was by the answer. Not because she was ashamed. She wasn't. But she was an adult. Her private life should be just that. But falling in love with Nicholas made that impossible. Before the day was over, everyone in Smith's office and the FBI who had a need to know would know that she had succumbed to temptation. Without understanding the situation, without caring about the facts, they would judge and condemn her for it. "I spent the night with him."

Only yesterday she had told Smith that Nicholas usually spent the nights with her, then had hastened to clarify that, of course, she meant only the evenings. This time no clarification was needed. His grim expression indicated that he understood exactly what she was saying.

For a long time he was silent, probably considering the consequences of her actions. When he spoke, his voice was quiet, nonjudgmental. ''We choose you because we think you'll appeal to Nick. We tell you to move in right across the hall, to spend as much time with him as possible, to get as close to him as possible, but now that you've done it, we'll have to censure you for it.'' He shook his head. ''It's not exactly fair, is it?''

He was being generous. There had been limitations on how close to Nicholas she was allowed to get, very strict guidelines that she had been well aware of and had disregarded. Going shopping with him had been fine. Encouraging him to kiss her and fondle her breast hadn't. Taking a walk through the neighborhood with him had been okay. Making out beside the fountain at the church hadn't. Going to dinner with him last night had been perfectly acceptable. Going to bed with him had been way out of line.

Grimly she focused on one word he'd mentioned. *Censure*. That was one of their options. They could keep it on a local level and give her a letter of admonition. They could refer it to the director of the bureau and give her a letter of censure, or they could fire her.

A month ago losing her job would have been the worst scenario she could imagine. It was all she had. It was her *life*. This afternoon it didn't sound so bad. If they fired her, she would close her savings account, add the money from her retirement account, buy a house and work hard at growing beautiful things. Flowers, shrubs, trees. Maybe, if she was very lucky, if Nicholas was very forgiving, a marriage, kids and a future.

He walked to the top of the stairs, his coat pushed back, his hands shoved in his pockets. ''However understandable it is, Lainie, what you've done represents a serious error in judgment. You should have come to me as soon as you recognized the problem. You shouldn't have let it go this far. The bureau will *have* to take disciplinary action. You'll be lucky if they don't fire you. In the meantime, they'll want you off this case."

"But you can keep me on. If you ask Sinclair as a personal favor…" She stood up and joined him. Down below, water lapped over the bottom two steps. Bits of pale brown foam drifted close to the river's edge, and a rat snacked on litter some visitor had thoughtfully thrown onto the rocks instead of in the trash can nearby. "Nicholas needs protection, and he trusts me. You'll never get anyone closer to him than I am. You'll never get anyone with more of an interest in keeping him alive than I have."

He acknowledged that with a nod.

"Let me stay," she said, quietly pleading, "and the day the case ends, I'll turn in my resignation."

He gave it a long moment's thought. In the end, he didn't give her an answer one way or the other. "I'll have to discuss it with Remy. We'll let you know." He gestured toward the bag she was still clutching. "Is that for me?"

She handed it over and told him what was inside and how Nicholas got it.

"It was delivered last night while you were with him?"

She nodded.

"Any idea what time?"

"He closed up the bar for Jamey at midnight. He found the envelope around seven forty-five this morning."

"If you had been alone…" He didn't add *as you should have been,* but she heard the words anyway. "What are the chances you would have heard something?"

"Slim. My apartment is over the storeroom and the kitchen. Nicholas's is directly above the bar and the kitchen." If there'd been any telltale sounds to hear, chances of hearing them from his place were better than from hers.

"What was Nick's reaction to the package?"

"He was troubled." Troubled enough to hide it from her this morning. Troubled enough—and worried enough about her safety—to give it to her this afternoon.

"Because this time the threat included you. Have you talked to him about accepting protection?"

"He says he can't."

"He doesn't trust us, and I don't know that I blame him. He knows from experience how easy it is to buy someone's loyalty. He saw firsthand a few years ago how easy it was for Jimmy to pay off Remy's partner. I wish he would change his mind, though." After a moment, he curiously asked, "If you quit, are you planning to stay here?"

"That depends on Nicholas. I'll have to tell him the truth at some point."

"Finding out that you're one of the enemy may be more than he can forgive."

She wished his outlook was a little more optimistic. After all, he'd known Nicholas a long time and had worked closely with him on Jimmy's conviction. It would have cheered her immensely if he'd said that Nicholas was a forgiving man, that everything would be all right.

What if her deception *was* more than Nicholas could forgive? What would she do? Where would she go? Could she stay on Serenity if he hated her? Could she leave it if he remained there?

She didn't have any answers, couldn't make any guesses. The only thing she knew for sure was that she didn't regret making love with Nicholas, and she surely didn't regret falling in love with him.

Saturday morning, like the Saturday before, was dreary, the sun blotted out in the eastern sky, the clouds heavy with the promise of rain. Nicholas wished they would drench Serenity in another long-lasting downpour, and he wished it would happen right now, before he and Lainie made it more than five feet from O'Shea's. Then he could pull her back inside the bar, secure the shutters and the doors, take her straight upstairs to the bed they'd left not long ago and keep her there for the rest of the day. They wouldn't have to make love, although of course they would. They could just hold each other. Talk. Sleep. Be lazy and enjoy.

But the rain didn't start to fall. It only continued to threaten, and Lainie was dragging him across the street to claim Karen's car, for which she'd already borrowed the keys. She'd used the weather as an excuse, but he suspected that Wednesday's late-night visit from Jimmy's thug was the real reason. A car offered protection that strolling along the sidewalk didn't. If he was honest, he had to admit that the idea made him feel more secure, too.

"Tell me again why we're going back to the junk store."

She scowled at him as she unlocked the driver's door and slid inside to open the passenger's. "A name like Vieux Carré Antiques does *not* belong to a junk store."

"No, it doesn't. It belongs to an elegant antique shop over on Royal. In fact, there used to be an elegant old shop over on Royal by that name. I'd forgotten about the place—they went out of business years ago—but a lot of the pieces in my house..." He trailed off. The house had been Jimmy's, never his, and a lot of its furnishings had come from the shop, until it had suffered a reversal of fortune—a reversal by the name of Jimmy Falcone. A reversal helped along by Nicholas. "So what is it you're looking for this time?"

She backed out of the space, circled the house and turned onto the street. "A nightstand for the bedroom and something else for the living room—a bookcase or desk or something."

"Why?"

"Because I want them. Besides, someday I'm going to have an old house, and these old pieces will fit perfectly in it."

It was the first time he'd heard her make a solid reference to the future, the first time she'd mentioned any desire at all for a house to make a home. Oh, she had talked one afternoon about fixing up the cottage at the end of the street, but the idea of starting a nursery on the grounds had interested her far more, he'd thought, than the house itself.

"Where will this house be?"

"On Serenity, of course."

He didn't ask how she thought she might buy a house, even on Serenity, on the salary Karen paid her. He doubted she'd thought that far ahead, but he had. He'd thought he might buy it for her—for them. She could have her flowers, and he could have her, and they would both be happy.

He smiled faintly. He hadn't been happy in so long that he'd thought he had forgotten how it felt. It felt *good.*

There weren't any parking spaces available in front of the furniture store, but Lainie found one half a block away and around the corner. She eased in between a delivery truck and a Dumpster, then they walked back to the entrance of the store. They hadn't gone more than ten feet inside when the blonde Nicholas remembered from last time moved to block their way.

"Excuse me," Lainie said politely, but the woman didn't move.

"You're not welcome here." Though the woman was looking straight at Nicholas, it was Lainie who answered, repeating her last words with a puzzled inflection.

"Excuse me?"

"You're Nick Carlucci, aren't you? I heard you'd gotten out of prison. I was hoping if you came back here that one of your old partners would kill you. No such luck, huh?"

The face wasn't familiar, and neither was the name— Lin—on the tag on her left shoulder, but Nicholas had a hunch who the woman was and why she hated him. If memory served, the owner of that elegant old shop had had a daughter—no, judging by this woman's age, probably a granddaughter—whom he was training to take over the family business. Unfortunately for her and for the old man, Jimmy had taken it first. "Don't give up hope yet." His voice was as quiet as hers was strident. "It still might happen."

The blonde's smile was cold and glittered. "If it does, it'll be one of the happiest days of my life."

Lainie was staring openmouthed at the woman. "Look, lady, if this is your idea of friendly customer service—"

"He's no customer, and if you're with him, you're not welcome, either."

"But—"

He caught Lainie's arm. "Come on. Let's go."

"But this is ridiculous. She certainly didn't mind taking my money the last time."

"Only because I didn't realize who he was. I never would have let you in the store if I'd known. Now I'm telling you for the last time—leave before I call the police."

Though Lainie was still sputtering protests, Nicholas pulled her outside and down the street. They returned to the car in silence, where she finally asked, "Who is she?"

He took the keys from her limp grasp, helped her into the passenger seat, then circled the car. As he pulled away from the curb, he started his answer. It was a long one. "Remember I said there used to be a store on Royal with the same name? I didn't make the connection before because it's so different now. It used to be one of the best antique stores in the city. It belonged to an old man named Landry. It had been in his family over a hundred years, and he intended to keep it there. He was teaching his granddaughter the business."

After a few moments of silence, he pulled to the side of the street, then gestured to the nearest storefront. "It was right there."

Lainie looked, her gaze sweeping over what was now an

upscale restaurant, catering to the tourist trade, then turned back to him.

"Jimmy collects antiques. He doesn't care much about them. He just likes owning beautiful, expensive pieces with a history of belonging to people with better breeding and more class than he'll ever have. He bought at Vieux Carré Antiques because they offered the best quality and set the highest prices." He fell silent for a moment, remembering the countless times he had accompanied Jimmy through those doors and the tables, beds, armoires, rugs and even dishes that had passed through the shop before arriving in his own house. The desk in his office, the bench at the foot of his bed, the crystal that had graced his dining table and the table itself... All had been old, sought after by people who valued them for their history, their workmanship, their uniqueness, and owned by a man who valued them only for their prestige.

"The old man had a bad year or two, developed some cash flow problems and turned to his best customer for help. Jimmy gave him a 'loan.' The old man paid back the principle, but the interest amounted to double that. He kept paying and paying, and eventually Jimmy wound up owning the major interest in the shop. He turned the place into a front for a few of his other businesses—did a little smuggling, a lot of money laundering. He and the old man fought about it all the time. In the middle of the last argument, the old man collapsed. He had a heart attack and died in his granddaughter's arms."

"Why does she blame you?"

He stared hard at the street ahead. Two weeks ago he would have answered plainly, bluntly, not caring how Lainie responded, probably hoping that his actions eight or ten years ago would repel her and make her keep her distance. Today, fearing the same thing, he found it harder to put the words together. "I was always with Jimmy when he visited the store. I helped set the terms for the loan. I delivered Jimmy's threats when the old man couldn't pay on time. I drew up the paperwork to transfer the business into Jimmy's name." He shrugged. "Why wouldn't she blame me? Along with Jimmy, I was responsible."

For a long time Lainie was silent. Her head was turned away from him, her gaze focused once more on the storefront. He couldn't see her expression. She couldn't see his shame.

While he waited for some response, the rain began, a few fat drops followed by a torrent. In a matter of minutes, the sidewalks, once busy with window-shopping tourists, cleared except for an umbrella here, a slicker there. It rained hard, the drops bouncing off the car, beating a rapid, unsteady rhythm that drowned out everything but his thoughts and Lainie's soft voice.

"Was she worth it?"

He knew immediately who she meant. He didn't hesitate in his answer. "Yes."

"You don't have any regrets?"

"I regret that I didn't succeed in sending Jimmy to prison. I regret that, to punish him, I had to become just like him. I regret the old man's death and everyone else's. But if I had to do it all over again, I would, because more than anything else in the world, I regret Rena's death. It was senseless, and it was my fault. I was too damn selfish, too damn ambitious, and it killed her."

His answer seemed to sadden her. It wasn't anything he could point to—her face was still hidden from him—but just a sense, a feeling surrounding her. Was she disappointed in him? Did she expect him to have learned from the past, to have become a better man who would make better choices given a chance? He wished, for her, that he *was* a better man, a more deserving man, but all he could be was what he was. Disreputable. Dishonorable. Dishonest. Manipulative. An ex-con. An ex-crook.

Finally she turned to face him. There was no sadness in

her sweet hazel eyes, no condemnation, no loathing. There was just gentleness, understanding, forgiveness. "You were never just like Jimmy," she disagreed, her voice as soft as her touch on his hand. "He does what he does out of a desire for money, for power and influence. He's an amoral, greedy bastard who doesn't give a damn who he hurts or destroys. *You* did what you did for Rena. For love. There's a tremendous difference."

He gave her words careful consideration, but he didn't agree. Maybe his motivation had been purer, his intentions nobler, but his actions had been as dirty, as despicable, as everyone else's. The end certainly hadn't justified the means. Jimmy wasn't rotting in some prison. The entire investigation, trial and subsequent overturning of his convictions hadn't been more than a minor inconvenience in the long run. He was still in business. He was still earning obscene profits. He was still breaking every law on the books and still getting away with it all, including murder. He was still above the law.

Nicholas hadn't accomplished anything. He'd thrown away his life for vengeance. He'd lived a life he'd hated with people he'd despised. He'd lost his dignity, his pride and his self-respect, and he'd sold his soul, all for justice, only to learn too late that there was no justice. Not for him. Not for Jimmy.

Certainly not for Rena.

Chapter 8

The rain continued through the day, a steady shower that occasionally turned into a downpour or even less occasionally stopped altogether. It was nine o'clock in the evening, three hours until closing time, and Nicholas was alone in the bar with only a handful of Jamey's regular customers. Three of them—Thomas Campbell and Virgil Heller, playing checkers and telling tall tales to Pat McCoy—he remembered from growing up on Serenity. The two old men had been regulars at St. Jude's with their families at their sides. Now their families had moved away and their wives were dead, and they were left alone in a neighborhood that was a far cry from the place they remembered. McCoy had been a few years behind Nicholas in school. He held a job and earned decent money, but for some reason he stayed on Serenity—probably the same reason Jamey had stayed, the same reason Nicholas had come back. It was shabby, run-down and worn-out, short on hope and long on despair, but it was home. That counted for something.

Nicholas was vaguely familiar with the other two customers, though not through any personal contact. Eldin Pierce sat facing the wall and nursing one more in a long line of beers. Jamey had passed on his sad story about a ground-floor apartment, an argument between punks on the street, a couple of semiautomatic weapons converted to full auto and a nine-year-old daughter, dead on the floor where she played. His wife had done her grieving, then returned to the job of being mother—and now father—to their remaining two children. Eldin had tried to drown his sorrows, but they were drowning him instead.

Jamey had filled him in on Ray Cook, too, who sat facing another wall. He bought the booze, like Pierce, but he didn't drink much of it. He just took a sip from time to time and stared morosely at the brick. His despondency could be traced back to a lost job and a wife and two kids who'd gone to stay with family in Mississippi. No one knew why he didn't follow. She had asked him to go—according to rumor, had offered the invitation repeatedly since she'd gotten a job and a place of her own. Maybe it was male pride that kept him here and miserable, because he couldn't support his family but she could.

Men had a lot to learn from women, Nicholas thought with a faint smile. The women in his life—his mother, Jolie, Rena and Lainie—had taught him more than all the schools and all the teachers in the world. He was looking forward to learning more from Lainie—about happiness, satisfaction, trust, the love between two mature adults, marriage and family. He was willing to spend a lifetime learning.

At the end of the bar the telephone rang, its electronic trill annoying. For years it had been a standard black model, updated once about the time he returned from law school from a rotary dial to a touch-tone. Recently, for convenience's sake, Jamey had updated again to an off-white cordless model. In his years with Falcone, Nicholas had come to distrust cordless phones for their lack of security.

Anyone with a decent scanner could pick up all the cordless calls in his area. Not that it mattered anymore. He wasn't conducting business over the phone or anywhere else that required security.

"O'Shea's."

There was a few seconds' silence, then a voice, low, raspy, indistinguishable. "So it's true. You're working as a bartender. So much for that law degree and all those years of experience. You're doing work any idiot could do."

Nicholas's fingers tightened around the phone. The voice could belong to any of a hundred people he'd known or a million he hadn't. There was no doubt, though, that it was one of Jimmy's people. "It's honest work," he said, careful to keep his own voice even, to show no fear. "You should try it sometime."

"What do you know about honest work? You're as unscrupulous as they come. Five years in prison didn't change that. You like to think you're different, that you're better, but you're just waiting for the next temptation to come along. You'll be just as weak and greedy as the others."

"You have a reason for calling besides maligning my character?"

"As a matter of fact, I do." The man sounded smug and self-satisfied. "Do you know where Lainie is? Do you know if she's all right?"

Ice spread through Nicholas, a quick freeze, as the line went dead. Over three hours ago he'd left her in her apartment. She would come down later, she'd said, then suggested with a slow, hot, provocative smile that maybe she would simply wait for him to come to her. So far, there'd been no sign of her, no sound from her.

She was in the apartment, and she was fine. She had to be. No stranger had come through the French doors. No one had gone past the bar and down the hall toward the stairs, not with him standing right there. But there was a back door, seldom used, and all those windows upstairs....

Still gripping the phone, he started down the hall. By the time he reached the stairs, he was running. He took them two at a time, pushed open her unlocked door—left unlocked for *him*—and burst into the apartment. "Lainie!"

The living room was dimly lit, but the overhead light was on in the bedroom. The instant he saw her there, lying back on a pile of pillows, a book open in her hands and a startled look on her face, the trembling started, sweeping through him. He crossed to her, dropping the phone on the mattress as he scooped her into his embrace, holding her tightly enough to make her breath catch.

"Nicholas?"

Only one other time in his life had he ever been so scared. Another rainy night, another city, another life. But Lainie was all right. She hadn't been hurt, hadn't been touched, hadn't even been afraid until he'd come rushing in. She was safe.

This time.

On the bed beside her the phone began a discordant beep, reminding him that he hadn't disconnected after the call. He felt Lainie fumble for it, then shut it off. Almost immediately it rang. Releasing her as quickly as he'd grabbed her, he pulled the phone from her hand.

As soon as he pressed the Talk button, he heard ominous, rumbling laughter, followed by the same voice. "Got your heart pumping, didn't I? You thought we'd slipped in the back door or climbed through one of those windows, didn't you? You thought you'd find her gone—or dead. Next time you might not be so lucky. Next time she might not be so easy to find…or so safe when you find her. Keep that in mind."

Slowly, when he was sure the man had hung up, Nicholas disconnected and met Lainie's gaze. "What was that about?" She was making an effort to sound unconcerned, but her voice was husky and less than steady.

"They know your name. They know you live here. They

know..." They knew the easiest way to destroy him was to kill her. For a moment he looked at her, then abruptly, knowing he had no choice, he got to his feet, threw open the closet door and yanked out the bags she'd moved in with.

"Nicholas, what are you doing?"

"You've got to get out of here. You can't stay any longer. It's too dangerous. They know now to use you to get to me. They'll kill you, and it'll be my fault, just like before, just like..."

Lainie stared at him, his words trailing off as he jerked open the zippers on the nylon bags, then carried the backpack to the dresser. Startled into action, she threw back the covers, got her feet tangled and had to waste a precious few seconds to free herself.

She was a few seconds too late.

Nicholas had already opened the right-hand drawer, grabbed a handful of socks and then become utterly still. She froze, too, at the foot of the bed, barely breathing. She felt sick inside, damning herself for breaking her own rule: confess before you're caught. Even under the best of circumstances, she'd known the truth would be difficult for Nicholas to accept, but if she'd come forward on her own, if she'd told him voluntarily, if she hadn't waited to get caught looking guilty as sin, maybe he wouldn't have been so shocked. Maybe he could have forgiven her. Maybe he wouldn't hate her quite so much.

But she was too late. A few lousy seconds, and she might pay for them the rest of her life.

Moment after moment passed—or maybe it was just seconds—before he dropped the socks, then slowly turned to face her, holding her pistol limply in one hand. "What is this?"

Suddenly cold, she hugged her arms to her chest. "It—it's a gun."

"I know it's a gun." His voice was loud enough, harsh

enough, to make her flinch. He made an obvious effort to control it. "What the hell are you doing with it?"

"It—it's for protection. Serenity's not the safest place, you know."

"Protection," he repeated. This time his voice was low, deadly, nerve-chillingly soft. "Karen doesn't carry a gun. Cassie doesn't. No other woman on the whole damn street carries a gun. Why do you? Who the hell are you that you need that kind of protection?"

She didn't have an answer prepared. If he'd found the other items hidden in the drawer—her badge and credentials—he would know exactly who she was and why she needed a gun. But he hadn't found the rest, so maybe— *please, God*—she could save this. Maybe...

Something in her face betrayed her. Fear. Guilt. Regret. Despair. Whatever he saw caused him to grab her with his free hand, shove her against the curved foot rail of the bed and bend her back until her feet barely touched the floor. Leaning over her, he pressed the barrel of the gun against her cheek. "Who are you? Why are you here?"

There was such dark anger in his face, such harsh mistrust, that even if she'd had a lie all sketched out, she couldn't have given it voice. The best she could do was whisper. "You know who I am, Nicholas. Please..."

He searched her face, then made a sudden connection that caused him to murmur, "Oh, God," before forcing her even farther back. His body was hard against hers, pinning her so she couldn't move, and only her toes were in contact with the floor. "That's how they knew your name. You're working for him, aren't you? Jimmy sent you here."

"No!"

"Damn it, don't lie to me! Is he paying you to keep an eye on me, to sleep with me, to do whatever it takes to get close to me?"

Now was her chance to tell him the truth, to blurt it out: *Yes, I'm being paid to watch you, but by the government, not Jimmy.* But once again, all she could work over the lump in her throat was a helpless plea. "You're hurting me, Nicholas."

His grin was full of menace, his whisper full of threats. "Oh, darlin', I intend to do a hell of a lot more than hurt you. Before I'm through with you, you'll be sorry you ever met me." He caressed her cheek with the cool metal of the gun barrel. "What was the plan? You were supposed to get to close to me—"

"No."

"Seduce me—"

"No."

"Make me fall for you. And then you would do it. It's perfect when you think about it. I was convinced that Jimmy would do it himself because it was personal, but, hell, what's more personal than being killed by the one person you trust more than anyone else in the world?" Another stroke with the gun. "When were you going to do it? Where? In bed? When I was asleep? Maybe when I was inside you—"

"I'm a federal agent."

His taunting words dried up, and he stared at her in shock. He released her, then backed away so quickly—as if he couldn't bear to touch her any longer—that she almost fell. "You're a—"

"I'm with the FBI." For a few more days, maybe a few more weeks. She wanted out as soon as she could get out, but she didn't think that would interest Nicholas. Right now, she doubted that anything beyond consigning her to eternal damnation interested him.

If there was anything good to be said about his reaction, it was that he didn't doubt her. He didn't demand to see her credentials. He didn't have any problem believing that she wasn't a hired assassin but an untrustworthy fed instead. It was hard to say, though, which he held in lower esteem.

He looked so stunned, so hurt. The part of her that loved him started to reach for him, to offer comfort, but the part that had betrayed him instinctively drew back. He might never welcome her touch again. He might never stop looking at her that way again.

"An FBI agent. So Kendricks decided to give me protection regardless of what I wanted." His voice was soft, bewildered, lost, but on the next words, as he laid her gun carefully on the dresser, it picked up an edge of anger. "Why did they pick you? Because you're pretty? Because you lie so well? Or because you don't mind prostituting yourself for the bureau?"

She ignored the compliment, because he didn't mean it, and the insults, because he did. "I'm sorry, Nicholas. I didn't mean for you to find out like this."

"How was I supposed to find out? Were you ever going to tell me?"

"Yes. As soon as I turned in my resignation." After the declaration of love that she'd planned to make and before the wedding she'd allowed herself a few dreams of, provided that he didn't hate her.

But he did. His dark gaze was narrowed and scornful as he studied her. "Your resignation. Right. You expect me to believe that you were going to quit your job to stay here on Serenity with me and raise flowers? A dedicated agent like you? A woman who'll do anything for the cause, even sleep with the subject of her investigation? That was why you kept running away, wasn't it? Sex was supposed to be the last resort, something to fall back on when all else failed."

"No. I kept running away because I was scared. Making love with you could cost me my job. The job was the only stability in my life. I was afraid to risk it, especially when you weren't offering anything to replace it."

"I'm still not offering anything, but you decided to resign anyway. How convenient. And just when did you make this decision?''

She hugged herself tightly, feeling a chill that had been absent only moments before. It came from his voice, from his anger, from his eyes. "Thursday. Smith said they would insist on removing me from the case for my unprofessional conduct. I told him I would resign the day the case ended if he could convince them to let me stay."

He flinched at her choice of words. *Unprofessional conduct.* It was a cold, ugly phrase that had nothing in the world to do with the sweet passion they had shared. It didn't belong anywhere in their relationship, but there it was, because of who and what she was.

Swallowing hard, she took a step forward. "Remember the other night, Nicholas? When you said that my background doesn't matter? That it couldn't affect the way you feel about me? That it couldn't make you not want me?"

The look that crossed his face was exquisite in its sorrow. "I was wrong."

His whisper hung between them, sending a shock through her. She had tried to prepare herself for this response, had acknowledged just how badly this whole mess could turn out, had even calculated that she had only one chance in four of coming out of it with her heart—meaning their relationship—intact. She must have lied to herself, though, because she *wasn't* prepared. Deep inside she had believed he would understand and forgive. She loved him, and she had thought that he might love her, too, at least a little. She had believed that he would deal with this and still want her, need her, love her.

Gripping the iron footboard for support, she sank down on the mattress. "Seems I'm not the only one who's been lying. I lied because my job involved staying close enough to keep you alive, and you lied because... Oh, yes. You wanted sex."

For a long, long time, the room remained silent. Lainie

stared at the floor, feeling as lost and weary as she ever had, and Nicholas seemed to be doing the same. All she could see in her peripheral vision was his feet, unmoving and still planted in the place where he'd backed away from her. Finally, in a voice that was flat and empty of life, he spoke. "Pack your bags and get out of here."

Her fingers were numb, but she gripped the iron rail a little tighter. "If you send me away, they'll just send someone else. Smith and Remy have no intention of sitting back and watching Falcone kill you."

"I'd rather have someone else. I'd rather have *anyone* else but you."

His words hurt, doubly so for the simple, emotionless manner in which they'd been spoken. She tried to ignore the pain and concentrate on what was important. "That can be arranged, but it'll take time. In the meantime, you're stuck with me."

Finally he moved, and she lifted her gaze to watch him. He walked as far as the wide door that led into the living room, then looked back. "Was any of it true? Growing up in Savannah, your mother and father, your marriage—any of it?"

"All of it."

"Right." His skepticism was cold. "What about not being able to finish college because you couldn't tolerate your father any longer? Or working as a waitress? Coming here to find something better? Choosing New Orleans because it was as far as your money would take you? Being short on cash when Karen offered you a job? Needing this apartment because you couldn't afford a place of your own on what she paid? None of that was true, was it?"

She swallowed hard before guiltily admitting, "Just the waitress part."

He stood there a moment longer, as if he needed to ask a few more questions. She would bet her heart she knew what they were. *Was any of the rest of it real? The kisses?*

The hours we spent together? The lovemaking? Did you mean any of it? Did you care at all? Or was it all just part of your job? It was just as well that he didn't ask, because right now, he wouldn't be able to believe her answers.

When he finally turned away, she got to her feet and walked to the same spot where he'd just stood. "For whatever it's worth, Nicholas, I never intended for any of this to happen. I never meant to fall in love with you, and I certainly never meant to hurt you."

Her words stopped him for a moment in the doorway, his back to her. After a time, he glanced over his shoulder and gave her another of those sad looks. "Yeah," he agreed, his voice distant and cold. "For whatever it's worth."

And then he was gone.

Lainie remained where she was until her feet began to ache and the muscles in her legs grew tight and tired. Finally she forced herself to turn back into the bedroom, to replace the pistol in its drawer, to return the backpack and the duffels to the closet. As she started to straighten the covers, she found the telephone there. She set it down just outside the front door, then went back to the bedroom, crawled into bed and curled up on her side.

He was angry—God knew, he had a right to be—but people got over being angry. When he recovered from the shock, when he calmed down and started thinking rationally, he would realize that what she'd done wasn't so terribly different from his own actions. He had lied and pretended to be something he wasn't in order to punish Falcone for Rena's death, while she had done the same thing in order to prevent Falcone from causing Nicholas's death. Surely he could understand the motivation and reasoning behind her actions.

But this wasn't about understanding. It was about feelings. It was about trust and betrayal. In his lifetime, Nicholas probably hadn't trusted more than a half-dozen people, but he had trusted *her*—more, he'd said, than anyone else in the world—and she had betrayed him. It didn't matter that she hadn't meant to or that she'd been trapped in a no-win situation. From the moment she'd met him, it had been too late to tell the truth and much too late to save herself from falling for him. But honorable intentions and desperate situations could never change the simple fact that she had betrayed him. He might never forgive her for it, and if he didn't, she might never forgive herself.

Sunday was a bright, sunny day. It was the one day that O'Shea's didn't open its doors at all, a fact for which Nicholas would be grateful if he could summon up the emotion. After the night he'd just spent, though, he was a little low on things like gratitude. Happiness. Hopefulness. Forgiveness.

He hadn't closed up last night until well past two, even though all the customers had gone home before midnight. He had stood behind the bar, doors propped wide, thinking morosely that it would be a perfect time for one of the drive-by shootings that gave Serenity its reputation. One of the resident punks could take mercy on him and put him out of his misery.

Of course it hadn't happened, and it wouldn't. Everyone on Serenity—probably everyone in southern Louisiana—knew that he was Jimmy's. He was safer from the usual thieves and thugs than anyone else in the city, with the exception of Jimmy, because no criminal who wanted to continue living would ever interfere with Falcone's revenge.

Of course, Nicholas thought with a bitter smile, if the old man found out the truth about Lainie, he would alter his revenge. There'd be no more late-night calls or visits, no more unsuspecting photographs, no more promises of death. No, he would leave Nicholas to live with his disillusionment. He would leave him to suffer the heartache of falling in love with the wrong woman.

No, not love. He didn't love Lainie, no more than he'd believed last night that she loved him. He cared about her in the way that any man would care about the woman he was having an affair with, but he didn't love her. His feelings for her were nothing compared to what he'd felt for Rena.

Even though he'd wanted to buy a house to share with Lainie. Even though he'd given too much thought to a future with her. Even though he'd caught himself a time or two watching Jamey with Karen and Sean and imagining himself with Lainie and a sweet baby with hazel eyes.

But none of that was proof of love. It was foolishness. Meaningless mental wanderings. Not wishes, not dreams, not destiny. Just an indication that he had too much time on his hands and too little going on in his life. Right?

Right. And if he ever persuaded himself...

Pushing away from the window where he'd spent the last hour, he grabbed a T-shirt from the closet and pulled it over his head, then left the apartment. He hadn't even managed to close the door, much less lock it, before the door across the hall opened.

A swift glanced showed that her night had been as restless as his own. Good. Since she was responsible for his problems, she should pay for them, too. He hoped she never finished paying.

He locked the door and pocketed the keys before facing her head-on. She was dressed, like him, in jeans and a T-shirt that fitted too snugly to allow for the concealment of anything, including that deadly little toy of hers. Of course, that was probably why she'd worn the waist pack every time they'd gone out. It hadn't held the usual women's stuff as she'd claimed but her pistol and the credentials she was required to carry whenever she carried the gun. All those times, he had walked beside her, sat across from her and held her in his arms, he had never guessed that she was armed, had never suspected that she was there to protect him. He had thought she was there because she liked him.

Idiot.

"Where are you going?"

Twenty-four hours ago he would have responded with a slow, lazy, kiss before issuing an invitation to bed. But twenty-four hours ago he had believed she was just Lainie Farrell, a little down on her luck but making the best of it. This morning he knew better.

"I'm going out—" He broke off, then asked, "What am I supposed to call you?"

"Nicholas—"

"Sorry. That name's taken already. I can't call you Lainie. That's a little personal for an ex-con and a fed, don't you think? How about Ms. Farrell? Or Special Agent Farrell?" His flippant remarks brought a layer of pain to her eyes that shamed him. He sobered and asked, "So what's the routine here? Do I have to check in and out with you? Do I just tell you where I'm going, or do you have to actually follow me?"

"You shouldn't go out alone."

Shouldn't, not *couldn't*. But if he left without her, he had little doubt that she would follow or notify some other fed to do so. He could lose a tail, of course. He intended to head for the Quarter, where he knew every nook and cranny, every alley and back way. It would take better than the FBI's finest to keep up with him there.

"I've been going out alone since I was six years old." He managed to pass without touching her and started down the stairs. He was halfway through the bar when he heard her steps echoing behind him. By the time he reached the first intersection, she was only a dozen feet behind him. Closing his eyes, damning both her and himself, he waited for her to catch up.

They walked in silence to Decatur, then to Jackson Square and beyond. He tried to avoid looking at her, and he knew she was avoiding looking at him. He would have known if she'd ever raised her gaze from the ground. He would have felt it.

He did feel it when they cut across from St. Ann to St. Peter in front of the cathedral and she laid her hand on his arm. Because it felt too damn good, he didn't shake her off or jerk free but let her fingers close around his forearm and pull him to a stop. He didn't look at her, though. Instead he fixed his gaze on a lone musician behind her, entertaining a small crowd with an Irish ballad.

"I'm so sorry."

He wanted to believe her, and maybe someday he would, but not today, not tomorrow, maybe not a long time after that. Not until he dealt with her deception. Not until he determined for himself just how much of these few weeks together had been real and how much had simply been Special Agent Farrell doing her job. He wanted to believe that pulling away from him, telling him no when she wanted—when he'd thought she wanted—to say yes had been business, while kissing him, coming to him and making love with him had all been personal. But he didn't know. He had trusted her, and she had lied, and now he would have to find some new trust before taking her word for anything.

"Yeah, sure." With a careless shrug, he turned and walked away, not looking back to see if she followed. He was past the entrance of Le Petit Théâtre when she caught up this time.

"I guess it was different—lying, pretending to be something else—when you were doing it with Falcone."

He didn't glance at her. "I didn't sleep with Falcone."

"You earned his trust and then betrayed it."

"I tried to send the most powerful organized crime boss in the state of Louisiana to jail."

"And I was trying to save your life."

"My life is none of your damn business. I told Kendricks and Sinclair that I wasn't interested in their offer of protection. I told them I would take my chances with Jimmy. It was *none* of your business."

"When you testified against him, you made it our business."

Abruptly Nicholas came to a stop, ignoring the tourists who had to step into the street to pass. He had assumed that Kendricks and Sinclair's interest in keeping him alive had to do with gratitude and his twenty-five-year-ago relationship with Jolie. But, of course, they weren't spending taxpayer money on sentimentality. Before he'd become a resident at the federal prison, he'd been a star witness in a federal courtroom. Witnesses against people like Jimmy Falcone were hard to come by, and Nicholas had been the best. If he died now, it would be one more powerful reason for other prospective witnesses to decline to take the stand.

Lainie wasn't here to keep him alive because anyone gave a damn whether he died. She was here to protect the future interests of the government if they ever managed to take Jimmy to trial again. With the possible exception of Jolie, no one thought his life was worth saving. They just thought his death was worth preventing.

That hurt a little more.

She stood a few feet away, her gaze steady on him. "I'm sorry."

"I bet you are. You screwed up on a regular basis since you took this case, and then you compounded it by telling Kendricks. Why the hell did you do that?"

"I had to," she said stiffly. "My actions reflected badly on him and the bureau as well as on me. My errors in judgment—"

"So far, you've managed to refer to it as professional misconduct, actions that reflect badly on the government and errors in judgment.'' Bitterness shaped his smile. "And here I thought it was just sex."

Her eyes grew cloudy, and her smile was just as hurtful as his own. "And I thought it was something more. I guess we were both wrong."

Suddenly he was more than hurt, more than bitter. He felt frustrated. Cheated. Mad as hell. "This whole mess was wrong from the start. They never should have sent you here. You never should have deceived me, and I never should have touched you. God help me, I never should have trusted you, and I won't make the mistake of doing it again."

"Nicholas, please—"

"Don't quit your job, Lainie. Go back to Kendricks and tell him you lied. Plead with him, beg, hell, sleep with him if that's what it takes—you're pretty damn good at that— but hold on to your job because, darlin', there's nothing for you here. You try to stay on Serenity, and I swear, I'll make your life hell.'' Which was only fair, because her mere memory was going to make *his* life unbearable.

With that he turned and started walking, heading nowhere in particular, just away. Damn her dedication and damn her duty, she followed. He crossed the street between cars, cutting it close enough to make the driver blanch, then worked his way into a large group of college-age kids. He maneuvered in front of one with the shoulders of a linebacker, then, at the last instant, slipped through the open door of a smoky, dark bar. Without slowing his steps, he headed straight for the bathrooms at the back—and the hall that led to an alley exit—pausing only briefly to watch the last of the kids go by with Lainie only a few steps behind. She didn't glance in the bar, but even if she had, she wouldn't have seen him in all the gloom and shadows.

He waited a moment longer, then opened the unmarked door that led into the hall. Once outside again, he stood in the narrow alley, at a loss. There was no place he wanted to go, no one he wanted to talk to. He could go somewhere for lunch, but he wasn't hungry. It was more tempting to go right back inside for a drink, but the way he was feeling, he might not stop. He could go home, brood in his empty apartment and wait for Lainie to give up looking for him and return, or he could wander around the city and wait for a better idea to strike.

Somehow, he didn't think he was going to get any better ideas for a long time.

Wondering why he'd left home in the first place, he headed that way again. When he got there, he found the bar locked up tight with the shutters closed. Even in her rush to catch up with him, Lainie had taken the time to secure the building. She was conscientious. Just as a good little FBI agent should be.

After he stepped into the dark bar and locked the door behind him, he leaned his forehead against the cool glass and groaned aloud. Here he had thought that maybe she'd been a hooker or an ex-con like him, maybe a nun or someone's wife, a lot of little someones' mother, but instead she was an FBI agent. He would have preferred any of the others over that…except the hooker. Or the wife. He didn't want to think about Lainie with other men, particularly with another man who had more of a claim on her than *he* did.

But he didn't have any claim on her. He was just her job, just a temporary assignment, spiced up with a little sex.

I thought it was something more.

He had thought so, too, but apparently he'd been wrong. More wrong than he could bear.

He went upstairs and took up his usual position at one of the windows. Time crept by with no sign of Lainie. When his hunger became too insistent to ignore, he ate a sandwich at the bar, then returned to the window, where he smoked enough cigarettes to force him to empty the ashtray. He had just stubbed out the last one in the place when the sound of a car drew his attention to the street. There weren't many cars on Serenity. Most residents couldn't pay the insurance or repairs on the only junkers they could afford, so they walked everywhere or relied on the city buses.

The car pulled to a stop in front of O'Shea's. It wasn't a regular on the street. It was too new, too sporty. Anyone down here who could afford a car like that would spend the money instead moving elsewhere. Of course, any number of FBI agents could afford a car like that.

Lainie got out and unlocked the door while the driver came around the car. Had she called for help in locating Nicholas, or had she taken him at his word last night and arranged for a replacement? Maybe this guy was going to take over the baby-sitting while she went back home to her life in Atlanta. It wouldn't be as much fun for Nicholas, but at least it would be honest.

Their steps sounded loud on the stairs, followed by the creak of her apartment door. Almost immediately, there was a knock at his own door. "Mr. Carlucci?"

He remained where he was, half sitting on the windowsill.

Another knock. "Mr. Carlucci, my name is Dolan. I'm with the FBI. Can I talk to you?"

He didn't break his silence. They couldn't be sure he was home. Lainie couldn't have seen him from the street below because she'd never looked up. For all they knew, he could be anywhere in the city. Hell, in the hours since he'd left her, he could have gone anywhere in the country.

There was a sudden thud on the door, a fist driven by frustration connecting with the wood with enough force to startle him. "Open the damn door, Nicholas!" He'd made the same request of her only a week ago, when she had almost kissed him in the bar before jumping up from his lap and fleeing to the safety of her apartment. He had banged it hard, too, and had sworn, but she hadn't relented.

He didn't have to, but he did. Leaving the window, he

crossed the room, opened the door only an inch or two, then returned to the sill. Slowly the door swung in—pushed by Dolan, no doubt. Judging by the emotion in her voice, Lainie would have shoved it hard enough to bounce off the wall.

The man looked to be in his early thirties. He was big, muscular, strong, but not particularly intimidating. The badge clipped onto his belt and the gun resting on his right hip helped improve that a little.

At his side, Lainie looked mutinous—and tired. If she'd spent the entire afternoon since he'd ditched her wandering around the Quarter, she should be tired. If he were a better man, he might feel guilty, but he hadn't had the most restful twenty hours or so himself, and it was her fault.

Dolan extended his hand. Nicholas didn't take it. If his refusal bothered the other man, it didn't show. "Mr. Carlucci, I'm Sam Dolan. I've been working with Lainie since she came to New Orleans."

So had he. The problem was, he hadn't known it until yesterday.

"You're not too happy with us right now. I understand that. What you need to keep in mind is that we're just trying to do our job."

"Oh, Lainie's been doing much more than just her job, haven't you, darlin'?"

She blushed. So did Dolan, who gave her a look and a nod of his head. Grudgingly she left the apartment, leaving the door open a few inches behind her. A moment later, her own door shut.

"Give her a break, would you? She's in a tough enough position as it is. She had a good record with the bureau until she met you. Now she's screwed. At best she'll get a letter of censure, which will pretty much end her career. She'll never get another promotion, and she'll never work another major case. At worst, they'll make an example of her and fire her. So lay off, would you?"

Nicholas shifted his gaze out the window. Across the street, the O'Sheas were gathered on the veranda—Jamey and Karen in matching rockers and Reid and Cassie sharing a newly hung porch swing with Sean. It was a nice homey scene, the sort that had never been part of his life, the sort that he'd begun to think maybe could be.

Deliberately he looked away from them, focusing instead on the empty building next door to Kathy's House. At least he knew now that Lainie didn't make a habit of sleeping with people involved with her cases and that sleeping with him had been her own idea, not her control agent's, Sinclair's or Kendricks's. But he had known that anyway, even when he'd accused her otherwise. He'd known because he'd known her.

Knowing didn't help much, though. There were still all those lies. So she hadn't had a choice. So she'd told the truth whenever possible. That didn't change the facts. She had come here under false pretenses. She had lied to everyone, especially him. She had made him fall in love with a woman who didn't exist, not really. It was a major leap from the ex-waitress, hard-luck gardener and all-around-handyman helper he knew to the well-educated, well-paid federal agent she really was. The other Lainie could belong on Serenity. She could easily stay here, making a home out of that run-down cottage at the end of the street, building a business with hard work and determination, spending her days with her hands in the dirt and her nights with him.

But the real Lainie, the one with the college degree and the salary higher than four or five residents of Serenity combined, the one who wore suits to the office and lived in a good part of Atlanta and was undoubtedly contributing to a profitable investment plan... She didn't belong here, and she certainly didn't belong with him.

He looked at Dolan. "You may find this hard to believe, but some parts of my life *are* personal. That means they're none of your business. Now, are you here for a reason?"

"Lainie says you want someone else moved in."

"She's wrong. I don't want anyone here." But that wasn't true. He wanted her. He wanted her so damn badly that it hurt.

"Things are already pretty rough for her. If you have her removed, it's going to get worse. Let her finish the case and salvage whatever she can. You don't have to spend a lot of time with her. Just let her do her job. Don't go out without telling her, and don't give her the slip when you do go out. Remember that she's trying to keep you alive. She's willing to risk her life to protect yours. Give her a little credit for that."

The last thing he needed on his conscience was Lainie risking her life for him. That alone was reason enough to send her away. He had just barely survived Rena's death. If anything happened to Lainie...

"Her job's not my responsibility," he said coldly.

"It is when you refuse to let her do it."

He stared hard at the interior wall, as if he could see through it, across the hall and through the next wall into Lainie's apartment. He wouldn't have to spend a lot of time with her, Dolan had said, but being with her wasn't the problem. Being without her—living without her—was. Lying alone in his bed while she lay alone in hers was a problem. Knowing that wherever he was, whatever he was doing, she was somewhere nearby but still out of his reach was a problem.

Knowing that he could very well put her life in danger was a major problem.

But maybe there was a solution. Maybe she could minimize the damage she'd done to her career, and he could be free of the government's attention for the first time in more years than he could remember. Maybe he could make a deal with her: he would let her stay—would let the FBI believe that she was doing her job by the book—and she would stay out of his way. It would benefit them both, and it should keep her out of danger. After the harm he'd helped do to her reputation within the bureau, it seemed the least he could do.

That brought him a moment's pause. There was something tremendously unsettling about knowing that, in having a relationship with Lainie—in doing nothing more than spending time with her, liking her, having feelings of both a sexual and a romantic nature toward her and acting on those feelings—he had helped damage irreparably an honorable career. He hadn't done anything that millions of men before him hadn't already done, but because of who he was, it would cost her dearly. It wasn't fair. She deserved better.

But she wanted *him*.

"I'll think about it," he said, then gestured toward the door. "Close the door on your way out."

Chapter 9

Lainie lay on the couch, staring at the ceiling. Her feet were propped on the sofa arm, her head butted against the opposite arm. A fold of teal sheet that had come loose was puffed out above her head, limiting her view, but it didn't matter. There wasn't anything in here that she wanted to see.

It had been a hell of a day. Her head ached, her feet hurt, and her heart was sore. She had seen more of the French Quarter and its environs today than she'd ever intended to see. She had wandered through block after block of shops, restaurants and bars, some of them seedy enough to make O'Shea's look like a first-class establishment. She had been met with suspicion, curiosity, a total lack of interest and, in a strip club on Bourbon, a proposition or two. She'd been worried sick, hurt and upset, and after the first two hours, her feet, in shoes not intended for endless traipsing, had started to blister. Then Sam had brought her back here and Nicholas had given her that bitter mocking look as he'd gotten in one more hurtful shot.

It was times like these when she missed her mother the most, when the unfairness of life smacked her between the eyes. Elaine Ravenel had had an extraordinary understanding of unfairness—and an extraordinary capacity for coping with it. The situation with Lainie's father must have been unbearable, but she'd given little sign of it. The first hint Lainie had had that something was seriously wrong was finding her mother in the garden that long-ago spring day. Before then she had always been all smiles and warmth, full of advice, encouragement and love whenever Lainie had needed them.

More than anything else, Lainie needed the love. She would give anything to have the kind of love the people around her enjoyed—from a friend, a sibling, a parent, a spouse, a child. It had been missing ever since her mother's death. Her father's love had been warped, and her brother's had come from a distance. If her husband had ever loved her, it had died an early death, and while the man she had almost married had been fond of her, there'd been no emotion more intense than desire. All her adult life, she'd been looking for someone to love her, and she'd dared to dream that Nicholas was the one.

Unless he was a more forgiving man than she'd given him credit for, she'd been wrong again.

Feeling queasy from lack of food, she slowly sat up and swung her feet to the floor. There was always sandwich stuff in the refrigerator, so Jamey could feed the occasional hungry customer, along with a half-dozen dinners in the freezer. She could fix a solitary meal and eat it in front of the television in the bar, or she could bring it back up here to this quiet lonely place and listen to the silence. The one thing she couldn't do was go out, not unless Nicholas went, too, and somehow she didn't think that sitting at a table across from her and trying to eat was high on his list of favorite things to do tonight.

Walking carefully because her feet were sore and quietly

because she didn't want to disturb Nicholas across the hall, she went downstairs. She settled on a sandwich because it was quick and easy and didn't stick on the lump that seemed to have settled permanently in her chest. She carried it into the bar, lit only by the single bulb in the hallway, and settled at a table against the far wall, where she ate staring at nothing more interesting than the shadows in the room, thinking of nothing more important than finishing the meal and getting through the next hour. If she survived it, then she would concentrate on the next one, and later rather than sooner it would be morning and time for her to go work.

If she still had a job. Now that Nicholas knew the truth, there was no reason to continue the charade with the O'Sheas. Because of their fondness for Nicholas and because they hadn't invested as much of themselves in a relationship with her as he had, they would take the news more kindly than he had, but they still might feel that she'd taken advantage of their generosity and betrayed their friendship. Sooner or later, they would want her gone from Kathy's House and out of the apartment, and then where would she go?

She felt the same anxious fear she'd felt twenty-one years ago when she'd left home. She had known she was going to Athens and where she would bunk for the first few weeks, but she'd had no answers beyond that. She hadn't known where she would eventually live, whether she would be able to find a job or how she could manage school and work and a poverty-level budget. All she'd known was that she had to go. She couldn't live one minute longer in her father's house.

Now the day was approaching when she would have to leave here. She didn't know where she would go or what she would do when she got there. Even though she was a mature adult with job skills, an education and a healthy savings account, she was more scared than she'd ever been as that eighteen-year-old. Of course, back then she'd been running away from the father she'd despised. This time she would be forced away by the man she loved. It was a big difference.

In the stillness of the bar, her sigh sounded big and so sad that it was blue. What she needed was a cold beer and a long, steamy hot bath. Her entire body was achy, the muscles tight from a full twenty-four hours of stress. Maybe a bath, a beer and sheer exhaustion would help her get a little sleep tonight—or maybe she would spend another night curled up in a ball, staring out the window, her eyes gritty and too dry for tears.

She popped the top on a bottle of beer taken from the cooler behind the counter, then returned to the table to replace the chair, legs in the air, and claim the napkin she'd left. She was halfway across the room when the lights went on, making her blink before she could focus on Nicholas. He stood motionless at the end of the bar, with the aspirin bottle she'd noticed the day she'd moved in clutched in one hand. She had thought at the time that he seemed more likely to give headaches than to suffer them himself. Her headache was her own—a consequence of stress, too many smoky bars and too much regret—but he'd given her a hell of a heartache.

He moved first, starting toward her, and she involuntarily backed a few steps away. He stopped a few yards away, with less than six feet and a world of anger separating them. "I have a proposition. Your pal Dolan wants you to stay here. He thinks maybe you can salvage something of your career if you stay and don't screw up anymore."

By "screw up," he meant have sex with him. As cold as he was right now, she didn't think that was even a remote possibility.

"You were right. If I throw you out, they're going to send someone else in. So I've decided that you can stay and pretend that you're doing your job."

"And what do you get out of this?" She was surprised that her voice worked, that it was mostly steady, a little cool and not at all pleading.

"You stay out of my way. You don't interfere. You don't tag along when I go out. You *don't* do your job, and I don't tell anyone you're not."

She shook her head. "I can't do that. It's not how I work."

"Oh, I've *seen* how you work, darlin'. Mostly on your—" As he broke off, shame flushed his face a deep bronze. Of course, her mind had already supplied the finishing touch to his insult. *Mostly on your back.*

"You didn't have any objections at the time," she reminded him, her voice a pained whisper.

"No, I didn't." He met her gaze, looked away, then back again. "At the time, I thought I was pretty damn lucky."

"But not anymore." His answer was no answer at all. It was enough to hurt. "I can't accept your proposition. I don't care about salvaging my career. As I told you, I'm quitting."

"You planning to get out before they fire you?"

"I don't care whether they fire me or censure me or throw a big parade in my honor. I don't want the job anymore."

"You want a house. And a nursery."

A month ago the idea of quitting her job had never entered her mind. She had been content with the idea of putting in thirty years, then retiring a white-haired old maid. If anyone had suggested anything different, she would have laughed. If anyone had suggested that she might ever want to start a nursery and live in a shabby, run-down house in a violent, run-down neighborhood, she would have been appalled.

Tonight she just felt wistful.

"I want a lot of things I know I'll never have."

"Am I one of them?"

She tried to look away, but his dark gaze trapped her. She had no idea what he wanted to hear—truth or a lie— or how he would react. Would he believe her, or would he mock her, scorn her, explain to her in very blunt terms exactly how little *he* wanted *her?* It didn't matter. He couldn't make her feel any more hopeless than she already did. "Yes," she said quietly, truthfully. "You come—"

Her admission was interrupted by the sound of breaking glass, mingled with earsplitting reports and dull thuds. Someone was shooting at them, spraying the front of the building with what sounded like an AK-47. Lainie had no time to react before Nicholas dove to the floor, pulling her down with him, maneuvering her underneath him. She struggled against him, pushing to dislodge him. "Let me up! I've got to get my gun…got to see… Damn it, Nicholas, let me go!"

His only response was to shift more of his weight onto her body, pressing her hard against the floor as the gunfire continued, the shots coming too quickly to separate, tearing through the shutters, sending slivers of wood and pieces of glass flying across the room. When the beer bottle she still held shattered in a spray of glass and foam, she jerked her hand to her body, squeezing it into the minuscule space between her chest and his. In her trembling fingers she could feel the rapid beat of his heart and knew her own matched it.

She whispered silent prayers as the gunman strafed the building from one side to the other. They should be moving, crawling along the floor until they reached the hallway. There was no way an AK could penetrate both the outside brick wall and the thick inner wall. But before she could make her voice work to give Nicholas the command to move, as suddenly as the shooting had started, it ended. The silence rang in her ears, and the trembling in her hands spread through her body. In all her years with the bureau, this was the first time anyone had ever shot at her, the first time her life had ever been in danger, and she was shaken.

One moment passed, then another, and Nicholas didn't move. Finally he raised his head to stare down at her. "Are you all right?"

Wide-eyed, she nodded, then raised her hand to his face. "Are you?"

He didn't pull away, but closed his eyes and rubbed his cheek against her palm. He gave her only a moment to savor the sensation, and then he was kissing her, his mouth hard, hungry and desperate on hers. He kissed her as if he might crawl deep inside her, as if he might imprint himself on her soul, as if the kiss might somehow save them both. It was exactly what she needed to calm her nerves, to warm the chill of fear that had swept over her. It was *exactly* what she needed to give her hope.

Too soon he pulled away, lifting himself off her, rising easily to his feet. For a moment he looked numb as he gazed around the room. Lainie stood up, too, dusting her clothes. Her first look around made her whisper. "Oh my God."

The bar was pretty much destroyed. Tables were splintered, legs shot off, chairs broken into pieces. Not one of the shutters or the French doors remained intact. Fragments of wood hung where the hinges attached to the wall, but the rest of the doors lay in pieces on the floor. The shelves behind the bar that had held rows of glasses and bottles of liquor were littered with glass shards, and a thin stream of whiskey dripped from one to puddle on the counter below. The space where they had lain was the only bit of floor that wasn't littered with chunks, shards and slivers of glass, making her curse the fact that she'd come downstairs barefoot.

Turning to Nicholas, she saw the blood that spotted his T-shirt and automatically reached out. It wasn't his, though. Her hand was marked with a half-dozen little cuts from the shattering beer bottle. When she'd tucked it between them, his shirt had absorbed the blood.

He still looked dazed, but anger was seeping into his eyes and the harsh set of his mouth. He turned in a slow circle, taking in all the damage, no doubt considering the damage those hundreds of bullets could have done to *them*. By the time he faced her again, there was nothing in his face but icy rage. "No more." The words were soft, no more than a whisper, followed by such volume, such intensity, that she flinched. *"No more, damn it!"*

Spinning around, he headed for the hall. Lainie stared after him, studied the heavy layer of glass and wood on the floor, then crossed it anyway. Safe in the hallway, she stopped to pull a shard of glass from each foot, then, ignoring the blood, rushed to the stairs. Halfway up, she met Nicholas on his way back down. Deadly determination marked his face, and her gun was in his hand.

"Nicholas, wait—"

He pushed her aside and was in the hall below before she caught her balance. Swearing, she raced upstairs, shoved her feet into the first pair of shoes she came to, grabbed her credentials from the drawer he'd left open, then took the stairs three at a time. When she rounded the corner into the bar, she was relieved to see a tall figure in jeans and a T-shirt standing in one door, but her relief drained away when she realized it wasn't Nicholas.

"What the hell happened here?" Jamey demanded. Reid was right behind him, and across the street on the sidewalk, she could see Karen and Cassie huddled together with nearby neighbors.

"Jimmy tried to make good on his threat against Nicholas. Did you see him?"

"Jimmy?"

"Nicholas."

Jamey shook his head. "I figured he was in here."

Shoving the credentials into her pocket, she pushed past

him and onto the sidewalk, staring down the street. Except for a few curious faces, it was empty. There was no sign of Nicholas. Trying to ignore the knot of fear in her chest, she returned to the bar, where she found the phone in pieces. In frustration, she pressed the heels of her palms to her eyes for a moment, dropping them away only when Jamey's and Reid's footsteps came close. "I need one of you to call Smith Kendricks or Remy Sinclair. Tell him Jimmy tried to kill Nicholas and—" She broke off, wet her lips, then finished. "Tell him that I think Nicholas is going to kill Jimmy."

It was three-fifteen in the morning. The police had come and gone, more than willing to relinquish a middle-of-the-night investigation on Serenity Street to the federal authorities. Only one New Orleans officer, Michael Bennett, had stayed, in part because he'd conducted more than his share of investigations into Falcone and knew as much about him as the feds and in part because of his friendship with Kendricks and Sinclair. While the evidence had been photographed, studied and gathered, at the table in the back hallway Lainie had been questioned to the point that she felt more like a subject than one of their own who had been a witness to—and practically a victim of—a violent crime. Of course, she wasn't one of them anymore. That had changed the first time Nicholas had kissed her.

Now they were all gone. Jamey and Reid had boarded the gaping doors with plywood from Karen's shed before going home. Jamey had asked her to spend the night at Kathy's House, but she'd refused. The other agents were all going out looking for Nicholas—an assignment from which she'd been pointedly excluded—but she would wait here in case he came back. In case he changed his mind. In case he didn't kill Jimmy.

She was so worried, so scared and tired. Sliding her chair back was a major effort. Standing up required pushing against the table—the one intact table in the place. If she could drag herself upstairs, she was going to collapse face forward across the bed, but she wouldn't sleep. Not tonight. Not as long as Nicholas was out there somewhere with her gun.

She was approaching the kitchen door when a tall man in a windbreaker stepped out. For an instant she panicked, then gave a nervous little laugh. Everyone here tonight, with the exception of Smith and herself, had worn navy nylon raid jackets. She'd left her own back in Atlanta. "My gosh, you scared me. I thought everyone had gone."

Then she remembered that the raid jackets were stamped FBI in gold on both sleeves and on the back, with the letters or a gold badge on the left breast. This man's jacket was just plain navy. Her smile faded, the hair on the back of her neck stood on end, and alarm rocketed through her.

He brought his left hand into view. The gun he held was pointed directly at her middle. "Would you come with me, Ms. Farrell?" He sounded so polite, so businesslike. If she refused, would he politely drag her out of here? If she tried to run, would shooting her in the back be just business?

She didn't have the option to refuse or the energy to resist. Instead she offered a smile and a mock-pleasant response. "Why, of course. How could I possibly refuse such a gracious invitation?"

So many years of being watched by the government and by Jimmy's own people had taught Nicholas a lot about moving around undetected. His clandestine meetings with Jolie five years ago had been easy to arrange, at least until, through Kendricks, the FBI had gotten involved. At the final meeting, Shawna Warren had led Falcone's men right to him, and he had barely escaped with his life.

He knew enough about the way the FBI did business to know that they were looking for him now. Ostensibly they wanted to stop him before he got to Jimmy. In all honesty, though, none of them would give a damn if he blew Jimmy's brains out in the most public of executions. They just wanted to be there to arrest him when it was done. It would look good in the papers, solving the murder of a major mob boss in record time. That it was Falcone who had died would be the icing on the publicity cake.

They didn't need to worry. If Nicholas survived to walk away—which was doubtful, considering that Jimmy was always surrounded by heavily armed men whose loyalty was bought and paid for—he would turn himself in. He didn't mind going back to prison. Living a long life on Serenity with Lainie would be his first choice, but knowing that she was safe, that she would never go through another incident like last night because of him, that she would never again be hurt, frightened, or damn near killed because of him, made a pretty good second choice.

The best way to ensure her safety was to remove the threat. That was why he'd spent the last hour standing in the corner of this shop, watching the street out front. The place was barely eight feet wide and maybe three times as long. Heavy brocade drapes hung at the windows and strings of beads dangled from above the door. The door was propped open with a brick, but what little fresh air it let in couldn't compete with the sickly sweet scents of incense that burned constantly on the table and permeated even the wood.

The shop belonged to a reader, an old crone dressed in a ragbag version of gypsy-style clothes who billed herself as Madame Helen. Promising answers to questions about love, life, money and the future, she claimed to know all and see all—and, for a price, she would tell all. For twenty bucks and no curiosity, she'd rented him this small corner, then settled into a ratty old recliner and fallen asleep.

It was nearly eleven o'clock. Provided his routine hadn't changed in the last five years, any minute now, Jimmy's limo would come around the corner and pull to a stop in front of the restaurant across the street. Jimmy and three or four of his bodyguards would go inside through the private side entrance while the driver went off to wait in a nearby lot, always prepared for a quick getaway. Since his routine hadn't changed in the ten years Nicholas had worked for him, there was no reason to think it had since.

The limo appeared, and Nicholas headed for the back of the shop. It took him more than twenty minutes to make his way unseen through the courtyard behind Madame Helen's shop to the back door, marked Employees Only, of the restaurant, but he didn't worry about the time. Jimmy was a man of habit, and habit made lunch a drawn-out affair. He usually discussed business over appetizers and multiple courses before finishing with dessert. The whole event took two hours, sometimes longer.

No one in the kitchen noticed him as he slipped through, though in jeans, a bloodstained T-shirt and the black leather jacket he'd bought off some kid last night—needed to hide the gun in his waistband—he definitely stood out. Sliding his hand underneath the jacket and wrapping his fingers around the grips, he made his way out of the kitchen and from one dining room to the next.

Jimmy favored the dining room in the distant corner of the building. The private entrance opened into a hall just this side of the room so he could enter and leave without notice. The central table was large enough to seat everyone he chose to invite, with small booths in the corners where additional guests could sit—or where bodyguards could watch those they were guarding without necessarily being privy to what was said. The arched doorway leading into the room was broad enough for comfort, but narrow enough that two men could easily block it. There were two men there now, faces he didn't recognize, but they certainly recognized him. The speed with which their hands went to the guns underneath their suit coats was proof of that.

He shoved past both men before they got their weapons

drawn, took up a place directly across the table from Jimmy and pulled out Lainie's gun, pointing it at the old man.

Jimmy lifted a bite of salad to his mouth and slowly chewed it, his gaze never leaving Nicholas's. After washing it down with wine, he stabbed another forkful, then said, "Nice to see you again, Nicholas. I would invite you to join us, but it seems there's no room."

He laughed at his own joke, as there was plenty of room. Fewer than half the chairs were filled. Today was no business lunch. There was only Jimmy, Vince Cortese on his left and the lawyer who had replaced Nicholas on his right. A couple of men were seated at the booth off to the left, and Vinnie Marino and Trevor Morgan stood off to Nicholas's right. Protecting the boss was a step up from the intimidation or drug running they usually handled.

"You look a little put out, Nicholas. You have some trouble at that dive where you work?"

"I hear Jamey plans to do some redecorating." The remark and the laughter that accompanied it came from Vince.

"What a coincidence," Nicholas said dryly. "They'll be doing some redecorating here, too, after today."

Jimmy gave an exaggerated sigh. "Before this goes any further and you do something you can't back down from, maybe you should take a closer look at my dining companions. Alex?"

Over in the corner, one of the men rose from the booth and dragged a figure out behind him. He was so big and she was so slim that Nicholas hadn't even realized she was there. Upon seeing her, he felt sick all the way through his soul. When Alex, still chewing on a crust of bread, raised a gun to her temple, Nicholas died a little inside.

At Jimmy's impatient gesture, Alex pushed her around the table, stopping an arm's length away from Nicholas, offering a trade—Lainie for the gun. Knowing that it meant Lainie's death as well as his own, Nicholas handed the pistol over, then caught her as the man shoved her forward. She was trembling uncontrollably when he wrapped his arms around her, and her face was white, her eyes reddened, weariness etched into every pore.

"I'm sorry," she whispered against his neck.

"It's all right." Of course it wasn't. Instead of Lainie living with his death on her conscience, he was going to die with her death on his. Once more, the simple act of loving him was going to cost a woman her life. She had already sacrificed enough for him. Her life was too much.

"They came to O'Shea's last night. They had guns."

And she'd been unarmed because he'd taken her gun. If only he'd been there... But it wouldn't have changed anything. He and Lainie would still be in exactly the same situation.

Jimmy stood up and leaned forward, his hands on the table. "Tell me one thing before Alex takes you away. *Why?* Why did you betray me? Why did you make this necessary?"

Still holding Lainie close, Nicholas answered for the first time. "Do you remember a girl named Rena Baker?"

Jimmy shook his head.

"I didn't think so. She worked at a place in Baton Rouge named the Bayou. You remember that, don't you?"

"Sure. It was a club I acquired...oh, twenty years ago."

"And when the owner told you he wasn't interested in selling, you changed his mind for him. Rather, you changed his widow's mind. Your boys shot the place up. They killed him, one of his bartenders, three waitresses and a customer. Rena was one of the waitresses. She wasn't important to you, but she meant everything to me." Everything, until he met Lainie. Rena had sent him down his self-destructive path. Lainie had saved him from it.

For her efforts, she was going to die.

Jimmy's reaction was understated. He didn't express disbelief that anyone could hold a grudge for twenty years.

He wasn't at all surprised that love could drive Nicholas to do all that he'd done. He understood vengeance. "I'm sorry the girl died, but it was just the cost of doing business." He said it so simply, the way any businessman might talk about expenses and losses. "You were part of my family, Nicholas. I loved you like a son. I'm very sorry you have to die."

When he gestured to Alex to take them away, Nicholas protectively moved Lainie to his other side. He had one last chance to get her out of this alive. It was slim, and it might possibly seal her fate, but he had to try. "How did you find out about Lainie?"

"We saw you together and asked a few questions. Everyone on Serenity seems to know Miss Farrell."

"Actually no one on Serenity truly knows her except me. Does she look like an out-of-work waitress who can't find anything better than a gardening and errand boy's job on Serenity?" He paused, giving Falcone a chance to study Lainie before going on. "She's an FBI agent, Jimmy. She was sent here to keep an eye on me."

"Sent by whom?"

Lainie answered, her voice steady if not strong. "Remy Sinclair is the case agent. He and Smith Kendricks came up with the idea. They brought me in from Atlanta because neither you nor Nicholas would know who I was."

"I don't believe you."

She fished in the hip pocket of her jeans, drew out a thin black case and tossed it on the table. It slid to a stop just in front of the salad plate. Jimmy opened it, compared the photograph on the credentials with her face, then closed it again with a decisive snap. For a long time he didn't say anything. He was weighing the pros and cons of each option available to him. If Nicholas were on the other side of the table, he would be vehemently advising the old man against doing anything to bring the full wrath and scrutiny of the government down on him, but the lawyer who was over there wasn't saying a word. He was just looking scared.

"Whatever else I did, Jimmy, I never gave you bad advice," Nicholas said quietly. "Last night you almost killed a federal agent. Now you've kidnapped her. If anything happens to her, Sinclair is going to camp in your back pocket. You won't be able to sneeze without him knowing it. Let her go."

"And, of course, I'd have to let you go, too."

He shook his head. "You let her walk out the door, and I'll go wherever Alex wants to take me."

"If I let her walk out the door, she'll go straight to the nearest phone and call Sinclair."

"Probably. But Alex and I will already be gone. You've got plenty of hiding places that they've never found. There'll never be any proof of what happens next." Beside him, Lainie started to protest, but Nicholas hushed her. Fear widened her pupils until her eyes were nearly black, and she was beginning to tremble again. The only time she'd said she loved him, he had doubted her sincerity, but he didn't have any doubts now. He didn't have any doubts about his own love now. Unfortunately it was a little too late.

It was the story of his life. Too little or too late.

Across the table, Jimmy reached a decision. As soon as he slid Lainie's credentials inside the breast pocket of his coat, Nicholas knew it wasn't the right one. "It's a simple fact—if I let her go, I can't kill you. I've been waiting a long time to do that, Nicholas. My reputation demands it. Sinclair can suspect all he wants, but there'll be no proof to tie her disappearance to me. No one saw her leaving Serenity last night with Alex and Mack. No one saw her coming in here with us. I doubt even the waiter could tell you anything about her, but even if he could, he wouldn't. He's Vince's cousin, you know." He gestured once more as he sat down. "Alex. Go with them, Vinnie."

Marino moved forward behind them. So did Trevor Morgan. "*No.* No one's going anywhere."

Nicholas glanced over his shoulder. The kid seemed edgy, his eyes darting from one person to another, but his grip on the gun was cool and steady. A quick glance around the room showed some measure of surprise on everyone's face—even Trevor's. For the most part, Jimmy looked annoyed, Alex a little scornful. Marino looked scared, though—*real* scared—and Vince was concerned.

As unobtrusively as possible, Nicholas began edging Lainie behind him.

"What the hell do you think you're doing?" Jimmy demanded, and Morgan turned the gun on him.

He parroted Jimmy's earlier words. "Something I've been waiting a long time to do. My reputation demands it." Then he pulled the trigger, holding it down, sending a spray of bullets around the room.

The last thing Nicholas saw before he and Lainie dove to the floor was Jimmy, sprawled in his chair, his head back, his mouth open, little blossoms of blood seeping across his shirt.

The restaurant doors were locked, business suspended for the day. The medical examiner's people had already taken away the bodies—five, in all—and the paramedics had transported the survivors to area hospitals. Hit once in the head and multiple times in the chest, Vince Cortese wasn't expected to live. The man with the raspy voice probably would.

Alex was dead. Vinnie Marino. The lawyer. Another man whose name Lainie had never heard. And Jimmy. Jimmy Falcone was dead. The cause of fighting crime in southern Louisiana had received a big boost, though not for long. With the old man gone, all the interests he'd controlled would be up for grabs. Others would take over, though hopefully not as crafty, as vicious or as cold. In a matter of days, it would be business as usual.

Like last night, a crowd had soon arrived—first New Orleans cops, followed by what must be every FBI agent in the parish, and Lainie felt as if she had spoken to every single one of them. Nicholas, at a table in the next room, had been put through the same wringer. Remy Sinclair had gone to tell him he was free to leave just before he stopped by Lainie's table to deliver the same message. She watched Nicholas walk out without a glance in her direction before she finally found the strength to go looking for Sam. "You got a piece of paper and a pen?"

He flipped to a clean page in the folder he held, tore it out, then fished a pen from his pocket. She sat down again, wrote a brief note, folded it in half and delivered it to Smith Kendricks, deep in conversation just outside the blood-splattered room. He broke off when he saw her, accepting the paper without question. After scanning it, he met her gaze. "Are you sure?"

She nodded.

"You know you don't have to."

For the first time in too long, she smiled. "Yes, I do."

He studied her for a long moment, then glanced toward the dining room where Nicholas had been interviewed. "I guess you do. Good luck."

"Thanks." She would need it.

She walked through the restaurant to the front door, where a somber man let her out before locking the door again behind her. She hoped she never had to set foot in the place again. Of course, with the future she had planned, it wasn't likely she would ever be able to afford such a place. All her money would be sunk into a house and a business. There would be none left over for fancy restaurant meals.

Stopping at the top of the steps, she sighed deeply. A house and a business. That was a big job to take on alone.

In all her dreams, Nicholas had been there to share the burdens and the pleasures, making it all worthwhile. After last night's kiss and the tenderness and protectiveness he'd shown her today, she had dared to hope that maybe he was coming around and finding some forgiveness in his heart. The fact that he'd left the restaurant without a word to her suggested otherwise.

So what was she supposed to do now? Move out of O'Shea's, for starters, and see about finding some way to help Jamey with the repairs. She could find a cheap motel, then invest a little energy tracking down the owner of the cottage at the end of Serenity. Sooner or later she would have to go back to Atlanta and close out her life there, and…

Gradually she became aware that someone was watching her, and the sudden ache around her heart told her who. Slowly she turned to see him leaning against the wall, a few feet to the left of the door. His hands were in his pockets, and one knee was bent, the foot flat against the brick. In the black leather jacket, with his eyes so dark and serious, he looked thoroughly disreputable. Thoroughly handsome and, oh, so dear.

He came to stand beside her on the steps, fixing his gaze on a store across the street. "So what happens now?"

She didn't know if he meant her plans for the immediate future or if he was speaking in general terms. She chose to believe the former. "I'm going home." To sleep. To recover. To plan and to pack.

"Share a cab with me."

She was more than happy to agree, for practical reasons as well as personal. She was tired. Last night as a guest at Falcone's estate hadn't been the most restful night she'd ever spent. Her blisters still hurt, and so did the cuts on the soles of her feet. She would have suggested a cab herself if the goon named Alex hadn't hustled her out of O'Shea's without so much as a nickel in her pocket.

They had to walk around the corner to find a taxi. Like before, the driver refused to take them any farther than the intersection of Decatur and Serenity. As they started down the street, Nicholas glanced at her. "You have any explanations for what happened back there?"

"You probably know that Trevor's brother Ryan used to run things down here for Falcone."

"I bailed them both out of trouble more than a few times."

"Maybe that explains why he didn't shoot you, too." Her smile was brief. "After Karen moved in over a year ago, Ryan started losing control. He got obsessed with her and her friendship with his pregnant girlfriend—Sean's mother. Apparently Jimmy decided he was causing more trouble than he was worth. A few hours after Ryan had yet another confrontation with Karen, he was found dead, shot in the head. No arrests were ever made. Officially there were no suspects."

"But unofficially?"

"Most people who had an opinion believed that Jimmy gave the order and Vinnie Marino carried it out."

"And Trevor shared their opinion."

"I guess so." They had reached O'Shea's. The glass, wood and brick fragments had been swept up from the sidewalk, but the four doors were still boarded over, giving it the look of any other abandoned business on Serenity.

Nicholas touched her arm and gestured toward the end of the street. Pushing her hands into her pockets, she walked with him past apartments and houses, empty storefronts and the Williams' grocery. When they reached the cottage, he pushed open the creaky gate, then followed her inside.

It was a beautiful place, even abandoned and neglected. There were so many thousands of places like it all across the South, standing empty and alone, slowly succumbing brick by board by windowpane to the heat, the humidity, to age and vandals and indifference. So many were beyond saving, but not this one. This beauty would be worth every minute of backbreaking labor and every penny.

There was no grass growing in the yard—just weeds that grew wherever they could, bare dirt where they couldn't and massive live oaks. Underneath the weeds and dirt was a walkway that led from the gate to each of the staircases. A dusty rose brick showed here and there as they approached the house.

Lainie tested each of the steps before placing her full weight on it. At the top, she gazed at the wrought-iron and brick fence across the front and the brick walls on either side. Run-down, overgrown and shabby, but definitely a beauty.

Without changing her view, she quietly spoke. "Tell me about Rena."

Nicholas stood a few steps below, seeing the same things she was seeing. He'd always liked the place, he'd told her one day. Had he ever dreamed, back when he was young and ambitious and able to dream, about sharing it with Rena? About making it a home and raising their kids and filling it with love? Probably not. One of his ambitions had been to escape Serenity forever. He never would have brought the woman he loved, the woman who had meant everything to him, back here to live.

Finally he looked at her, his expression as open as she'd ever seen. "What do you want to know about her?"

Everything. Nothing. Just one thing. "Why do you blame yourself for her death? You didn't even know Jimmy then."

He walked past her and onto the broad gallery, where he rested his hands on the weathered gray railing. She wondered if he needed the support of something solid and strong in order to tell the tale. *She* was solid. *She* was strong.

"After we moved in together, Rena and I agreed that she

would drop out of school and work to pay my expenses. As soon as I graduated from law school, we were going to get married and, if she wanted, she would finish her degree then. At the time, she didn't want to. All she'd wanted was a house and babies. And me.''

He added the last as an afterthought, as if he couldn't quite imagine a woman as special as Rena wanting him. Lainie understood. *She* wanted him more than anything.

''She worked as a grocery store checker during the day and a waitress at night. She'd started out in a restaurant, but the tips were better in the bar. She hated the job, though. She didn't like her boss and didn't trust the people he did business with. She wanted to quit, but the money was good and I was taking such a heavy load that I couldn't help out. I convinced her to stay until school was out for the summer, when I could work, too. It was the only thing we ever argued about. She was afraid, but, for me, she stayed.''

Stayed to see her fears come true, to die in a feud that had nothing to do with her. Stayed to become one more of Jimmy Falcone's innocent victims. And, of course, Nicholas blamed himself.

''She was an adult, Nicholas. She could have quit the job against your wishes. Maybe you would have gotten angry, maybe you would have argued again, but you would have resolved it. She wouldn't have lost you over it.''

''I know the arguments. Hell, I'm a lawyer. But I also know that if she hadn't been in the club that night, she would be alive today, and she wouldn't have been in the club that night if she hadn't wanted to please me. Any way you look at it, it's my fault. I'm at least partly responsible for her death.'' His fingers tightened on the rail. ''But...''

Lainie tested the balustrade that protected the landing where the two stairways met the porch and found that despite age and neglect, it held firm. She leaned against it and faced him.

"I've done twenty years' penance. Even Father Francis, who was the hardest, most unforgiving man I've ever known, would think that was sufficient. Rena would think it was way too much. She would think I was twenty years' past due for getting on with my life. For *having* a life. For falling in love, getting married, having a home, raising a family and all those things that would have made her proud. She would think I was an idiot for losing so much, for wasting so much time."

"What do you think?" She had to force the words out because her chest was too tight to allow for more than the shallowest of breaths.

"I *am* an idiot. Saturday night I thought I had the luxury of time. Though I was too angry to admit it, I knew I loved you and nothing in the world was going to change that. But I thought I could nurse my hurt feelings and wounded pride for as long as I wanted, that I could push you away and make you suffer because I was suffering. I thought I could indulge myself, then eventually get over it, and we could pick up where we left off. Then Sunday night you almost died, and today you came close again."

Finally, with great effort, he released his hold on the rail and came to her. He didn't stop until he was right in front of her, his hands on either side of her. "If there was one lesson I should have learned from Rena's death, it's that there are no guarantees. We might have fifty years together, or maybe only ten, or not even one. However long it is, the key word is *together*. However many years or months or days I have left, I want to spend them with you, Lainie, because I was right about two things—I *do* love you, and nothing will ever change that." He drew a breath, then bluntly asked, "Will you marry me?"

She resisted the urge to smile with delight. "I think I should tell you first that I'm out of a job."

"You can work here with me."

"What would we do?"

"You can open a nursery. I'll work on the house."

"Fixing the house won't take forever. Then what would you do?"

"Have you taken a close look at the place?" he asked dryly. "When it's done, *if* it's ever done, I could work for you or...or I could see about getting my license reinstated. This time I could do it right and help the people who deserve it."

His words made her feel incredibly warm inside. "You know, I've been having this serious urge lately to hold a baby in my arms, to create a little hope for the future."

The corners of his mouth twitched just a little. He knew what her answer was going to be. He knew she couldn't imagine anything more perfect than spending the rest of her life with him. "Funny. I've been having the same urge."

"I wasn't very good at this marriage business before."

"That's because you didn't try it with me." He moved a breath closer. "Answer me, Lainie."

"You know I love you."

"I know."

"I need to tell you—"

He brought his hand to her mouth, stopping her words. "Tell me yes," he commanded, then, without waiting, kissed her gently, sweetly, tenderly. It left her legs a little weak, her head a little muddled and her heart achingly full. "Tell me."

For a long time she simply looked at him—at his handsome face, his dark eyes, his intense expression. Then she smiled a big, happy, full-of-love smile and gave the answer he'd asked for. The only answer she could give. "Yes."

Yes. A thousand times yes.

* * * * * *

Available in February 1998

ANN MAJOR

CHILDREN OF DESTINY
When Passion and Fate Intertwine...

SECRET CHILD

Although everyone told Jack West that his wife,
Chantal—the woman who'd betrayed him and sent
him to prison for a crime he didn't commit—had
died, Jack knew she'd merely transformed herself
into supermodel Mischief Jones. But when he
finally captured the woman he'd been hunting,
she denied everything. Who was she really—
an angel or a cunningly brilliant counterfeit?"

"Want it all? Read Ann Major."
—Nora Roberts, *New York Times*
bestselling author

Don't miss this compelling story
available at your favorite retail outlet.
Only from Silhouette books.

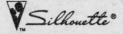 *Silhouette*®